SWAN SONG

For Zak,
Best Wishes.

Stant

D1472255

ABOUT THE AUTHOR

Stewart Kellerman, a former editor at the New York Times and war correspondent for United Press International, writes books and blogs about the English language. He has reviewed books, written on literary subjects, and reported from Southeast Asia, the Middle East, Latin America, and Washington. He is the author of two other books, *Origins of the Specious* and *You Send Me*, both written with his wife, Patricia T. O'Conner.

SWAN SONG

A Novel

STEWART KELLERMAN

RUSHWATER PRESS

P.O. Box 50151
Sarasota, FL 34232, USA

PUBLISHER'S CATALOGING-IN-PUBLICATION DATA
Names: Kellerman, Stewart, author.
Title: Swan song : a novel / by Stewart Kellerman.
Description: Sarasota, FL: Rushwater Press, 2019.
Identifiers: ISBN 978-0-9801532-8-6 (pbk.) |
978-0-9801532-9-3 (ebook)
Subjects: LCSH: Friendship—Fiction. | Old age—Fiction. |
Retirement communities—Florida—Fiction. |
Swindlers and swindling—Fiction. | Cape Canaveral (Fla.)—Fiction. |
Jewish fiction. | Humorous fiction. |
BISAC: FICTION / Humorous / General
Classification: LCC PS3611 .E4355 S83 2019 | DDC 813.6—dc23

Printed in the United States of America
www.rushwaterpress.com

10 9 8 7 6 5 4 3 2 1

FIRST EDITION, 2019

Book design by Simon M. Sullivan

COVER ILLUSTRATION: Souvenir postcard of Times Square,
circa 1937, from the collection of the author.

For Pat

AUTHOR'S NOTE

The people who populate *Swan Song* are no one you know, and everyone you know. They make us laugh, and then they break our hearts, simply because they are universal and at the same time so utterly individual. To create such characters without making them stereotypes is a rare achievement.

The Space Coast, and Satellite Beach, really exist, but places like the House of Aloha, where Selma has her hair done, and Golden Chopsticks, Sid's favorite Chinese restaurant, are imaginary, along with Pelican Pond, their gossipy retirement community.

Of course everybody comes from somewhere, as Selma says, and although the Waxlers and their friends are fictional, they do "come from somewhere."

On the cover of this book you'll see a photograph, taken in Times Square around 1937, of the author's mother and her two best friends as young unmarried women out on the town. The 21-year-old Edith Greene, flanked by her companions Jeannette and Charlotte, were a threesome when they were young, just as the characters Selma, Kitty, and Rose are in this book. Edith, like Selma, played the ukulele. And Edith and her husband, Allen Kellerman, did move to Florida when Al retired, just like Selma and Sid Waxler. But there the similarities come to an end.

While the real-life Edith and Al Kellerman do not appear in this book, they did contribute to it. They sat patiently through long interviews, describing to the author what it was like to grow up in New York City in the early 20th century, how young people worked and played and courted, how they raised their young families, and how they eventually coped with the challenges of retirement and a new way of life.

I was lucky enough to know Edith and Al, my husband's parents, who were gracious, kind, and loving people. They died before they had a chance to read this novel and publicly declare that they are NOT Selma and Sid and that their sons are NOTHING like Dewey and Zoot.

—*Patricia T. O'Conner*

ACKNOWLEDGEMENTS

Many of the people who helped make this book are long gone, including my parents, Edith and Al Kellerman; my brother, Larry Kellerman; my aunts Frances Zaklad and Millie Goldberg, and my old neighbor (and Radio City ballet girl) Edith Siday. I learned about the gossip business from my friend and former colleague Frank Swertlow, and about the jazz world from my sax-playing buddy Rick Steinberg. But my main helper and main inspiration was my main squeeze, Patricia T. O'Conner.

CHAPTER I

THE SPACE COAST

I was always fussy about my hair, but I had to tighten the purse strings when things fell apart. To save a few pennies, I'd take my own colors to Annette's House of Aloha: Miss Clairol, an ounce of Topaz and an ounce of Moon Haze. I still had beautiful hair, as nice as when I was a schoolgirl. Maybe a little nicer, if I say so myself. I waved naturally, which I didn't as a girl. Believe it or not, I hadn't permed since I was in my twenties and unattached.

Annette used to set my colors with two ounces of L'Oreal, but I made her switch to Clairoxide after the Disaster. It was sixty-five cents less and my dear friend Kitty saw something in *Florida Today* about how this big shot at L'Oreal had been a Nazi during the war.

If I needed a good treatment, Annette would shampoo me with Wella, first the conditioner, then the conditioning shampoo. My boys used the stuff, too—Dewey, my oldest, and Zoot, number two—but only the shampoo, the one with cholesterol.

Annette knew a terrific trick. She'd rub in a tiny

amount of conditioner as she applied my color. This was so the tips shouldn't dry out. She learned that in Pawtucket, where she had a unisex before moving to the Space Coast.

Of course, everyone in Florida came from somewhere. Sid and I used to live on Kimball Terrace, the dead-end block next to Yonkers Raceway. We had a detached brick with a flagstone patio in back and a finished basement. It took Sid half a summer vacation, but he put up the paneling downstairs all by himself, a very nice wormy cherry.

I discovered Annette soon after moving to Satellite Beach, where we bought when Sid retired from teaching radio and television at Gompers, his vocational high school in the Bronx. This was a few weeks into 1981, not too long after the Reagans got to Washington.

I was still a mere bobby-soxer of sixty-five, barely old enough to get my senior discount at Mercury Marquee (Sid used to call it the Sin-a-Plex). He was sixty-six, nearly four years younger than Reagan at the Inauguration. Day in and day out, Sid was carrying on about that cowboy in the White House. Little did he realize, but Reagan wasn't the rustler we had to worry about.

To be fair, it was Kitty who found the House of Aloha, Annette's beauty parlor in Spaceport Plaza. Annette was between Reliable Realty—don't get me started on that—and Golden Chopsticks, Sid's favorite Chinese restaurant. He was very picky when it came to Chinese, wouldn't touch anything but the most boring dishes from the chow mein school.

Spaceport Plaza, by the way, wasn't exactly a mall, but one of those older-style shopping centers on A1A where you had to step outside to go from store to store. All the shops were stucco, pink stucco with little aquamarine awnings in front—Spanish style.

Kitty had always been the pioneer. She discovered Pelican Pond, our retirement village in Satellite Beach. She bought first, then I did, and Rose brought up the rear. Rose was forever last, the sweetest person in the world, but a faint heart who was always waiting for Kitty and me to show her the way.

We'd been together through thick and thin. The Three Musketeers—that's what everyone used to call us when we were growing up on Livonia Avenue in Brooklyn. We wouldn't let anybody separate us. We had plenty of aggravation from our husbands, let me tell you, but we insisted on finding three houses close to one another in Yonkers. Rose lived down the street from me on Kimball Terrace and Kitty was one block over on Halstead.

Kitty was the brave one. I remember when we were in tenth grade at Thomas Jefferson and she took Rose and me into the city for Chinese at the Singapore. This was the first time any of us had tried Chinese food and Rose was acting like Daniel in the lion's den.

"What the hell are you afraid of?" Kitty hollered for the whole room to hear. "Christ Almighty, it won't jump up and bite you. You're supposed to be doing the goddamn biting."

I should have warned you about Kitty's mouth. All ears were burning at the tables around us. Even the Chinese waiters were getting an earful. Well, Rose may have been a crybaby, but I wasn't exactly Selma the Lion-Hearted when I saw the menu.

I couldn't tell my egg foo from my mu shu in those days, let alone the more exotic stuff—octopus suckers, chicken toes, eye of newt, for all I know. I kept asking our waiter if the dishes had onions. I didn't like cooked onions. I could eat raw onions chopped up with tuna and other things, but not cooked in my food.

Onions never agreed with Sid, either, raw or otherwise. He was of the opinion—and not just an opinion in his case—that onions give you gas. Sid always had an opinion, too many of them in my opinion. We wouldn't have been in such a state if he'd listened to me.

I wanted to be on the pond, but Sid knew better. Kitty and Leo had already bought a lovely Hacienda, one of the higher-quality waterside villas. Rose and Sol were still hemming and hawing, but it looked as if they'd take the plunge and get a Hacienda, too.

Sid had other ideas. The way he figured it, we'd be throwing good money away to be on a pond, especially an artificial one, when we didn't even have a canoe. He wanted us to get a Chalet, the cheaper unit with a breezeway instead of a garage. The Chalets were over by Tropicana Trail and the traffic congestion. As an added attraction, you had a lovely view through your picture window of Luna Lanes, the bowladrome across the street.

"Everyone wants to be on the pond," Sid argued as we examined the prospectus in Yonkers. "You have to pay top dollar there. Why should we go into debt to be on the water?"

"But that's where I want to be, on the pond next to Kitty and Rose."

"We shouldn't tie ourselves down with a mortgage at our age, Bubbie. If we buy away from the water, we'll have our home free and clear. And we can put the left-over into a nest egg."

"I don't want an ugly bowling alley in my face. I don't even like bowling. And what are we going to do with a nest egg? Sit on it until we hatch chickens?"

"I'm sorry, but I'm not a high roller like some other husbands I could mention. I had to slave in the school system all my life."

"You'll be getting a very nice bundle from your variable annuity when you retire, $22,215 in cold cash, as you never cease to remind me. Why can't we use this manna from heaven to buy a Hacienda? We'd need to borrow only ten thousand more."

"It doesn't make sense to pay double-digit interest rates to be on a phoney-baloney pond. Who needs water?"

Listen to him, Sid Waxler, the Answer Man. Let him speak for himself. You should have seen me as a girl. I used to slice through the water without a splash, just like the girls in *Billy Rose's Aquacade*. Even in Florida, I could have swum circles around the tadpoles sunning themselves topless by the pool of the Econo Lodge on A1A, the place with the turquoise tiles.

As soon as we got to Pelican Pond, I joined Aquacise at the Olympic pool. Maybe I shouldn't be the one to say this, but I was a sensation. Loretta Liebowitz, our lady lifeguard, said I had more natural talent and enthusiasm than the rest of the class combined, though that might have been a slight exaggeration.

Sid used to take me to Orchard Beach in the summer, back when we had the one-bedroom on Sedgwick Avenue in the Bronx, our first home together. We used to suntan in section twelve, where the musicians congregated. Sid would lie back on a beach towel, his eyes closed, as I serenaded the crowd with my mandolin, an old Gibson.

Sid wasn't much of a swimmer—more of a splasher, actually. I have a picture from the old days. He's at the beach, holding Dewey on his shoulder. Dewey in diapers, such a tiny thing. Sid's hair is stuck to his head like a wet washcloth. He's a stringbean, standing there in his trunks. They were navy, the trunks, but you can't tell from the picture because it's a black-and-white.

Sid's hair was still as black as ever when we got to Florida, but he never appreciated his good fortune. I worked so hard to get my color right and he didn't have to lift a pinkie. It wasn't fair. He was still a stringbean, too. I'd like someone to explain that. I had to struggle every day of my life to keep my girlish figure. Sid, on the other hand, could stuff whatever garbage he wanted into that big trap. Not an ounce stuck to his bones. This had to be the metabolism or something, maybe hormones. At night, I'd look at his tiny little size-thirty belt draped over the armchair in our bedroom and feel like strangling him with it.

As usual, Sid had his way about the Chalet. We got it for $74,895 plus closing costs, just about what we cleared from selling the house in Yonkers. And he insisted we put the entire $22,215 from the school system into a one-year CD at Sun Bank, the branch on South Babcock in Melbourne. It had the best rate around, fifteen percent compounded, and you got a pocket calculator for opening the account.

Sid moved the rest of our money, a few thousand from Yonkers Savings, into a joint checking account at Southland, the bank with the drive-in window around the corner on A1A. It was across from the Econo Lodge and next to Oinkers, the barbecue place on the ocean. You could get a platter of ribs for three ninety-five, a platter big enough to hold a ten-pound turkey.

For some reason, it made Sid feel good to have that nest egg in the bank. You would have thought it was a Fabergé from listening to him. But what were we saving for? Unless I was mistaken, burial shrouds were still being made without pockets.

My God, the aggravation we went through over that money. I get sick thinking about it. I curse the weasel responsible for what happened. His bones should be broken and trampled into the earth. Excuse me, but a bitter heart makes you say such things.

Well, I gave in on the Chalet, but I insisted on a kitchen with room for our Inca gold dinette set from Yonkers. That's why we bought a Chalet Luxe, the two-bedroom end unit with a bath and a half and an eat-in kitchen. It was equipped with new Hot Point appliances, wall-to-wall carpeting, and a tiled Neptune green tub in the master bath that you stepped down into.

Sid liked the idea of the spare bedroom that came with an end unit. I furnished it with twin beds, in case the boys decided to do Sid and me a big favor and pay us a visit. Not that Dewey, the snob, or Zoot, the hipster, would stay with us—let alone Fleur, Dewey's socialite wife.

All we got from the children was grumble, grumble, groan. Mostly they complained that the only thing we did was complain about them, which I couldn't figure out, since there was no way to get a word in edgewise with all their complaining. I have a question, Dr. Brothers. If we were such rotten parents, how did they turn out to be so perfect?

Well, I'm not the only person to tumble into the generation gap and crack my skull. Kitty emerged black and blue from raising Myra, her little sweetheart. And Rose had a concussion or two, thanks to Becky and Zach, the sweetness and light of her life.

I remember when I worked for Ansonia Shoes before the war. It was just off Herald Square, which was why you could always find me in Macy's at lunch time. I was the steno in the office, but I did a lot of other things— the sales floor, the cash register, the account book.

I sent the checks to Mrs. Wolfowitz, the boss's wife, when she went to Grossinger's over the summer. I even filled in when the model was sick. I wasn't a model size— she was a four and I was four and a half—but I'd squeeze my foot into it.

The point is, we got the most beautiful stuff at cost from Binghamton and the other shoe places upstate. I rated beautiful shoes and made sure my friends had them, too. No wonder I had such good friends. You have to be a friend to have one.

Well, maybe I should have put up more of a stink about the pond, as if that would have changed Dr. No's mind. He could be very stubborn, ignoring me till I wilted like a warm salad. He was just as obstinate about the Disaster, but I don't want to talk about that.

CHAPTER 2

PIÈCE DE RÉSISTANCE

I was an excellent mixer and got right into the swing of things at Pelican Pond. There was Healthercise with Wanda twice a week, then Aquacise on Wednesdays with Mrs. Liebowitz, and Pelican Pluckers every Sunday, our mandolin orchestra.

I did "Young at Heart" for my Pluckers audition. I may have been a bit rusty, but everybody could see I knew which end of the pegbox was up. Without being asked, Skippy Holzer offered his chair to me and moved back to the second mandolins. He was a fine musician, but he was having a hard time with his fingering because of miner's elbow, a bursitis. Actually, he used to be a telephone installer in New Paltz before retiring.

There were nineteen mandolins, six mandolas, and three mando-cellos in the orchestra. Three other mandolins plus a mandola and a mando-cello—the mandolin's big sister and big brother, you know—could join us at a moment's notice. With an orchestra of seniors, you had to arrange for substitute players.

We had an interesting conductor, Bernstein, who used

to teach music education at Parsons Junior High in Flushing before retiring to Florida. He looked like the picture of Paderewski in one of Zoot's old music books, balding in front with an overgrown vegetable patch in back.

Bernstein had been comfortable when he retired from the school system, thanks to his wife, Mildred. She used to work for the IRS in Garden City. They put most of their savings into a Château, one of the high-priced private homes on Society Hill. It was similar to a Hacienda, but you had a third bedroom, a den off the Florida room, and a fenced-in yard with space for a pool.

We had our concerts in the Cabaret on the first and third Sundays of each month—from two to three in the afternoon, admission free. On the other two weekends, we rehearsed in the Wellness Room of the Club House, the squat building next to the Cabaret.

The Arthur Godfrey Cabaret—no one used the formal name, though—was the centerpiece of Pelican Pond. It was a white wooden building, round like a wedding cake, with gingerbread carvings on the gables, windows, and doors. At three stories high, it was visible from every home, even the Sandpipers on South Patrick Drive—the rental units off in Timbuktu for retirees who couldn't afford to buy.

We did the most interesting stuff. At my first concert, Bernstein's granddaughter, Carlee, was visiting from Great Neck and played the vibraphone solo. This was a couple of weeks after I got to Florida. There was a packed house, but it might have been because Mercury Marquee, the sixplex at Moonwalk Mall, had nothing good that weekend.

Our main attraction was *Winkle, Twinkle*, an arrangement of the "Twinkle, Twinkle" tune for mandolin orchestra and vibraphone. I know exactly what you're thinking, but you shouldn't jump to conclusions. It was quite an interesting piece in its own way. Well, maybe I would have chosen a marimba for the solo, but Bernstein liked the effects you get with a vibraphone.

We received a standing ovation, especially Carlee, the soloist. She had to come back for three curtsies and two bows. She was six or seven, a honey blonde in braids. Bernstein once told us she was named for his maternal grandparents, Carl and Leah, who were gassed in the camps.

She wasn't a real soloist, of course. All she had to do was tap out the tune one note at a time with a single mallet—twinkle, twinkle, tink-tink-tink—at the beginning and at the end of the composition. In between, the rest of us did all the work, turning the song inside out and upside down until we had our pièce de résistance.

I still remember a word or two of French. Miss Lazarus would be proud of me—my French teacher at Thomas Jefferson—or rather Mlle. Jeannette, as we were supposed to call her. Danny Kaye went to school there; his wife, Sylvia, too, though a few years before yours truly. Rose also took French, but Kitty insisted on being different and studied Spanish.

At that first concert, my two friends were sitting just below me in the audience. Rose would clap timidly after each piece, but Kitty preferred to shout olé at the top of her lungs as if I were fighting a bull instead of a musical score.

The audience for these amateur productions was very informal. Kitty was in peach Pucci pajamas and Rose in baggy Bermudas with a lady-bug print. From the stage, I could see Rose hunched in her chair, knees pointed up at the ceiling like two missiles poking out of their silos.

Rose's youngest, Becky, had bought her the shorts on Maui. Becky always liked bugs. I remember when Rose and I took the children to Radio City in the fifties. Becky insisted on carrying a brown paper bag with her and holding it on her lap. Inside, she had a short-horned grasshopper that hopped around all through *Ivanhoe*.

Rose—Rose Moskowitz—was taller than she looked, five-eight on her Florida driver's license, but she wouldn't extend herself. I'll never forget the sight of her slumping into gym class in high school, back when she was still Mossman.

Miss Ducey, the gym teacher, used to scare Rose half out of her wits. She'd point a knobby finger at her, then point it at the posture poster on the wall.

"Straighten up that crooked spine, young lady. Do you want to turn into a pretzel? Stomach in! Shoulders back! You won't steal anyone else's space if you stand up straight."

I once thought Miss Ducey was the meanest person in the world. Little did I know. She was a cream puff compared with a party I won't mention, may he drop dead and be buried in a toxic dump.

Not that I had a concern in the world those first few weeks in Florida. Who had time to worry? When I wasn't signing up for one activity after another, I was off with my friends exploring the Space Coast.

To orient yourself, Satellite Beach is on the Canaveral peninsula—a barrier island, actually—between the Atlantic Ocean and the Banana River. It's just off the mainland from Melbourne and a dozen miles south of Cape Canaveral on A1A, the road that runs along the Space Coast.

In fact, A1A becomes Astronaut Boulevard at the Cape. There was a place over there called the Astroburger, a drive-in with waitresses on roller skates that looked like Minuteman missiles. You could order a Sputnik for a dollar and a quarter. It was really just a hamburger with an olive on a toothpick. The olive was supposed to be the Sputnik.

We had our own temple at the retirement community, Beth Shalom, not a building like Young Israel in Yonkers, but a room in the Club House, the room with double doors next to where we played cards. We even had our own rabbi—Nathanson. Actually, he was only a part-time rabbi, semi-retired because of a liver problem. When he stared at you for talking during services, it really was with a jaundiced eye.

There were so many activities at Pelican Pond, from Japanese Bunka to Ballroom, Conga, and Boogaloo. The sailors had slips for Sunfish at Las Brisas, the boat house on the artificial pond. Everyone wore captain hats like that guy on *Gilligan's Island*. If you owned a bigger boat, you could keep it across South Patrick at a dock on the Banana River.

I wouldn't have missed Aquacise for the world. We did the aquatic finale from *Bathing Beauty* in February, the movie with Esther Williams and Xavier Cugat. I'd go to the pool at all hours to practice my routine. The other girls may have joked about putting a phone in the cabana for Selma, but Loretta—Mrs. Liebowitz, you know—had the highest regard for my attitude.

"You're the class dynamo," she told me after my second or third practice. "I'm counting on you to be out here each and every Aquacise to share your energy with us."

She didn't have to twist my arm. I always loved to swim. People used to say I was another Esther Williams. Not in the produce department—who could compete with those cantaloupes?—but I had nothing to be ashamed of. In fact, I was often mistaken for Bette Davis, especially in three-quarter profile, though my hair was a little lighter than hers.

I talked Rose into coming with me to Aquacise a month after we got to Florida. My God, she acted as if the water were treated with sulfuric acid instead of chlorine. I'd be surprised if she spent more than five minutes in it. From then on, she'd detour around the tennis courts to avoid coming within sight of the pool. I tried to get her to go back, but she always had an excuse.

One time it was sacroiliac syndrome. She strained her pelvis while dusting and went to a chiropractor to have the hip bones and sacrum realigned. Another time it was an ingrown toenail. She saw a podiatrist because the skin was perforated and foot bacteria could invade the soft tissue. Then she had an allergic reaction to mulberry pollen, which resulted in a sinus infection. The ear, nose and throat man gave her an antibiotic, but that only led to another complication.

"The amoxicillin is tearing my stomach up, Selma. It

destroys the natural bacteria and makes you feel like you're in a plane at forty thousand feet. But how can you fight a bacterial infection without antibiotics? If I don't use it, I'll keep reinfecting myself with my own mucus."

Rose couldn't wait to join What Ails You, the worry-warts. They met in the Card Room at the Club House to analyze each new ache or pain. There used to be just one large room for cards, but Rose and her friends got management to divide it with an accordion door into smoking and non-smoking.

Well, I held her off as long as I could, but she finally dragged me to a meeting of What Ails You in March, a couple of months after we got to Florida. The health-niks were discussing hypercalcemia. Everyone had the symptoms rhymed and memorized—bones, stones, abdominal groans, and mental moans. I never went back. I preferred to spend my time on more pleasant things.

Healthercise, for example. I could do fifteen push-ups, thirty knee-bends, and forty sit-ups. Wanda Schlachman, the exercise lady, gave me six gold stars and two silvers. Only Kitty had more, but she used to be a professional dancer.

Needless to say, Rose wouldn't go near Healthercise, either. She avoided Wanda like the plague. I don't know where she got that from. Wanda was the nicest person in the world. She was a tiny little thing, not much taller than Dr. Ruth. She was well up into her eighties, but she had more voltage than Florida Power & Light.

We had Healthercise in the Wellness Room of the Club House. If you were on Leisure Loop, the path that wound around Pelican Pond, the Club House was a few dozen steps after tennis en route to the Olympic pool, where we had Aquacise. There was also a heated—the kidney-shaped pool on the way to croquet. We had our own golf course, too, eighteen holes, three of them on the water, including one with an alligator.

Kitty and I went sailing on the pond in the spring. You had to sit through a lecture before you could take out a Sunfish—the boat on the leeward tack had the right of way over the boat on the windward. Once was enough for me—all that bobbing up and down upset my stomach.

Of course, Kitty wouldn't get seasick. Nothing fazed her. Three days after joining Gray Panthers, she became leader of the pack. That woman had a mouth on her. She acted as if the Founding Fathers wrote the Bill of Rights with her in mind. She'd take us on another cavalry charge every week, whether it was for opening the school auditorium at Satellite High to retirees or extending the senior discount at Mercury Marquee to all matinees, not just on weekdays.

Kitty may have been a head shorter than Rose, but she made up for it with excellent posture, which was only to be expected from a ballet girl at Radio City. Helen Hayes once said she wanted to be the tallest five-footer in the world. Well, that could have been Kitty talking.

Not everyone remembers this, but there used to be both ballet girls and Rockettes at the Music Hall. The ballet would come out between the movies and do a hop, skip, and a jump from *Swan Lake* or one of the other classics. It wasn't easy work. There were four or five shows a day. If it was a very good movie, the girls might have to do six.

In the old days, you could see a plié in theaters all over town—the Paradise, the Roxy, the Brooklyn Paramount. It was nothing like the Bolshoi, just show business pure and simple. There were hundreds of ballet girls in the city. From what I could tell, most of them had their noses up in the air. Not Kitty, but a lot of them acted like ballerinas. These girls couldn't work steady in real ballet, so they jumped at the chance to pirouette around the stage before a movie or a live show. Well, everyone has to eat. It's hard to hold your nose in the air on an empty stomach.

CHAPTER 3

ROCK OF GIBRALTAR

Back in the Garden of Eden, there was a worm in the apple. Man may be a social animal, but you couldn't tell from watching Sid those first few months at Pelican Pond. All he wanted to do was hide at home like Rip Van Winkle and let life pass him by.

"It's time to come out of your cocoon," I pleaded until I was hoarse in the throat.

"One social butterfly in the family is enough, Bubbie."

"You worked hard all your life, Sid. You deserve a little fun."

"I don't want fun. I want peace and quiet."

"You'll have enough of that when you're six feet under."

"Will you please, Selma?"

The nonsense I had to put up with. A month after we got to Satellite Beach, I asked Sid to take me to *Annie Get Your Gun* at the Cabaret, but he was more allergic to culture than a vampire to garlic. So maybe the Cabaret wasn't the Copa, but it had the best shows on the Space

Coast. People came from all over—Titusville, Coco Beach, Tortoise Island. Once I met a couple from Kissimmee. They lived down the road from the Tupperware museum.

The Cabaret was so popular that management put up a neon pelican on A1A by the plastic pig for Oinkers. The beak pointed the way to Pelican Pond. The entrance was three blocks west of A1A on Tropicana Trail, between the two pelicans made out of concrete and chicken wire.

The featured entertainers were quite interesting in their own way. I'm not talking about the amateurs who performed in the afternoon for free—Pelican Pluckers, Sharon's Singalong, the Sweet Adelines, and so forth. The established artists took over at night, stars like Jonathan Winters, Julius LaRosa, and Red Buttons. Okay, so they might have been warmed-over meat loaf, but we weren't exactly nouvelle cuisine ourselves.

I remember trying to get Sid to go with me to the Pinky Lee variety show that February. I begged him on bended knee—literally, and I had the sore knees to prove it.

"He's doing Eddie Cantor songs, Sid."

"I saw the movie, Bubbie."

It would have been easier to move the Rock of Gibraltar. In the end, I had to tag along with Kitty and Rose and their more lifelike husbands, the spare tire in the trunk.

Sid wasn't interested in Healthercise, either. He preferred his own exercises. His favorite was pullups. He'd pull on the lever of his La-Z-Boy to make the back go down and the footrest go up. Oh, here's something interesting. I once read that two guys named Ed invented the La-Z-Boy. It was in 1927 and made them rich. They were cousins from Michigan. I know just who they had in mind.

"Please, Sid, you'll like Healthercise if you give it a chance. Wanda is wonderful with the gentlemen. We have three others, including the rabbi. His doctor says it's good for the liver."

"For the umpteenth time, no. My gorgeous wife does enough exercise for the both of us."

Sid's mouth was the only organ getting any exercise. With a box of junk food in one hand and the remote in the other, he'd stretch out in his recliner and stare at the TV, a twenty-one inch Motorola on the credenza in the living room.

"What else do we have to eat, Bubbie?"

"Eat? You just finished lunch two hours ago and you've been stuffing yourself with Doritos and Fritos and Cheetos and God only knows what else ever since."

"My stomach doesn't have a wristwatch."

"Poor hungry man. You can't wait until supper?"

"I eat a balanced diet."

"Maybe two balanced diets."

I should have let sleeping dogs lie. As the Chinese say, be careful what you wish for.

In April, Sid dragged me to Save-a-Lot in Spaceport Plaza to buy a swively whatnot, something like a Lazy Susan, so he could twirl the living-room TV around and watch from the kitchen. He didn't want to miss a thing when he went for more Twinkies, not one commercial for Polident, Miracle Ear, or Depends.

His favorite channel was CNN, the cable news. All I got from him was Reagan this and Arafat that, Ayatollah, Ayatollah, Trump, Trump, Trump!

"I don't get it, Bubbie. If Isaac and Ishmael could live in the same house four thousand years ago, why can't the Arabs and Israelis live in peace now?"

Once Reagan sent someone down to Florida from Washington—the assistant deputy to the deputy assistant—to talk to us about the new Medicare changes. All the other seniors were going to the temple to hear him, but Sid had other ideas.

"Why should I waste my time on that dreck, Bubbie? These phoney politicians and their flunkies are all the same, whether they have donkeys or elephants stuck next to their names."

In other words, he was interested in current events, but only if he didn't have to get off his behind. Do you want to know how hard it was to get him out of that chair? Here's Exhibit A.

It was Columbia's maiden voyage, the first space shuttle. This was in April or May, if memory serves, though the service isn't as good as it used to be.

To mark the occasion, I got The Friends together, the three couples from Yonkers. It was the first of Selma Waxler's space brunches, which were to become a tradition on the Space Coast.

I made brown-eyed Susans, my special recipe, as a treat. You get the brown eye by baking the cookie with a chocolate kiss on top. Everybody raved. I had to refill my Venetian serving tray three times to keep up with demand, the tray with gondolas for handles. Mr. Wolfowitz gave it to me as a wedding present, along with a twenty-dollar bill. This was an extraordinary thing. You never got wedding presents at Ansonia. The other girls were amazed.

As for Sid, he was proof of Newton's first law of motion—a body at rest tends to remain at rest. He refused to budge and join us in the Florida room for brunch. He just sat there in the living room, staring popeyed at the TV. With the countdown about to begin, I approached the Immovable Object with a fresh batch of cookies hot from the oven.

"Please come join us, dear," I whispered so the whole world wouldn't hear. "Do you want everybody to talk?"

"Let them talk. I'll have another cookie, Bubbie. You really outdid yourself this time."

"Thank you, Sid, but keep your voice down. Why do you have to watch the liftoff on TV when you can walk twenty little steps and see it live through the jalousie windows?"

"The view is better on TV. At least it would be if the hostess with the mostess weren't blocking the screen."

No one is deafer than a stubborn man. Sid wouldn't leave the house all spring, except to go to Winn-Dixie for more garbage to stuff down his throat. Everything you weren't supposed to do, he did.

It wouldn't have been so bad if he'd gone out to eat once in a while, but that was asking too much. He'd rather gobble a bag of Doritos at home than take me to the Burrito Brunch at Pancho Villa's House of the Sizzling Fajita, the place on A1A with the neon sombrero. Kitty and Leo went there every weekend. They couldn't stop raving about it. Even Rose liked it, though Sol felt the food was too Tex and not enough Mex for his discriminating taste buds.

The result of all this was plain for everyone to see. As I got younger, my husband was going in the opposite direction. In a few months, his lovely hair went from black to salt-and-pepper to white. With a husband like that, who needed a picture in the attic?

Before long, his infinitesimal waistline wasn't so small anymore. He could barely buckle that nothing of a belt. He punched a new hole and another and one more until he ran out of leather. Finally, he had to go to Burdine's in April for a new belt, a thirty-four. He needed a thirty-six in July and a thirty-eight in October. If it kept up like this, he'd soon be shopping at Big Boy's in Moonwalk Mall. Instead of a calendar, I could have kept track of my first year in Florida by counting the number of belts hanging out of service on the inside of Sid's closet door.

I think four belts had been retired by the time we got the letter from Sun Bank in early 1982. The news inside—our one-year CD was coming due in a few weeks—gave me one more chance to make my case for living next to Kitty and Rose.

"Isn't it time we moved up to a Hacienda?" I asked that night after serving the tuna croquettes and sweet potatoes. "There's a new for-sale sign in front of the house two doors down from Kitty, the one with magenta tiles on the roof."

"Not the Hacienda again. I thought we settled that last year."

"Please, dear, it would mean so much to me."

"The answer is still no, Selma. You're making me cranky."

At first, Sid wanted to move the money into another CD at Sun Bank, but then he learned the new rate would be a whole percentage point less than the old one. Maybe that accounted for the change in his TV viewing habits.

Instead of Arafat and the Ayatollah, he was now watching the bulls and the bears. If he wasn't tuned to Dorfman and the other fortune tellers on cable, it was Irving R. Levine and company on the network news. You know, the McClellan Oscillator and the Elliott Wave, the Phillips Curve versus the Fiomucci, blah, blah, blah. After a week of all these upticks and downticks on TV, I wanted to scream.

It was now the last week of January 1982, a few days before the CD was coming due. The $22,215 nest egg was about to hatch, and the Waxlers would soon have a $25,809 chicken in the pot.

Not that I was thinking of chickens or eggs that morning when I met Kitty and Rose at the House of Aloha. We were celebrating our first anniversary in Florida by treating ourselves to Glamour Girl Day. If you had the works, Annette would give you half off on everything, and throw in the manicure and pedicure for free. Oh, you got lunch, too. Mr. Moon, the headwaiter at Golden Chopsticks, or Yu Wa, his brother-in-law from Hong Kong, would come over from next door with tea and dim sum.

Well, on the way out of the House of Aloha, Annette gave us all copies of *The Orbiter*, our weekly newspaper. There was a very nice item about Annette and her staff of professionals, right above an ad for Glamour Girl Day. The writer called her a well-known leader in the hair- and skin-care business on the Space Coast for over ten years.

Sid's nose was glued to the TV as usual when I got home. I think he was listening to the technicians on FNN, something about how the market was long on the shorts or short on the longs. In other words, the Dow was oversold versus the S&P or vice versa.

I tried to say something about going to the Cabaret— Kitty and Leo had invited us to join them for Joey Bishop—but he just turned up the volume. I think one of the technicians was talking about the Kraft macaroni-and-cheese index. It was supposed to be a classic recession food. When sales are up, the economy is down.

What was the use? I went over to the couch and opened *The Orbiter*, but I couldn't tune out the TV. The technicians had moved on to the Dough Jones index, which tracks the size of the hole in a Lender's bagel. If you use more dough, that's a sign of good times and therefore a bullish indicator. It was at this point that my eyes fell on a story in the paper.

"Listen to this, Sid. They have an interesting item on the Community Spotlight page about this fellow at Reliable—Arlee Sparlow."

"Reliable?"

"You know, the realtor down the road. The Lions had their annual pancake breakfast and gave him a pin for public service."

"Oh, you mean the place in Spaceport Plaza."

"He's having a talk at eight tonight on how to manage

your money. It's free. He volunteers his time for adult education at Satellite High."

I couldn't get over the change in Sid after dinner. He was like that cartoon where the lump of mud becomes a monkey and the monkey becomes a man and the man gets up and walks and then he's on a skateboard and wearing a Walkman.

Without any encouragement on my part, he struggled into his mocha leisure suit, which had been languishing in the closet since we got to Florida. I wanted to pinch myself. After a year of hibernation, the bear was coming out of his den to smell the flowers.

"How do I look, Bubbie?" Sid said as he took a deep breath and pushed the last button of the jacket through the hole. "Do I meet with your approval?"

I stepped back and gave him the once-over. The leisure suit had been swimming on him when I got it on sale at Cross County in Yonkers, but the buttons were about to pop now.

"It may be a bit snug, Sid, but it's very nice all the same. You always looked good in mocha."

I was so happy to see him coming to life again. Whoever said God moves in a mysterious way had something there. My most fervent wish was about to be granted. Little did I realize. Once the genie was loose, I wouldn't be able to get him back into the bottle.

CHAPTER 4

A GENUINE HUMAN BEING

Arlee Sparlow was at the door of the school auditorium, giving each new arrival the glad hand. He was dressed in white from head to toe, very tropical: silk shirt, linen suit, suede shoes, and holding a Panama hat—Our Man in Havana.

"A pleasure, sir," he said, shaking Sid's hand, then turned his charms on me. "I see you've brought the little lady."

He was quite nice in a southerly way. He didn't you-all us to death, but he never passed up a chance to yes-sir or thank-you-ma'am. There was something about him—I don't know the word for it—whatever a realtor has that corresponds to a doctor's bedside manner.

He held out a hand to me. When I offered mine, he took it and touched his lips to my finger tips. Thank God my nails had been done that morning at Glamour Girl Day. Theresa tried something new, Iron Hoof. It was originally for horses, but worked on people, too.

"And how are you this evening, ma'am?"

"Charmed, I'm sure, Mr. Sparlow."

"Arlee, please. Everyone calls me Arlee, ma'am."

He moved off to introduce himself to the Pontifacios—Annette and her husband, Rocky. There was an aura about Arlee. He made everyone feel like his closest friend. He had a thousand closest friends. He wasn't exactly handsome, though he looked nice enough to me.

He tapped the microphone to make sure it was on, then began with tidings of gloom and doom—inflation, deflation, recession, depression. In other words, déjà vu all over again, soup kitchens and pushcarts, people selling apples on the street, the sky is falling.

"It doesn't take an IQ of a gazillion to figure out what brought you fine folks here. You labored diligently all your lives, only to find yourselves locked in a cage with inflation. The lion may be satisfied now, but he'll be mighty hungry before long."

I was expecting a nervous little guy like Depew, the fast-talker from Century 21 who sold us our Chalet, but Arlee was as smooth as molasses. He was in his fifties—a six-footer, give or take an inch—with a drawl that got thicker as he spread the molasses on.

"I can tell you ladies and gentlemen didn't just fall off the watermelon truck," he said. "You're not interested in any old get-rich scheme. But if you're here, you must realize you've been sitting on dead center for too many years."

He had such personality and mannerisms, like Robertson and Falwell and those other fellows on the religious channel. Rocky found it mesmerizing, but not even Mesmer himself could have kept Annette spellbound. She dozed off somewhere in Act 1, Scene 2.

What do you expect? It was Glamour Girl Day, and she'd been shaking her kishkes from seven in the morning until seven at night.

Bernstein, the conductor of my mandolin orchestra, was sitting across the aisle from us and up a row. He should have let Annette work on his wild and woolly hair. From the rear, where you didn't see the bald part, he could have been Albert Einstein's twin brother.

Mo Bialer, the owner of the only decent deli on the Space Coast, was next to Bernstein, on the side away from us. I spotted Heshy Liebowitz, Loretta's husband, in the first row. Heshy always waited for her by the cabana after Aquacise. He was hard of hearing and had to wear a Miracle Ear. He used to be a Whirlpool repairman.

"With the help of modern medicine, people are living longer now," Arlee was saying, his hands wrapped around the microphone stand. "But if you sit back and do nothing, you'll outlive your savings. Did you ever see a duck swimming in the pond? From the shore, it looks like the duck's doing nothing, but under the water it's kicking like hell, if you'll pardon me, ladies."

He had something to say on each investment opportunity, most of it negative, but still quite informative, especially about mutuals, the loads and the no loads. I already knew about the front loads, but it never dawned on me that some of them could get you on the way out, too—the rear ends.

"A stock fund may be perfectly fine in a bull market, but just wait until the Dow drops a few hundred points and then try to cash in those blue chips. The turnip is out of blood. As for treasuries, the T-bill may be safe, but it's an old stuck-in-the-mud investment. And the long bond is shark and tuna territory. You better be one of the sharks or stay out of the water."

There was a five-minute intermission, supposedly to stretch our legs, but Arlee used the occasion to shake whatever hands he'd missed the first time around. He was also passing out his business card and résumé to any interested parties, which meant every gentleman in the audience.

"Should he be doing this?" I whispered to Sid.

"Doing what?"

"Using an adult-education class to drum up business."

"A big doer like him doesn't have to obey Robert's rules of order."

Annette's husband, a scrawny little guy, came over to see Sid. He was wearing a T-shirt with a picture of the Roman Forum on the back and the name of his restaurant, Rocky's Villa Romana, on the front.

"This fellow is a straight-talker, isn't he?" he said. "He makes a lot of sense."

"He's a genuine human being," Sid agreed. "Now they're all blow-dried and look like the guy who sells John Hancock life insurance."

Arlee returned to the stage and resumed his litany. He shot down the various investment opportunities one by one, like sitting ducks in the amusement park. He saved his biggest gun, the bazooka, for FDIC bank accounts—insured money markets, passbook savings, and certificates of deposit.

"If you keep your money in the bank, inflation will grind you down. Does this sound a little frightening, my friends? Of course it's frightening! Lord, it makes me want to get up on my hind legs and howl."

It wasn't until he came to the last duck that he held his fire. Not surprisingly, this was real estate, where he had a vested interest. Now, I was the last person to hold that against him. If it were up to me, I'd have been the proud owner of a Hacienda instead of a CD.

"The senior citizen living on a fixed income is facing a critical challenge. How do you get a rate of return that exceeds inflation? The answer is wealth creation. Ever since Adam and Eve, more wealth has been created in real estate than everything else. Lord have mercy on the fool who plays it safe in this economy. No, sir. Playing it safe is like paying the cannibals to eat you last."

My mind must have wandered because the next thing I knew, Arlee was explaining the fine points of a VA repo for five hundred down and positive cash flow. You had to look at the comps, eighty versus seventy-five—a buy at seventy-five, but a maybe at eighty.

"I believe in giving it to you straight," he said, unscrewing the microphone for the grand finale. "I don't drink French Chablis, just hundred-proof J.W. Dant bourbon."

He came to the edge of the stage, holding the mike in his hands and looking down on us. He had a way of speaking to the whole audience while at the same time making each of us feel like the most important person in the room.

"If you have a lick of sense, you can succeed. The only thing holding you back is lazy thinking. You have to tell your brain what to do instead of letting it tell you. Listen to me, brain, wake up! Come on, feet, step over to the telephone! Okay, fingers, dial that number!"

He had everyone—well, all the gentlemen—singing his praises by the end of the evening.

"Nobody ever handed this guy something on a silver platter," Bernstein said to Sid on the way out. "You can tell he learned his business in the trenches."

Sid nodded. "He's very down to earth, a roll-up-the-shirtsleeves type person."

"He reminds me of myself when I was all spit and vinegar," Mo Bialer said, rubbing his mushed-in nose. Did I mention that he used to be a prizefighter? I'd have had a nose job, but Mo was proud of it.

Sid's mouth was going a mile a minute when we got home. Leveraging and cash flow, appreciation, depreciation, tax abatements, multiple listings. My head was spinning.

"Bubbie, do you remember the three keys to success in real estate?"

"Location, location, location?"

"No. You weren't listening. The comps, the demographics, and the mechanicals. If all three are good, you're sitting pretty."

I let him drone on. Why not? Sid finally had an interest in life. He was a new man or, rather, the old one again. Who could ask for anything more?

Well, now that you mention it, there was something more. In bed that night, I leaned over to give him a goodnight peck and before I knew it he was kissing me back. There are certain things you never forget, and I don't mean riding a two-wheeler. I was so happy that I got up in the middle of the night and did a two-step all the way to the toilet. You know, dancing on the deck of the *Titanic*.

CHAPTER 5

BENEVOLENT CAPITALISM

Sid was up and about the next morning while I slept on contentedly. I may have been in the arms of Morpheus, but I was dreaming about somebody else. As for the man of my dreams, he was fast at work on his first million by the time I padded into the living room in my daffodil housecoat and matching slippers.

He didn't notice me for a while. He was sunk in the sofa, a cup of instant coffee in one hand and the real-estate pages of *Florida Today* in the other, searching for a handyman special with good comps, demographics, and mechanicals.

There was a new ring on the drum table nearest him. We'd originally bought them for table lamps, but Sid sawed two inches off the legs in Yonkers to make a pair of end tables for the sofa. This was when we replaced the Stern's table lamps with torchères from Abraham & Straus.

"You're up early, Mr. Trump," I greeted him, holding my tongue about the coffee stain.

"You have to be an early bird, Bubbie. You can't make money lying around in bed."

"No?" I said. "Go tell that to the strippers at the House of Babes on A1A."

I couldn't believe the change that came over Sid the next few days. He was running around like Roger Bannister and the four-minute mile. He got up at dawn when the paper landed on our doorstep, then wolfed down his breakfast while he devoured the real-estate ads. He left the dishes for me as he raced off in the Toyota to check out the listings or stop by Reliable Realty. When he got home, Mr. Paganini invariably played another rhapsody to Arlee Sparlow.

"He's very big on the Space Coast, Bubbie. You should see him in action. He knows all the right buttons to push to make the power structure work for him."

Sid had such enthusiasm, you wouldn't believe. He reminded me of the young man I'd met at Gay Blades. You know, back when the dinosaurs still roamed the earth. In those days, you could get worn out listening to him.

It was a terrific place, Gay Blades, where I used to ice-skate with Kitty and Rose in the '30s. I don't remember exactly how much it cost to get in, but the subway was still a nickel, the same as the trolley, and the deposit on a Coke bottle was two cents.

I did a very good tango, but I hated to jump and always kept one foot on the ice. Kitty was a fine skater, too, though she didn't have much time for it after she began dancing at Radio City. Rose, for her part, would mince around the rink as if her skates were too tight in the toes.

I was usually the late one. You could blame Mr. Wolf-owitz for that. He'd keep me at Ansonia until he locked up, complaining all the while about the mentality of his customers. I was a good listener, but the person he really needed to talk to was Sigmund Freud.

"This ladies' shoe business is making me crazy in the head, Selma. How can a smart woman spend more on a meal she eats in an hour than on a pair of shoes she'll wear for years?"

When Ansonia closed for the day, I'd walk over to the garment district to pick up Rose. She kept the books at a place on Seventh Avenue, Sam-Al Accessories, fine hosiery. Once Al asked me out to lunch, but I preferred to spend my break at Macy's. Anyway, I was over twenty-one—old enough to know better than to waste my time on a married man with three small boys, the youngest in diapers.

The rink was a few blocks from Sam-Al, over by the old Madison Square Garden, if I remember, and up a flight of stairs.

Rose and I were taking a break when it happened. You weren't supposed to carry food onto the ice, but nobody minded if you stayed next to the railing. She was drinking hot chocolate and I was having a cup of frozen custard.

Rose, the Ancient Mariner, was carrying on as usual. Her sinuses were acting up again, but it was hard for me to hear a difference. Rose always had a sniffle or a stuffed-up nose. She would have made a good Miss Adelaide on Broadway, if not for her stage fright. Be that as it may, another medical procedure had come to her attention, something in The Mirror about an operation where the doctor inserted scalpels into your nostrils to clean out the passages.

"He has to cut slits across all four sinuses to let them drain, Selma. Unfortunately, the septum is broken in the process. If it doesn't heal properly, you can whistle the rest of your life."

"Please, Rose, I'm eating!"

"You can get hard clusters of mucus in the sinuses and eustachian tubes. Possibly even hearing loss and chronic vertigo, with permanent disability from labyrinth disease."

Anyway, there we were, Rose and I, standing by the railing at Gay Blades and minding our own sweet business, when all of a sudden who should skate into my life but Sid Waxler.

He thought it was a big joke—a bump in the night, that's what he said. But I wasn't laughing, not with half a cup of custard on my new lamb's wool sweater. It was from B. Altman's, a lovely mock turtleneck with a trellis of wild roses running down the front.

To be fair, Sid turned out to be a perfect gentleman. He wiped that idiotic grin off his face and went to buy me a new custard. He couldn't be more sorry. He'd pay for me to take the sweater to a fine French cleaner; the skirt, also, for the inconvenience he'd caused.

I couldn't get over his outfit—plaid suit, striped shirt, checked tie. It made you dizzy. He always had a good sense of color, but he was bad at geometry. I used to get cross-eyed from staring at him until he agreed to let me coordinate his clothes.

I must have told him I worked for Ansonia because pretty soon he was going on about Johnston & Murphy, his favorite shoes. He always loved wing tips. Before long, it was Johnson & Johnson and then this place in upstate New York—Johnson City, if I remember. Pretty soon, he's giving Rose and me a lecture on big business.

"So they build a company town in the middle of no-where, right down to the barbershop, five-and-dime, and bungalows for the workers. That's called benevolent capitalism, ladies."

Sid's mind was bouncing around like a pogo stick, from capitalism to paternalism to isms I can't even re-member. His father, a victim of classism, had a little two-by-nothing business in the fur district. There were only two of them, an inside man and an outside man. Sid's father was Mr. Outside, the one who took the sam-ples from store to store.

"I used to help my old man after school, sorting skins and going to retailers with him. But I didn't want to be a furrier and kiss the buyers' behinds all my life. I asked myself one question: What is your personal goal in life? I didn't have to think twice. I wanted to be a radio man."

He couldn't stop talking about radio. Maxwell this, Hertz that, vacuum tubes, amplitude, frequency, phase, modulating the carrier. I got a kick out of his enthusi-asm. He was a true believer, never mind that song—they told Marconi that wireless was a phony.

He learned all about crystal radios from a book at the public library. There was a branch on a Hundred-and-tenth, a few blocks from his family's railroad flat on the Upper East Side—or, rather, East Harlem. It was an

Italian neighborhood then, a rough place for a Jew to grow up. If you went down the wrong street, you didn't come home with a whole head.

Sid used to take the El down to Cortlandt Street, the radio district, when he was a boy. That's where you went to buy parts if you wanted to make your own radio. He'd stick his nose up against the glass storefronts—Milo, Terminal, Leotone, Leeds—and drool at all the gadgets.

For me, the interesting part was what Sid got on his homemade radio—from KDKA in Pittsburgh, the first commercial station. It was Dempsey-Carpentier, the heavyweight championship. Carpentier was the Frenchman that Dempsey knocked out in the fourth round.

"I'm not a boxing fan like some other fellows, but it was a very big event in the neighborhood," he said. "Everyone wanted to listen, all except for a few ladies. They were afraid to put the headphones on."

Did I mention Sid had wavy hair like Don Ameche's? As he waxed ecstatic about making his first radio, he could have been Alexander Graham Bell at the end of the movie when he shouts, "Watson, come here." Or did I see that movie later? Anyway, you know what I mean.

Sid began working for Blan the Radio Man while he was still in high school. He got a full-time job in the stock room when he graduated, then moved into sales a few months later, parts and supplies. He was good at thinking up things, too, so customers with special problems would go to him. He was considered a rising young man on Radio Row.

"Blan is a nice spot to learn the business, but I don't intend to stay there forever. One day, I'll open my own place on Cortlandt—Waxler Radio & Electric. All I need is to accumulate enough capital for the merchandise— the inventory, as we say—and the commercial lease."

I think Sid was the assistant manager at Try-Mo, another radio place, by the time we got married. To be honest, running off to Tarrytown wasn't so romantic. There was a sign on the justice of the peace's wall: Don't Throw Rice!!! Yes, with three exclamation marks. In fact, we didn't even have rice; we forgot it in our hurry to get on the road before the morning rush hour.

We thought we were such hot stuff. I love you, the sky's the limit. We took off in the Studebaker, our first car together, a blue runabout with a jump seat in the rear. It wasn't exactly Nancy Drew's blue roadster, but I loved it. This was in 1940, when Fanny Brice was on the radio, the year before Pearl Harbor.

We drove to Niagara Falls without stopping so we'd be there for the first night of our honeymoon. I still remember the people we stayed with—the McGarrys. They had a big shingle house that was broken up into rooms. If you used the bathtub, you had to clean up with scouring powder. The tub had claw feet. All the shine was off the porcelain, but it was white enough for us.

The next morning, we took a ride under the falls on the *Maid of the Mist*. The water sprayed the deck, but the crew gave us oilskin slickers to protect our clothes. In the old days, cloth was soaked in oil to waterproof it, so the water would run off. I still have pictures of us in the slickers. My bangs are soaking wet and Sid is blinking in the spray. The most beautiful sight was the rainbow in the sky.

We took a tour of the power plant that used the water from the falls to make electricity. I'd have skipped that, but wild horses couldn't hold Sid back. You had to watch for falling rocks when you climbed down to the plant. The mist tickled your nose at the foot of the falls. I think it was the St. Lawrence, the river flowing by.

The guide told us a generator broke down one day and the workers had to take the thing apart. Inside they found an entire Model T stuck in the machinery. It must have been sucked down from above the dam.

We spent three days there, then drove to Howe Caverns in Cobbleskill. I was mixing up my stalactites and stalagmites until Sid taught me a little trick: When the mites go up, Bubbie, the tights go down. That was the first time he ever called me Bubbie. It's a term of endearment in Jewish, you know, like sweetie pie or my little chickadee.

We also went to the Thousand Islands, like the dressing. It's where we saw Bolt Castle, a very sad story. This Bolt fellow came over from Germany and made a fortune. When he fell in love and got married, he decided to build a castle for his wife. Unfortunately, she died before the castle was finished and the poor man didn't have the heart to complete it.

You can still see the ruins, the most beautiful staircase. I have a photo of Sid on a stone bench with his hands clasped around one knee. A turret is in the background. He's wearing a tie and hat, a homburg with the brim snapped forward, and trying to look like a man-about-town.

As it turned out, Sid never did get his own place on

Cortlandt. He was a radio operator in the Pacific fleet during the war, then went to City College on the GI bill. Try-Mo wanted him back after the war, but Sid thought it would be safer to get a teaching degree. We now had Dewey—he was born just before Bataan and nursed until Corregidor—and Zoot was on the way.

Do you know the school where Sid taught was named for Samuel Gompers? He was a Dutch Jew, the head of the cigar makers. In the old days, there were thousands of people making cigars by hand in New York City, but then the machines came along and replaced them.

CHAPTER 6

A STRING OF FINE PEARLS

I may not be a mind reader, but I know exactly what you're thinking. Sid is supposed to withdraw our nest egg from Sun Bank and wave goodbye as Arlee Sparlow flies off with every last cent to join Gauguin in Tahiti. Well, my dears, you couldn't be more wrong.

Actually, Sid did withdraw the money when our CD came due at the end of January 1982. But he moved all $25,809 of it into a money market at Southland, where we had our checking. He wanted it to be handy for when he was ready to take the plunge.

Southland was happy to have our additional business and gave us a six-inch, black-and-white Sony in appreciation. (You needed a magnifying glass to see the picture.) We also got Checking Plus for our old account, which would let us write checks for up to $1,500 over the balance.

The bank was in a white wooden building with columns in front that made it look like a plantation house. There used to be two hitching posts by the drive-in window until Kitty's maid, Birdella, an excellent worker from Palm Bay, mentioned something to her. The jockeys had already been painted white, but Kitty and Birdella picketed in the driveway for three days until the bank agreed to replace them with a pair of extruded-plastic flamingos.

The Bible teaches us that he who maketh haste to be rich shall not be innocent. All I can say to that is amen. Not that I was thinking of such things come February. I was happy to see Sid happy. If only he'd stop treating me like one of his students at Gompers whenever I brought up the subject of buying a Hacienda near my friends.

"We have to put our money to work for us, Bubbie. You can't just pull down the shade and make inflation go away."

"We don't even have shades, Sid. We have blinds."

"I'm only pointing out that we shouldn't put ourselves at the mercy of a government pension. If we lock ourselves in an iron lung, we'll forget how to breathe on our own."

Now for the $64,000 question: Who do you think was Sid's speech writer? Yes, sirree, he'd sponge up Arlee's words each day, then squeeze them out for my benefit. Sometimes he'd even drag me to Spaceport Plaza to get the gospel first hand.

Arlee was always the perfect gentleman, holding the chair for me and observing the other niceties. As soon as he saw me coming through the door, he'd roll down his shirtsleeves and grab his white suit jacket from the coat rack on the wall—a rack of antlers, actually. He always

45

wore white suits, whatever the season. I think he got them from a Cuban fellow in Miami, a custom tailor around the corner from the jai alai frontón.

I took Arlee a bag of homemade hamantaschen when we visited him the day after Purim—it was late February that year. He couldn't thank me enough. He loved the prune-filled ones best, but Sid wouldn't let him enjoy them in peace.

"She won't stop nit-picking me," he said. "She's a nay-sayer. This property is too rickety, the other one's too noisy. Tell her, Arlee, she doesn't understand."

I cut in before Arlee had a chance to tell me anything.

"You're darn right, I don't understand. I wouldn't live in any of those dumps if you paid me a million dollars."

"Nobody's asking you to live in them. Explain it to her, Arlee. Real estate is an investment where you have to nurture value back into a property."

Arlee brushed the crumbs off his pants and made a T sign, like the coach does when he's asking for a timeout.

"You're absolutely right, ma'am. Take this property on Poinsettia Place in Coco. It's a poor excuse for a house in the present condition, but once it's restored, goodness, you won't recognize it. Real estate is like a string of fine pearls. It grows more valuable with the years."

"My mother used to say pearls don't make a necklace, Mr. Sparlow—the thread does."

"Arlee, if you please."

What a talker. I'd look for any excuse to escape the sales pitch. Healthercise, Aquacise, Pluckers. I'd even go to Hooshman, my Iranian dentist, for a cleaning. He had a good hygienist, Jolene. She was left-handed, but that didn't make a difference. Of course my favorite hideout was the House of Aloha. I could tip my head back in the sink and let Annette wash my cares away.

"You've got such beautiful hair, honey, and your skin is as soft as a baby's behind. Does Sid ever call you Doll Face?"

"Stop making me laugh, Annette. You're a real artist, even when you're just shampooing me."

"Don't give me that. All I have is good beauty skills from doing a lot of hair."

The House of Aloha was a hole in the wall with only two beauticians' chairs, one manicure table, and a bubble-top dryer. Annette had the chair in front, next to the cash register and the bronze hula-girl floor lamp. She wasn't much older than my boys, but we hit it off right away. One look from her and I would open my heart as if we'd known each other since Adam and Eve.

"What's wrong, Selma? Don't tell me it's Sid again."

"God only knows why I'm bothering with this. He has eyes for only one person, and it's not yours truly. Maybe I should be having my head examined instead."

"Just leave your head to me, honey. How about new lashes? If you want to look your best, you can never afford to have tired lashes."

If I were in her shoes, I'd have lost ten pounds. She was always falling out of her clothes. Everything was two sizes too small, all of it except for Annette herself and her Madame Pompadour. You should have seen her do the hula. No, on second thought, maybe you shouldn't.

Do you know hula dancing used to be very popular after the war? There was a band leader named Johnny Pineapple. Once I took a hula lesson with Sid in the mountains. I can still do it. Sid learned the first part, where you wave to the earth and the sky, and then he got lost.

But back to business. All Sid wanted to talk about that spring was the two-bedroom on Poinsettia. Arlee thought we could get it for $27,895. It needed a little TLC, but the place was a steal. Sid took me to Coco to see it after our Seder at the temple. To be honest, it looked like a dump.

"Try to have an open mind," Sid said on the drive home. "Imagine the possibilities."

"I do have an open mind, but I don't have a drafty one."

Like a starfish on an oyster shell, he wore me down. In the end, we didn't have to pay the full asking price. And Sid arranged for us to assume the old mortgage, an FHA at eight percent, which meant he had to withdraw only $20,410 from our money market for the closing in April.

Sid decided to do the TLC himself to save money. I'll bet he spent ten hours a day on Poinsettia Place, hammering and sawing, painting, hanging sheetrock, the whole kit and caboodle. Even so, he had to withdraw another $5,405 from Southland to pay for the material, leaving us with only a few dollars in the money market.

He painted the shutters lavender. It was the exact same color as the streamers that used to fly from the Maypole on Stone Avenue when Kitty, Rose, and I were little. One year we made costumes out of crepe paper—Kitty was Mother Goose; Rose and I were her little geese. Well, the paint on the house was barely dry before three hungry buyers were bidding against one other.

"Lord, I've got them fighting like a pack of wild dogs with a bone," Arlee called to say.

We ended up getting $43,750, almost a thousand over our asking price. This was in May 1982, not quite a year and a half after our arrival in Florida. After the legal fees, broker's commission, termite inspection, and all the other dribs and drabs, Sid walked away with a net profit of $7,352. The only thing he'd lost was twelve pounds. He was so busy fixing up that old dump that junk-food stocks nearly crashed on Wall Street.

All right, my fears about the handyman special had come to naught. Everything went like clockwork and now we had $33,225 in the money market. Southland even raised our Checking Plus line to $2,500 and gave us a Visa Gold card with a $5,000 credit limit. So there! I was wrong and Sid was right. I'm big enough to admit it. But I couldn't help thinking of what my father used to tell me when I was full of myself. Even a broken clock is right twice a day.

CHAPTER 7

THE THREE MUSKETEERS

Kitty looked like the Hanging Gardens of Babylon that June when she met Rose and me for lunch at Mo Bialer's Jewish Riviera. She was wearing her Princess Galitzine palazzo pants and a Lilly Pulitzer blouse that had more orchids than a hot house.

As usual, Kitty was making a political as well as a fashion statement. Pinned to the collar of the blouse was her Porky Pig button: It's Not Kosher to be a Male Chauvinist Pig. Her daughter, Myra, had gotten the button from another divorcée in her empowerment group and given it to Kitty for Mother's Day.

Liberated or not, Kitty could be as vain about her appearance as any girl in *Earl Carroll's Vanities*. Of course, I was the last person to criticize her on this point. The Bible tells us beauty is vain, but I don't buy any of that. If it's a sin to take care of yourself, I'm a sinner.

Mo Bialer, the owner and maître d', led us to a booth in back, the one next to the mural of Mayor Koch climbing up the side of the Empire State Building. You know, like King Kong, except he had Bella Abzug in his arms instead of Fay Wray. I guess that was supposed to make it a New York deli, two politicians with big mouths.

Mo handed us the menus. You wouldn't believe it to look at his pot belly, but he'd been a lightweight in the ring. The high point of his career came when Barney Ross knocked him out in the second. Mo was a good puncher, but he broke his hand on the champ's head.

"The soup is mushroom and barley, ladies. I have some very nice brisket today and the pot roast is nice, too, also the stuffed cabbage."

Mo had a deli on Fordham Road in the Bronx before retiring to Coco Beach. After a year of watching the palm trees sway, he came out of retirement and bought the lease from the widow of the previous owner. It used to be called Delancey Street. Rose heard somewhere that Fleishman, the fellow who had it before Mo, died of a malignant melanoma—on his crotch, of all places. I don't know, maybe he was a nudist.

"How are your blintzes today, Mo?"

"Fine, Selma, how are yours?"

"Listen to him," said Kitty. "He thinks he's Henny Youngman. Well, I don't find these prices very amusing. This is nuts—six ninety-five for the brisket?"

"It's a very big sandwich," Mo said.

"Maybe bigger than my appetite."

"Come on, Kitty," I said. "Don't give him a hard time."

"Oh, what the hell! If I have to pay six ninety-five, I'll have the pastrami."

I ordered the blintzes with sour cream. Rose was having an allergic reaction to poison ivy and had only a cup of soup. She'd been pulling up weeds in a flower box and forgot to wear gloves.

"I got it in my eyes and nasal passages," she said. "If you have chronic postnasal drip, this is a nightmare. I had to get a cortisone injection to suppress the immune system. It's a miracle drug, but you have to watch for cortisone rebound."

Rose dressed like an old lady in mourning whenever her spirits were low. This time, it was a faded black knit dry-cleaned to death at Lady DuBarry, Sol's old business in Yonkers. She hadn't even bothered to put on the Pucci pin he'd just gotten her at the Kennedy Space Center. It was red, white, and blue, like the emblem Pucci designed for Apollo 15.

"I'm nervous about Sol," Rose said. "He's been blowing up like a balloon since we got to Florida. It could be low-thyroid function. You have to take dried cattle thyroid or thyroxine, the synthetic. If the autoimmune system is involved, it may be Hashimoto's disease. Or is it Kawasaki's?"

As far as I could see, Sol just ate too much. He'd never been the runt of the litter. The only time I ever saw him skinny was when he got home from the war—he and Leo had been with the Fifth Army in Sicily—but it didn't take him long to grow back into his civvies.

Sol had joined Lox et Veritas, the big eaters of Pelican Pond, right after Mayflower unloaded the cartons. In a few months, he was looking like a sumo wrestler on a binge in the Ginza. I don't know about the others, but Sol was a gourmand, not a gourmet, no matter what he thought. Miss Cowper, our old English teacher, always insisted on the distinction.

If he wasn't eating, Sol was ruining the meal for everyone else by lighting up a cigar. Not at home, of course. Rose wouldn't let him smoke in there even if cigars had more vitamin C than grapefruits. She didn't want his ashes messing up all her mahogany furniture. She was very fastidious, too much so in my opinion.

Well, it didn't take a genius to see that there was something on my mind, too. You had to put a cage around Kitty to keep her away from a bowl of pickles, but even she noticed.

"Why the long face, Selma?" she asked, spearing the last half-sour in the bowl. "Did somebody take away your bag of M&M's?"

I tried to smile, but it was like smiling with chapped lips.

"I've had it with being ignored, Kitty, especially when the other woman isn't even a woman. Do you want to hear the latest act from *Les Misérables*? Now Sid has his eyes set on a dilapidated town house in Eau Gallie. It's next to the Oracle of Delphi."

"The what?"

"You know, that new Greek restaurant *The Orbiter* liked so much."

Instead of sympathy, all I got from Kitty was her joke about the Greek tailor. You rip-a-dese, you men-a-dese. She thought she was hilarious. Before long, she was doubled over and choking on her pastrami. Well, if worse came to worst, there was a sign for the Heimlich maneuver on the wall next to Mayor Koch.

"Leo's driving me nuts, too," she said after taking a sip of Cel-Ray soda. "He's a perpetual motion machine. All he wants to do is run from one hardware store to another, checking out the merchandise: What's new? What's old? What's selling? Who's talking deals?"

The truth is Leo retired from the hardware business too soon. He wasn't ready to hand over the three Seligman's Home Beautiful stores to Myra and put himself out to pasture. I think it bothered him most that the business was more successful than ever with Myra in charge.

She'd always been handy with tools, even as a child. She was only ten when she made *Light Queen Esther's Crown* for the Purim festival at our temple in Yonkers. You had to throw the ball into Esther's mouth to make the crown light up.

When Leo wasn't tripping over his size-twelve shoes at Ace or True Value, he was on the phone with Myra. He still knew the location of every nut and bolt in the inventory, and he wanted a status report on each one. Leo couldn't understand why she didn't appreciate his help.

"Poor Leo," Kitty said. "He's like a broken record: He built that business up from one single store all by himself. Now, all of a sudden, she's the boss and he's the sidekick. Where does she get off treating him like Gabby Hayes? And so on and so forth."

Mo came back with our checks and complimented

54

Kitty on her blouse. He said Ruby Keeler had one just like it in *Footlight Parade*, and that got her talking about her career as a dancer. I have a wonderful story to tell you about her, Kitty Seligman, though she was still Nussbaum back in those days.

CHAPTER 8

ISN'T IT ROMANTIC?

It was the Depression and Kitty was taking dance lessons for twenty-five cents each, thanks to the WPA. I was still at home with my mother, but Kitty was living like a gypsy on the Upper West Side. She had to share a bathroom with eight other girls and got only half a shelf to herself at the bottom of the fridge—or was it still an icebox?

This was before she'd ever danced at Radio City. What happened was she heard something from somebody, a friend of a friend who had it from another friend, an Armenian girl, if I'm not mistaken. One thing led to another and, lo and behold, Kitty had a show.

She filled me in over lunch at the old Automat on Broadway, the one in the Forties. That's where Kitty ate all the time. She used to love the codfish cakes and creamed spinach, but if things were tight, you could have coffee and a roll for only a dime.

"We're doing ballet, Selma. I'm getting thirty-five bucks and a pair of brand-new toe shoes every week.

Christ, I almost crapped in my leotards when I got called out."

I looked around to see if anybody was listening. It could be embarrassing being with somebody who had a mouth like that. Anyway, I congratulated Kitty on her new job, only to find out that she'd already borrowed on God only knows how many weeks' wages to buy a sable wrap at Best & Company.

Sable, no less! I made an innocent remark about how much it must have cost her, and she jumped down my throat. Everybody in the Automat heard.

"I'll thank you to mind your own business, Selma. It's my money. For Christ's sake, why should I dress like a farmer from Oshkosh?"

"Keep your voice down, Kitty. So where will you be tripping the light fantastic?"

"You won't believe. It's the old Apollo at Times Square, where Merman, Durante, Bolger, all the big names played. Of course, we're just the opening act, the warm-up."

"Well, who else is on the bill?"

"The only thing they told us is we'll be doing a scene from *Sleeping Beauty*. You know, real class."

I didn't see Kitty for a week while the ballet girls rehearsed at a dance studio near Columbus Circle. They didn't actually set foot in the Apollo until opening night when one of the producers picked them up at the rehearsal studio and dropped them off at the stage door around back.

I had a double-entry class that evening and couldn't

go—Mr. Wolfowitz wanted me to fill in whenever the bookkeeper was out. So I didn't know what I missed until the next morning when Kitty called the shoe store to acquaint me with the details.

It turns out the ballet girls were given a dressing room upstairs—"Our own goddamn dressing room!"—so they didn't see any of the other acts until Kitty and the rest were called down to take their places.

"There were six of us to one side and six to the other as the overture began. We bourréed out and the audience went wild. I never heard such a racket. You would have thought one of the girls had fallen out of her tutu."

Kitty laughed, a belly laugh like the ones Sid used to make before the Disaster robbed him of his sense of humor, among other things. I could hear her put a coin in the box—there was a pay phone in the hall where she lived.

"So, we were breaking in threes to turn before going off stage," Kitty went on. "There we were, en pointe, and—Christ Almighty!—you'll never imagine what we saw waiting in the wings."

She left me hanging for a few seconds.

"Boobs! There were boobs all over the place! Do you know what the famous Apollo Theater now is? A burlesque house. They put us on to warm up the crowd for a bunch of strippers."

"No! I don't believe it."

"Believe me, Selma. Christ, we practically fell off our toes. Now I could make out what the audience was hollering. Take it off! Take it off! My God, we finished turning and got the hell out of there."

As the ballet girls ran off stage and the strippers ran on, the orchestra switched gears—from Tchaikovsky to the bump-and-grind.

Well, three of the girls left the show as soon as they learned what it was. They had boyfriends and the ultimatums came: Quit immediately or the wedding is off or the engagement is over or everything is finished. Nowadays, there's worse every night of the week on cable, but it was different then.

I'd like to report that the experience taught Kitty a lesson. This wasn't the case. I would have been out the stage door as soon as the truth dawned on me—or at least as soon as I'd paid off the sable wrap. Kitty saw things otherwise. Not only did she stay, but she took up cigarettes. Not smoking, mind you, just cigarettes. The smoke made her wheeze, so she walked around with a long cigarette holder and an unlit cigarette.

Kitty was still at the Apollo when she met Leo. He was working at his father's hardware store in Manhattan, learning the business from the ground floor. It was called Seligman & Son in those days. They met one weekend on the Broadway trolley. He was an Ichabod Crane type, all neck and arms and legs. I think he tripped into her as the car made a jerky stop. Kitty couldn't wait to tell me about him.

"He's scrawnier than a turkey that nobody wanted for Thanksgiving. Don't ask me why, but I'm nuts about the guy. As soon as he took his glasses off and looked at me, zing went the strings of my heart."

Naturally, Leo wanted to see Kitty dance, which was the last thing she needed. She tried to put him off—she didn't want him to find out about the strippers —but she was running out of excuses. What she finally did was tell him she worked across the river at a show in Hoboken, but that didn't put an end to it.

"Now he wants to come to Hoboken and see me dance. I keep telling him no. Why should you go all the way out there? I'll meet you when I come out of the Tubes. So every night, I run into the subway after the show, race downtown to where the trains come in from Jersey, then run upstairs to meet him. I'm ready to collapse, and he's all raring to go."

As luck would have it, she got a call from Radio City after a few weeks of this—she and the Armenian girl had auditioned to be extras. Now Kitty didn't have to sneak around anymore and Leo could wait for her with the stage door Johnnies. This was 1935 or '36, if I remember, a few years after the Music Hall opened.

It so happens that there was also a little monkey business involved when Rose met Sol. Actually, I was the one who brought the two love birds together. The Bible says there's nothing new under the sun, but I never heard another story like this one.

What occurred was I had a blind date with Sol a month or two before I met Sid. He was nice enough, but he was overweight even then and every pore of his body reeked of cigar smoke. He was already beginning to lose his hair, too, though he was only a few years older than Sid.

I met him through the Perlmutters, who owned the candy store downstairs. We couldn't afford a phone at home until I went to work for Ansonia, but they used to let us get calls in the store. Mr. Perlmutter would go into the alley and yell up if there was someone on the line for us.

You can't imagine how poor we were when I was little. If we were lucky, there might be a quarter of a chicken on Friday. I'd get the leg and skin and my parents would share the rest. There was no hot water and the toilet was in the hallway. But we did have an icebox to keep things cold in the summer. My mother would buy a nickel or dime block, depending on how hot it was. The water used to drip down the drain all night as the ice melted.

As I was saying, the Perlmutters knew Sol's family and served as the matchmakers. He took me into the city to see a Bette Davis movie—*Jezebel*. People were always telling me I looked like her. In fact, three people in the theater tapped my shoulder to remark on my profile. I could have passed for her in a crowd scene if I painted my lips up to the nostrils and brushed on a tube of eye liner.

After the movie, we went for egg creams at Auster's. Sol's cigar was smelling up the place and Mendy made him put it out. He was the Auster who could play Rimsky-Korsakov on the violin and piano at the same time. He used his toes for the piano part.

"Now this is an egg cream," Sol said after licking his lips. "It's the most famous egg cream in America. People come from all over to get the formula, but it's a family secret. They seal the back off when the syrup is being made."

As he walked me home from the subway station in Brownsville, Sol tried to educate me about the dry cleaning business. There were four methods of stain removal—

solvent action, lubrication, chemicals, and digestion. The spotter starts with the solvent and moves on from there to the next one, ad nauseam, until the stain breaks down. I yawned in hopes he would change the subject, but Sol wasn't the man to take a hint, if there is such a man.

"Do you know why dry cleaning is called dry, Selma?"

I shook my head, which only encouraged him. The dry cleaner, he said, uses a liquid with no water in it, a solvent called perk, something that can be both dry and liquid at the same time.

"Unlike water, the universal solvent, perk doesn't make your colors bleed or run," Sol said. "And it won't shrink the fabric or wash away pleats."

Why is it that talking has to be a one-way street for the male of the species? As we reached my building on Livonia, Sol took me by the elbow and leaned forward. I gritted my teeth, but instead of kissing me he stubbed out his cigar in the planter we had by the front stoop.

Well, Sol called me a couple of months later, but I was already seeing Sid. Anyway, Sol wasn't my idea of young Lochinvar—or Rose's either, or so I thought, which only goes to show.

I'd already given Rose the lowdown on my date with Sol, leaving no stone unturned. She was very sympathetic, agreeing that smoking was a disgusting habit and giving me a lecture about smoker's cough and other complications involving the upper-respiratory system.

So what do you think happened when I told her Sol had called me again and I'd turned him down? You'll never guess. She suggested I pass her number on to him! You think you know someone and then a thing like this happens. I guess she felt left out, the last fish out of the water.

Sol took Rose to the 1939 World's Fair at Flushing Meadows on their first date. He wanted to see the GM Futurama—he always liked science—but she was more curious about the girls buried in the ice. You could see them shaking in there from the cold. As Rose and Sol came out of the subway on the way home, he was expounding on jelly stains.

"I'll bet you don't know why dry cleaning is called dry," he said as they turned onto Sutter Avenue. "It's because—"

"Because the dry cleaner uses a liquid without water in it," Rose interrupted. "That's how something can be both dry and liquid at the same time."

So two hearts went pitter-patter. And love turned out to be the universal solvent.

CHAPTER 9

THE PROPHET OF DOOM

Sid was a true believer. He and Arlee saw everything alike, two eyes in the same head. And like all true believers, Sid wanted to convert the world. He should have gone to work for the Jehovah's Witnesses, the ones who knock on your door the moment you get in the tub.

It was autumn when we went to Mercury Marquee with Rose and Sol for one of the *Star Wars* movies. I think it was the one where Luke Skywalker learns that what's-his-name, the fellow in the mask, is actually his father, or maybe it was the next one.

We were in their Ford Taurus later, guys in front and dolls in back. Sid had lost a good twenty pounds, but Sol looked like King Kamehameha after a big luau. He'd grown from a Portly to an Xtra Xtra Portly at Big Boy's since arriving in Florida a year and a half ago.

As we got to the Indian River, Rose was going on about how the world was full of troubles—I think Princess Grace had just died from the car crash—and then Sol said something about how he'd rather eat himself to death than go all of a sudden like that. If I remember, we were on the Eau Gallie Causeway when Sid began pestering Sol about real estate.

"In this economy, you can't just roll over and play dead, Sol."

"If I want to gamble, I'll drive up to Dog Track Road in Sanford and bet on the hounds."

"It's not gambling if you look at the entire equation. You examine each property very carefully and consider the market: Are we at the apex? Are we on the downside?"

"My money is very happy where it is in the Windsor Fund, Sid, or it would be if I could only get my hands on all of it. Garfinkle was late again with the interest payment."

Did I mention that Sol had sold Lady DuBarry, his dry-cleaning business, to a young fellow named Garfinkle, the spotter at Chez Paulette in New Rochelle? It was an installment sale, but Garfinkle was having trouble with the payments.

Sid was still going strong—he was like a Jerry Lewis telethon—when we stopped by Mo Bialer's for a snack on the way home.

"Use your imagination, Sol. A man of your experience can do better than a mutual fund."

"I want to put my feet up and watch the grass grow. I washed my hands of aggravation when I retired. Or I thought I did. Garfinkle always has an excuse. It's Reagan's fault or Wall Street or whatever. The truth is he doesn't know his ass from his elbow. I can't wait until the three years are up and I'm rid of that albatross."

Mo stopped by the booth to talk to Sid about a property in Rockledge. I think Mo's bad hand was hurting him—that happened whenever it was going to rain— and he was complaining again about how hands weren't made for hitting people in the head, especially not somebody like Barney Ross with a rock for a head.

All of us had sponge cake and decaf except Sol, who ordered a pastrami sandwich—or tried to. Rose was usually the Cowardly Lion, but she had a voice on her when the subject came to health.

"Do you want to eat yourself into the grave, Sol? Stop acting like a child in a candy store."

"I'm tired of being a grown-up. For forty years, I had to get up at dawn and open the shop by seven. It's time to enjoy myself. I want to hear my arteries hardening."

"Look in the mirror, Sol. Tell me the truth. Do you like what you see?"

"I don't want to be a movie star. Maybe what Hollywood needs is more large, bald, fat men. In other words, reality."

Rose kept at him until Sol changed his order from pastrami to babka. He ate the cake in about two seconds, then stuck a cigar in his mouth and waited for the rest of us. Rose was reminding him that Mo didn't allow cigar smoke at the tables when all of a sudden Sol saw Bernstein sitting in the booth in front of ours.

Bernstein was on a renal diet, but he always came to the Jewish Riviera the night before his dialysis and ordered a hot pastrami sandwich. It was the worst thing for him, a killer, but everything would be flushed out of his system the next day, so why not?

Anyway, Bernstein took a bite of his sandwich and chewed it very slowly. He was in heaven. I don't have to tell you where Sol was. He looked like Tantalus, the guy who stood in the midst of plenty, but wasn't allowed to have any of it. Sol couldn't contain himself.

"What's that garbage you're putting in your mouth?" he shouted over to Bernstein. "I hope you're not going to tell me that's a pastrami sandwich."

"It's an excellent sandwich." Bernstein picked up his plate and held it out to Sol. "Here, smell that aroma. Ambrosia!"

"Get that dreck out of my face. You call that pastrami? That's not the pastrami I grew up with." Fortunately, Mo was in the kitchen and didn't hear. It was just sour grapes, of course.

Bernstein withdrew the plate to the safety of his own booth and took another bite. His hair was standing on end as usual, as if he had a finger stuck in the electric outlet.

"I don't know where you grew up," he said to Sol over his shoulder, "but I have a feeling your memories of pastrami are better than the original."

Didn't somebody once say a wise man eats to live, but a fool lives to eat? Well, food got us off the subject of real estate, be it ever so briefly.

A few weeks later—November 1982—Sid had a tête-à-tête with Leo at one of my space brunches. It was another shuttle, Columbia this time. Somebody from Mission Control was discussing Goddard, the father of modern rocketry, when I turned on the TV in the living room.

I'd made lasagna for brunch. I got the recipe from Annette—it was her father-in-law's favorite. I was able to buy most of the ingredients at Albertson's, but Rocky let me have the fresh mozzarella and Italian sausages from his kitchen at cost. The thing that made Annette's recipe so special was you added a cup of red wine to the tomato sauce.

"I'll stick with hardware," Leo was saying as I carried out the hot dish with my pelican potholders—Rose made them for me at Chat-n-Sew. "I promised Myra to plow my share of the profits back in the business."

"You can't put all your eggs in one basket," Sid said. "Especially not when America is suffering from Reaganitis."

"It's what I know best. I had a heart-to-heart talk with Myra to make sure she was serious. In ten years, I said, do you see yourself in the hardware business? I knew her answer would be yes, but I had to ask."

"Real estate is something you can depend on in troubled times, Leo. The retail business is like musical chairs. You don't want to be left without a chair when the music stops."

Sid's mouth was so busy, I had to reheat his plate twice in the micro. Leo was craning his neck around, looking for somebody else to talk with. Unfortunately, Sol was in the bathroom and Rose was lecturing Kitty and me about a new orthopedic shoe for hammertoes.

"I know what you're saying, Sid, but I promised Myra. I just wish she'd pay more attention. You try to tell her something and she doesn't hear a word. If she knows so much, how come every guy she dates turns out to be a toches cowboy?"

Kitty's ears perked up. "What a load of crap," she said. "Give her a little time, will you?"

Leo ignored her. "My life would be complete if I could see Myra settled before I pass on," he said to Sid. "Speaking of which, how's that boy of yours, the musical one? Does he intend to settle down anytime soon?"

"Zoot's doing just fine, thank you."

"Myra likes jazz, too. She has all the Ella Fitzgeralds, two shelves of them."

Poor Sid! People kept changing the subject on him. Anyway, he flipped two more handyman specials in 1982, the town house in Eau Gallie and a condominium on the water in Palm Bay. He made $6,750 on the town house and $8,775 on the condo.

For the uninitiated, flipping is when you buy a place, fix it up and sell it for a quick profit, then buy another to flip, and so on and so forth, until you get to the pot of gold at the end of the rainbow.

Everything was moving so fast, too fast for me to take it all in. It was like that scene in *I Love Lucy* where the conveyor belt speeds up in the candy factory and she can't keep up and has to stuff the chocolates in her mouth.

If only Sid had paid half as much attention to me as he did to his cockamamie investments. It was a chilly winter for yours truly. You didn't have to read Kinsey to know this wasn't normal.

Once Sid came into the bathroom—the one attached to our master bedroom—while I was soaking in the tub and singing "How Deep Is the Ocean." I think he was looking for his aftershave. I had an idea. I lifted myself out of the Mr. Bubble, rising from the foam like Aphrodite, but he didn't give me a second glance, or a first.

I worked hard to look good. A thing of beauty may be a joy forever, but only on the days you work at it. Every day was a struggle. And what did it get me? I could have been made out of cellophane from the way he stared right through me.

"I don't know why I'm bothering with my estrogen," I told Kitty on the way to the House of Aloha one day in November. "I might as well let myself wither away."

"Stop whining, Selma. An old broad like you should have had her fill of sex by now. You ought to heave a sigh of relief and be done with it."

"An old broad? In case you've forgotten, my dear, I'm six months younger than you."

"Excuse me, Baby Snooks. Consider yourself lucky. You could have been born a rabbit and you'd be pregnant for life."

Financially speaking, Sid seemed to know what he was doing. He made a nice profit on each real-estate deal. By the middle of December, we had $48,847 in our money market at Southland. Crabbe, the bank manager, wrote to say he was extending us Ready Credit in gratitude for our patronage. Now we could borrow $10,000 just by writing checks. This showed his confidence in us, not that we had any need for more credit.

I was also growing confident in Sid's business acumen, even if I still had a question or two about where all this was heading.

"Do we need so much, Sid? Why can't we stop while we're ahead?"

"You can't turn back the clock, Bubbie. If it were up to you, the human race would still be crawling on all fours."

"All I know is it's wrong to be too greedy."

"Why do I waste my time trying to explain things to you? You're a prophet of doom. You fought me every step of the way. Where would we be now if I'd listened to you?"

"In a Hacienda on the pond near my friends, where I wanted to be in the first place."

A couple of days before New Year's Eve, Sid invited Arlee over to our place for coffee and cake. Sid wanted to celebrate a successful year of investing and plan for the next one. I was going to bake applesauce nut bread, but Arlee insisted on bringing a strawberry shortcake from Chez Gourmet at Moonwalk Mall in Melbourne.

"You shouldn't have," I said.

"Just a trifle for the pretty lady."

"Here, let me take your jacket."

Arlee hesitated, then handed it over. Maybe he was embarrassed by his suspenders. There were green turtles going up one shoulder and brown pelicans down the other. Be that as it may, all our profits were now in the bank and Sid was itchy to buy a more substantial property.

"I'm ready for a multifamily, Arlee, instead of just hopping from house to house."

He had his eye on an apartment building in Melbourne Beach. Unfortunately, the down payment would take every penny in our money market. And where would he find money for the TLC, except from our joint checking account?

"I don't like the sound of this," I broke in. "Your eyes are getting too big for your wallet."

"We can't play it safe, Bubbie. We have to go out on a limb and shake the money tree."

"I was always led to believe that money doesn't grow on trees, Sid."

"That way of thinking will get us nowhere. Tell her, Arlee—it's the right thing."

Arlee put his cup down and collected his thoughts. I took a breath and waited for the worst—the two of them ganging up on me as usual—but I had a pleasant surprise.

"I don't want to throw cold water on you, Sid. I like a man who's full of himself, but a mistake gets mighty expensive in today's marketplace."

"My pockets are deep enough, Arlee."

"Trust me, Sid. You know what the cowboys say: there ain't no horse that can't be rode and no man than can't be throwed. I have an idea. Just give me some time to let it percolate."

CHAPTER 10

'ONE FINGER SNAP'

If I remember from Miss Cowper, it was Shakespeare who said a thankless child could sting you sharper than a serpent's tooth. I'm no expert on reptiles, other than the two-legged variety, but I have more than enough knowledge of ungrateful children.

A few days after Mr. Sparlow's visit, our youngest boy, Zoot, honored us with his presence. He had a gig in the vicinity and managed to fit Sid and me into his busy schedule. What happened was the *Royale*, a ship sailing out of Cape Canaveral, had a jazz cruise for New Year's with three bands—Dixieland, be-bop, and blues. You left Port Canaveral before dinner on New Year's Eve 1982 and returned after brunch on New Year's Day 1983.

It gets a bit complicated here, but all you need to know is that Zoot's booking office in New York arranged for him to be a sub in the be-bop band. The tenor, a guy from Yonkers named Digger Landman, had to have root canal. As luck would have it, Zoot had a few hours to spare from the time his ship docked at the Cape to when People Express was leaving the Orlando airport for New York.

I wanted him to spend the night with us. It hurt to see the boys' room going to waste, especially since I was changing the sheets regularly on the twin beds and dry-cleaning the embroidered spreads, the matching pair my mother made for us when we moved to Yonkers.

But Zoot had better things to do, a gig in Philly with a hip lady who played with both hands at the same end of the piano. She drove for the Hound—the upper Allegheny route—when she wasn't doing jazz music.

Well, Zoot graciously permitted us to wine and dine him at Bernard's Surf, the restaurant in Coco Beach with its own fleet of fishing boats. Sid loved the food there, but he couldn't keep his hands off the onion rolls and would have gas all night long.

It's a good thing the dress code was casual. Zoot had on a pair of jeans from the Civil War and a faded work shirt with holes at the elbows. If ever there was a creature of habit, that was Zoot. His Earth Shoes must have been resoled a dozen times—you couldn't buy them any-more—and his red beard was down to his bellybutton.

Anyway, Zoot ordered the seafood platter. God only knows where he found room after all the stuff they serve you on a ship; maybe he had a tapeworm. No sooner was the food on the table than Zoot and his father were at each other's throats. This time it started when Zoot told us he'd bought a new tenor.

"You paid over five hundred when you traded up from the Mark VII to the Yamaha three months ago," Sid said. "You were raving about the Japanese technology."

"Hey, will you get off my case? So the Yamaha turned out to be a crappy horn, but this new Yanagasawa is definitely there. Whatever they put in the metal, the stuff is right on the head."

"Zoot, you have to grow up one of these days and be more responsible. If you saved your money, you wouldn't have to worry about where the next meal was coming from."

"Give me a break. I'm more into make-it-now, spend-it-now. I made plenty on this gig. You should have heard me. I did this Herbie Hancock tune, 'One Finger Snap.' It was a modal thing with a few changes, but the pace was furious. The bass player was staring at me like I was a monster."

Sid couldn't exchange five words with either boy, Zoot or Dewey, without the atom splitting. Well, it didn't take long for Sid to bring the conversation around to another one of his pet subjects, the benefits of employment in the school system.

"You could start at thirty thousand with your master's in music. If you want, I'll call Guerrini, the new principal at Gompers. They had something on him in *New York Teacher*."

"Look, I get off on what I do, okay? I worked with some great people on the boat. The drummer's been gigging around for over twenty years. He played with Freddie Hubbard; he played with Kenny Burrell. Man, he's been with everybody."

I have an idea. Maybe if Zoot had been more successful at playing jazz, he wouldn't have worked so hard at playing the part. Anyway, he was swearing he was just a finger snap away from the big time when he noticed me trying to change the subject.

"Hey, Mama, how's it shaking?" he said.

"I don't want to butt in, Zoot, but Leo was just asking us the other day if you ever see Myra. She's running the three hardware stores by herself now."

"Not that again," he groaned, rolling his eyes and reaching for the bread basket. "Will you two stop busting my chops?"

When the boys were babies, my mother used to tell me that raising a child was like cooking a fish—too much poking would spoil it. Well, that may be true, but I was always a poker.

"She has a nice smile, don't you think?" I said.

"I would too if I had a hundred thousand bucks in my mouth."

"Don't be such a smart aleck," Sid jumped in. "Hardware is a good clean business, nuts and bolts, a nice inventory. She even likes music. You have a lot in common."

"How many times do I have to tell you? I'm not interested in a ball-buster like Myra Seligman or her damn hardware stores. And I don't need a matchmaker, you dig?"

"There's an old Jewish saying," I said. "A man without a wife is like soup without meat or vegetables. In other words, plain water."

The great musician pretended to be deaf. You know, Beethoven. It was obvious we wouldn't convert him that day. He could date a dozen girls, but he didn't know how to be close to one. It was like rock-and-roll, where the dancers never touch. I prefer the fox trot myself.

Did I mention that Myra was an only child? She was named for Kitty's brother, Ronnie—actually, Myron—

who died when his B-25 was shot down in the war. I don't want to stray too far afield, but the reason Kitty had just Myra was the RH factor. In those days, the doctors couldn't do anything. Actually, she had a second, a boy, but he had brain damage and lived only three days.

When Zoot was born, the doctor had to use forceps to pull him out. His head looked like a tube of toothpaste squeezed in the middle, but it straightened out in a few days. That's the way things were done then. I don't think there was any brain damage, but you never know.

One day Zoot came home from band class at Mark Twain, his junior high, with an old instrument turning green, his first saxophone. Smell it, Mom, smell it! He acted as if it were eau de cologne. In eighth grade, he played at a jitterbug dance and wore that old suit Sid had at Gay Blades. He rolled up the cuffs and folded over the sleeves, but it was still too wide and baggy. That's when he began calling himself Zoot—before, he was Nathaniel, for my father.

If only I could have taken him apart like a watch to find out what made him tick. He was so talented. You should have heard him at our twenty-fifth wedding anniversary in Yonkers. We had it at Patricia Murphy's, the room in back that the restaurant used for special occasions. The appetizer was stuffed cabbages and the entree was chicken Polonaise.

Zoot got the band, a bass player and a pianist in addition to himself. He did some jazzy tunes like "Embraceable You" and "Anything Goes," but he did them his way. There were so many wonderful songs, oldies ... memories, memories. He did the anniversary song, the one in three-quarter time, but then he switched to society time, a slow two, actually a medium fast four: Oh, how we danced on the night we were wed....

It was like a movie, 20th Century-Fox. For weeks, people would call me up to say how great it was. The food, the dancing, the entertainment! We were so proud of Zoot, such a talented boy and so very serious about his music. He'd practice for hours, until his lips were black and blue.

One summer he sold records at Sam Goody. All the customers loved him. He would have been a great success at music, too, if he'd put half that effort into selling himself. Well, who knows? Maybe he was afraid to try to sell himself and find out nobody was buying.

CHAPTER 11

YOU NEED A BIG SHOVEL

Not too long after we welcomed one prodigal son to the Space Coast, the other phoned Sid and me from *The Hollywood Reporter*, where he'd just begun doing the gossip. The lady who owned the paper didn't like people to tie up the office lines with personal calls, but Dewey had a mind of his own. A tongue of his own, too.

"She's a graduate of the Simon Legree School of Business," he said. "She acts like the paper's a plantation and we're her field hands."

This didn't sound like the start of a beautiful friendship, but it was Dewey all over again. He was incapable of staying in any job long enough for his desk chair to get warm. One year, he had to attach seven W-2 forms to his tax return.

Well, Dewey kept us on the line for over an hour with the latest from his gossip column, *Snoop*. He dropped so many names that I couldn't keep track. It was Robert E. Lee's birthday, a holiday for trash collectors in Florida, but there was more garbage on the phone than in the overloaded can stinking up our breezeway.

If I remember, Dewey had met Jackie Collins at a swanky place with calypso dancers and an all-girl saxophone band. She was going to put him in *Hollywood Wives*, or maybe the book after that. Joan Collins, the sister, snubbed what's her name or vice versa at Spago. And Zsa Zsa was getting divorced again—for the seventh time, what do you know?

"It's the shortest romance since Ernest Borgnine married Ethel Merman," Dewey said. "You have to scratch your head and ask: Does this dame have her act together?"

Seven husbands? My mother once said something about a couple living down the hall on Livonia: They both have love, he for himself and she for herself. She was a very sweet woman, but I'll bet that's where Dewey got his sarcasm.

Anyway, he tried to call Begelman the producer for an item in *Snoop* and the big shot was always too busy—at least that was the story. Dewey got the secretary ten or twelve times, but Begelman was never available to pick up the phone.

"I have more class under one fingernail than Begelman will ever have and I return my calls," Dewey said. "I'd like to see the look on his bloated face when he reads *Snoop* tomorrow."

"Begelman?" Sid asked. He was on the extension in the master bedroom.

"David Begelman. A thief, a forger, whatever. So what does the judge do? He sentences him to make a documentary on drugs. You and I would be in jail and Begelman makes a movie."

As usual, it didn't take long for the nitro and the glycerine to combine.

"I don't know why you waste your talents on such dreck," Sid said. "Is this what we sent you to NYU for? A master's degree in communications and you write a gossip column."

"I'm sorry if I haven't lived up to your expectations. It's great to know I've had all those wonderful talents and opportunities, and still haven't amounted to anything."

"I didn't say that. Your mother and I are very proud of you."

"You have a strange way of showing it. I work for *The Hollywood Reporter*, not *The Washington Post*. Begelman is big news here. It's the same as being at Justice and covering Ed Meese. You need a big shovel."

Sid switched gears at this point, reminding Dewey that we had a wonderful guest room with two twin beds just waiting for him and Fleur to bless with their presence. For an answer, we got that old line from Sam Goldwyn.

"In two words, im-possible. I'm wearing out my Rolodex right now and Fleur is decorating a beach house in Malibu. They want an indoor waterfall you can turn on from a remote in the Bentley. So we're up to our eyeballs. It's a grind if you're trying to put something away."

My ears perked up at that. Dewey and Fleur were saving for something.

"Dare I ask?" I said. "I hope this means you two will soon be having good news for us."

"Is that all you have on your mind?"

"The clock is ticking, Dewey. What is Fleur now, thirty-five? It's time to get serious."

"As I told you the last time and the time before that, we don't intend to contribute to the population explosion. I ought to make a tape so you can listen to it on instant replay."

"Where would you be if your father and I thought that way? Do you know what I think? You're two selfish people who don't want to inconvenience yourselves."

I know, I know. When a son gets married, he divorces his mother. As it turned out, Dewey and Fleur were saving for the down payment on a house of their own. They were renting in Marina del Rey, but Fleur wanted to get into the housing market before being priced out.

"You can't imagine what a house in any acceptable location goes for now," he said. "We saw one the size of a hat box last month, twelve hundred square feet in Brentwood, two small bedrooms, one and a half baths, very dark and very little yard. Guess how much?"

"A hundred thousand?" Sid asked. "One and a quarter?"

"You must be kidding. Six hundred, and it was gone in three weeks. What gives here? If you figure it out, call me."

Did I mention that Fleur was the financier of their household? She considered herself another J. P. Morgan. Dewey was good at spending money, but Fleur was in charge of saving it. She had their Visa with a bank in Arkansas, the money market in Texas, and a CD in Maryland.

It took Sid a good minute to react to what Dewey had

been telling us about the housing market in Southern California. Sticker shock, I guess.

"Help me understand this," he finally said. "Why would anybody in his right mind want to live in Los Angeles and pay those prices? I could find you a mansion on Riverside Drive in Indialantic for two-fifty. All the big operators live there."

"Be serious. You sound like Joe Six-Pack. Fleur and I are not going to live in a house in Dogpatch designed by a dropout from the Bob Jones School of Architecture."

"I didn't go to Harvard and I didn't go to Yale. This is the way I sound. And what do you know? You wouldn't recognize a real town if they put up a billboard to welcome you."

"Fine," Dewey said. "You can live in a hick town next door to the guy who wears a polyester suit and hoses down his driveway once a week. Not me."

He had to hang up then and take another call. I think Begelman was finally getting back to him. I'd love to have been a fly on the wall for that one.

Oh, Dewey, he was always sticking his nose where it didn't belong. In his case, the child really was father to the man. He was only eight when he found *Love Without Fear* on our night table in Yonkers. He wouldn't stop asking questions. I decided to let him read it, but that only raised more questions. Sid finally shut him up by promising to let Dewey watch the next time we did it. He was kidding, of course, but I don't believe in lying to children.

Dewey was already a big gossip by the time he got to Mark Twain. He used to come running home from school with news bulletins about all the spoiled brats in class. This one had that; that one had this. Of course, Dewey always had to have whatever it was. I could never understand that attitude. The grass is greener on the other side of the road only until you have to mow it.

I was no better at analyzing the hidden recesses of Dewey's mind than Zoot's. One thing for sure, I had nothing to do with his name-dropping. I'm the most down-to-earth person in the world. It didn't come from my mother, either. One year she knitted him a pair of wool socks, and he acted as if he were too good to wear them. You should have heard her let Little Lord Fauntleroy have it.

"You know what we used to say in the old country about people like you? On the outside, even horse droppings are shiny."

CHAPTER 12

WHO'S THE CABOOSE?

Do you know the Sherlock Holmes story where the clue is the dog doesn't bark? Well, I had no such reticence when my partner in wedded bliss brought up Arlee Sparlow's latest scheme at the end of January, our second anniversary on the Space Coast.

"How would you like to make a lot of money and live it up on the Gold Coast, Bubbie?"

"The Gold Coast?"

"That's what Arlee calls Riverside Drive, where all the big fish live. Some day we could have him as a neighbor. He's on Riverside, right off Waccabuc Road."

Just what I needed, Mr. Sparlow for a neighbor. Sid could keep his big fish. Do you know what our waiter Yu Wa once told us when Mr. Moon bawled him out at Golden Chopsticks? The big fish eat the little fish, the little fish eat the shrimp, and the shrimp eat the dirt.

As to what this was all about, Arlee had a friend, a builder who owned two lots on Lorelei Drive in Indialantic. I think they were in Korea together; one was the radio operator and the other carried the machine gun. Well, this fellow, Ray Earl Sloat, was in difficult straits. He got the lots cheap, but he had to borrow heavily to develop them for town houses. Then he used up all the money and his wife left him—she ran off with the accountant.

To make matters worse, Ray Earl's credit was very bad and the bank was going to foreclose unless he found a partner, somebody with good credit and a lot of cash to spare. I'll give you one guess who that somebody was supposed to be.

"Who needs the Taj Mahal, Sid? I learned at my mother's knee that you shouldn't hang your hat where you can't reach it."

"That way of thinking will get us nowhere, Bubbie. Just let me take care of this. Somebody has to be the locomotive and somebody the caboose."

"How dare you call me a caboose? I'll have you know I'm a size six, which I ought to be after all my hours of Healthercise. And let me tell you something else, Sid Waxler: I intend to be part of this train, and I don't mean the rear end."

I was beginning to wish he were still vegetating in his La-Z-Boy. If Sid wasn't nagging me about the town houses, Arlee was. I got it from all sides, like the Israeli Army when it was fighting on too many fronts at the same time.

Arlee would put that maddening smile on his face whenever he saw me coming in the door at Reliable Realty. He reminded me of Nu-Face, the store at Spaceport Plaza that installed shiny new doors on old kitchen cabinets.

"We have to pull together in the same direction,

ma'am. If you tie your horses to opposite sides of the cart, you'll get nowhere."

"Do you know what my mother used to say, Mr. Sparlow? If everyone pulled in the same direction, the world would keel over."

"Please, it's Arlee, ma'am. Now, I'm sure you had a fine mama, but I don't want us to become immobilized here by a deadlock situation."

Of course I had a fine mama. And "fine mama" doesn't begin to do her justice.

My mother was the most self-sacrificing person in the world. She had to work sixty hours a week when she came over on the boat in 1907. Not that she ever whined about those days, before Dubinksy improved things for the ladies' garment workers. She was a sewing-machine operator on Second Avenue, doing hem linings twelve hours a day. For that, she got $12 a week. The boss was very nasty and searched the girls to make sure they didn't take anything home, or at least that was his story. He was probably a dirty old man.

She was living with relatives in Williamsburg—the Coopers—until my father came over to marry her a few years later. He was from the same village, the carpenter's son. It was one of those places that were always changing. One day, it was Russia, then it was Poland. I don't know what it is now. Anyway, he didn't have a kopeck to his name, but somehow she managed to save enough in that sweatshop to send him $50 for the trip on steerage.

She didn't have to sew in such awful places for long— not her, an artist with needle and thread. When I was in first grade, she was already working with fine silk on Pitkin Avenue, lingerie with appliquéd flowers. Later, she was the assistant forelady at a millinery shop in Manhattan. While I was in high school, she was making party dresses for little girls on Sutton Place, pink and blue taffeta. She was quite successful in her own way, but money never seemed to stick to her, at least not in those days. If she put a few dollars away in East New York Savings during the good years, a lean year would come along and take it away.

She was the soul of goodness and kindness. Everyone loved her. My friends called her Tante Zissel even though she wasn't really their aunt. Do you know what Zissel means in Jewish? Sweetness. They wanted to change it to Zelda on Ellis Island, but she wouldn't let them. She had a hard life, but she never complained, and she was always ready to help somebody more in need.

When Kitty was eight, she wanted to take dance lessons from Madame Ludovika, a retired ballerina in East New York. They were only ten cents each, but her mother wouldn't waste a penny on such foolishness. Oh how Kitty jumped for joy when Tante Zissel offered to pay! And how she sobbed when Mrs. Nussbaum found out and sent her back with the dime. No matter. Kitty found a way to get her lessons. I admired that about her. Where there's a will, there's a way.

You couldn't keep Kitty away from us—the Greengrass family. It made more work for my mother, but she treated Kitty like a daughter. Kitty's apartment was in back of the building, the quiet side. We faced Livonia, which meant the rooms shook when the New Lots train went by on its way through Brownsville, our neighborhood in Brooklyn, but you didn't notice after a while.

Rose would stay over once in a blue moon, but Kitty usually spent one or two nights a week with us, even after the Nussbaums moved to Stone and Dumont, next to the library. I remember you were able to take out six books at a time, but only two could be novels.

It meant sharing the sofa with Kitty when she stayed. I never had my own bed as a girl. The sofa was big enough for me, but Kitty and I needed to squeeze in. Once we had a fight and she put two chairs together in the kitchen. But we almost never fought. We were like sisters, maybe closer. I never heard of sisters who were such good friends.

In fact, I used to have an older sister—she had ash brown hair like mine—but it's a painful story. We shared the sofa before she died of the Spanish flu when I was two years old. Her name was Malka, but everyone called her May, for when she was born.

Once a month, we had a carp swimming in the bathtub. A lot of people preferred pike or pickerel for gefilte fish, but my mother used only carp. She liked a fatty fish. She'd buy it live from Gorelick's, the fish store down the street. She was very good in the kitchen and shared her knowledge: As long as it's fresh, Selma, you can buy the cheapest. Actually, she would have used my Jewish name, Sheyneh, which means pretty.

If Kitty was spending the night, she'd help me wash vegetables for the soup you boiled the fish in. After my mother clubbed the carp and cleaned it, she wrapped the head and bones inside the skin and dumped everything into the pot—with onion, celery, and carrot. It was the only thing I'd eat with cooked onions.

One evening, Kitty was chopping a carrot for the pot when she noticed blood dribbling down her leg. She was the pioneer in this, too. My mother knew what to do. She sent me for her sewing basket, then got out a piece of cloth and improvised a napkin for Kitty.

In the old days, we made our own napkins, at least the girls in our social circle did. I don't know about the Vanderbilts and the Rockefellers. This must have been the first time I heard of menstruation, though my mother never used that word. She called it di Tsayt—the Time. Kitty got Myra a little book when her time came. *Now You Are a Woman!* It gave you pointers, what to do and not to do. It's a bad time to get your hair permed and you should take a shower instead of a bath.

God only knows why I got into all that, except to avoid returning to Chez Waxler, where Sid was still putting me through the wringer night and day. He'd stick the legal papers for the town houses in my face every five minutes and I'd tell him to go away.

If things got bad enough, I could lock myself in the toilet and take a bath. I'd turn the faucet as far into the red as it would go, then dump in half a box of Mr. Bubble. I loved a hot bath, the hotter the better. I wanted to feel like the lobster when you throw it into the pot. Of course, sooner or later I'd have to come out and Sid would be at me again.

"Arlee says we can't just throw our money in the bank and let it grow, Bubbie. It's not like feeding the chickens."

"He doesn't know everything, Sid. The world was created by someone bigger than Arlee."

"Women just don't understand these things."

Well, you're damned if you do and you're damned if you don't. In the end, I agreed. It was late February, about a month after our second anniversary in Florida, that we went to Reliable Realty and signed the papers. Sid and I were now partners with Ray Earl Sloat.

CHAPTER 13

CULTURED MARBLE

You know what they say about sausages. If you like them, don't watch them being made. I could say the same about town houses, at least those that Sid and Ray Earl were putting up in the spring of 1983.

This was the deal. Ray Earl would provide the land, plans, and expertise; Sid would come in with $25,000, the cold cash, and sign at the bank for a construction loan. The two of them would then share the perspiration and the profits in equal measure. At least that was the way things were supposed to work out.

I never did like Ray Earl. I met him only five or six times, but he had liquor on his breath each time. He reminded me of Wormley, the drunk we had living up the block in Yonkers.

Well, I put my foot down about one thing. Ray Earl would come to the door for Sid, but I wouldn't ask him in. A man like that shouldn't be allowed to associate with respectable people.

He was sharp—that is to say, sharp in the bad sense of the word. He was always trying to use somebody or put something over on someone, like when Tom Sawyer tricked the other boys into whitewashing the fence for him. Sid ended up doing all the work. He went over to Lorelei Drive every day to ride herd over the contractors and workmen.

"They're good fellows, Bubbie, but you have to watch them like a hawk. One of them was about to drive off with a trunkful of ceramic tile. You can't catch everything, but if you're careful, they don't steal too much."

Ray Earl should have shared the burden, but he was always in a bar or at home sleeping it off. The few times he showed up on Lorelei Drive in March or April, it was to second-guess Sid's better judgment. He'd say Sid was doing too good a job, buying the higher-grade material—five-eighths sheet rock instead of the three-eighths—when the cheaper stuff would do.

"He's going to nickel-and-dime me to death, Bubbie. If he had his way, we'd be putting up crappy vinyl-sided modulars that would fall down before we could find buyers. He ought to be selling lemons at Eli Potts's used-car lot. Every second, he's trying to pull something."

It turns my stomach to think of that Sloat person. In this case, you really could judge the book by its cover. He was as ugly on the outside as on the inside. He had a pushed-in pig's face with blood vessels all over his nose, or should I say snout, from all that liquor.

I wasn't impressed with Ray Earl's expertise, either. He was supposed to be the one with the know-how, but Sid had all the good ideas. This so-called expert wanted to put a triplex on each lot—that's what the land was zoned for—but Sid knew better.

"It's like this, Ray Earl," he explained over the phone. "If we convert the two lots into one, we can build eight units, four on each section. No, wait. Give me a chance to explain. Of course we have to get a variance to make it into one parcel. Yes, I realize that means going to the zoning people and filling out a lot of forms and waiting a long time, but I can handle it all."

Ray Earl was right about one thing. It took forever to get the variance. He wanted to grease a few palms, but Sid put an end to such talk. He got it done without anything crooked.

Sid had three or four other good ideas. Ray Earl wanted to incorporate the usual way, which would have resulted in endless red tape with the IRS. But Sid made it a subchapter S, the right way. I don't know how, but it would save on taxes as well as red tape.

Not surprisingly, the drunk liked that idea. He hated to pay taxes. This is what he once told Sid: The tax return is only your first offer. He should have been married to the Helmsley woman—you know, only the little people pay taxes.

Sid got Leo to put in a good word with one of his friends at Vern's Home Improvements—Bluford, if I'm not mistaken. He provided the cultured-marble vanities for only three percent over cost. I think Ray Earl got the blueprints for almost nothing from a guy he knew in Palm Bay, an unemployed architect, but Sid had to make dozens of changes.

Sid insisted on the nicer shower-and-tub units and fireplaces with fragrant-cedar mantels. He thought of so many nice features. All Ray Earl ever did was make things difficult.

"I feel like an alligator wrestler," Sid complained. "He's the meanest, most slippery person I ever had to deal with."

The fireplace was a big selling point, quite unusual in Florida, which may be why the town houses sold so fast. Yes, they were a great success. I was wrong again. Arlee found buyers for all eight houses in a matter of weeks. You have to give the devil his due.

People were tripping over one another to make an offer. One fellow, a salesman for Atlantis Elevator, agreed to pay two thousand more than the asking price. Of course, the houses were priced to sell, only $55,000 for an end unit, the most expensive model.

We could have done even better by taking paper— mortgages, you know—on two houses, but Arlee felt a fast nickel was better than a slow dime. Actually, it took another six weeks for us to get our hands on any of this fast money. It was frozen while the lawyers argued over reimbursing Sid for his expenses. Ray Earl didn't want to give him a penny.

"He's a psychopath, Bubbie. He'll tell you a different story today, tomorrow, and the next day. He should be hospitalized."

It was a constant shouting match, especially when Ray Earl was on a binge, which was all the time. One day the drunk went too far.

I came home from Aquacise in April to find Sid and Ray Earl butting horns like two billy goats. They were over by the breezeway, their faces all red, and the veins popping out on their necks. I was afraid Sid would have a stroke.

"Who the hell are you calling a chiseler, Waxler? I don't need to take any more shit from you and your kind. Why don't you go back where you come from? And take all your shit-eating, piss-complected Shylock friends back there with you."

"Get off my property, you stinking Nazi bastard," Sid shouted. "Go bury yourself in a hole where you belong and don't come back here again."

The nerve of that drunken pig! He stunk from high heaven. Where did that crook get off calling us Shylocks? He was the money-grubber. He rolled in the slime and dared call us names and criticize our complexions. Dear God, what makes them hate us so much?

The hatred is everywhere. Once I was having lunch with Kitty at the Automat. This was a few months after her mother got the telegram about Ronnie's plane going down. There were two gentile girls at the next table, talking about how it was all a Jewish war—our Christian boys were dying just to save the Jews. I could see Kitty was holding her breath and counting to ten. When she finally spoke, her voice was so quiet I hardly recognized it.

"Did either of you two lose a loved one in the service?" she asked.

The girls shook their heads.

"Well I have," Kitty said, raising her voice with every word. "My brother Ronnie—Ronnie Nussbaum—a Jewish boy who died to save bigots like you. So shut your goddamn mouths or I'll shut them for you. Christ, I never heard such pure, unadulterated bullcrap in all my life."

She was still swearing like a stevedore five minutes later, though the girls had long since run off, leaving their coffee unfinished on the table. I wonder if they still feel the same way, wherever they are.

My heart still pounds when I think of the time my mother's brother came over from Europe after the war. He looked like the skeleton in a doctor's office, and that was the least of it.

We got him got him home—Sid and I were living on Sedgwick Avenue in the Bronx—but Uncle Simcha didn't want to talk. He would have sat there in silence if my mother hadn't insisted on hearing what had happened to the rest of the family. Her mother had been a very stubborn woman. We'd offered to send her a ticket, but she wouldn't leave.

Well, my uncle was chopping wood outside the village when the Nazis came and rounded all the people up. They had to dig their own grave, one big ditch for everybody to fall in, then the Nazis shot them down like animals. He watched it all from the woods: his mother, his wife, his three children, friends, neighbors, the whole village. He couldn't help them.

He lived in the forest for two months, eating wild berries, but a farmer turned him in, a Polish neighbor. I don't know why the kind-hearted Nazis didn't just kill him on the spot. Instead, they did him a big favor and sent him to the camps. What it must do to you to be in places like that!

Uncle Simcha ate two portions of everything I cooked—the pot roast, the boiled potatoes, the beets. He still looked worse than poor Yorick, but the meal helped loosen his tongue.

"Dig up a Jew or a gentile after a couple of years and their bones will look the same," he said—my mother was helping us with the Yiddish. "But tell that to an anti-Semite. It won't mean a thing. They suck the prejudice in with their mother's milk."

You didn't have to be hit on the head with Plymouth Rock to see that Ray Earl Sloat was a dyed-in-the-wool anti-Semite—or, in Sid's words, a two-bit Hitler who stank like the corpse of a rotting pig. From then on, he and Sid didn't speak—the lawyers did all the talking.

In the end, it worked out fine—fine for everyone but Ray Earl. He was driving on the Bee Line when his jalopy skidded off the road. *The Orbiter* said he flipped over in a field of skunk cabbage. That's where he belonged. He was drunk, naturally. His blood-alcohol level was 0.2.

His wife, the one who ran off with the CPA, returned home from Coral Gables and demanded her share. She had a lot of nerve. Sid wanted to get it over with and he gave her a little more than she deserved. Actually, I had nothing against her. She wasn't like Ray Earl. She may have been disloyal, but she didn't hate us or want to eat you alive.

Sid ended up netting $62,762 on the eight town houses. He took me on a tour before handing over the last set of keys to the new owners at the end of May in 1983. He was so proud as he pointed out the workmanship. Look at this storm gutter, Bubbie, the ducting is real copper. And see that Air-Flo window over there—the thermal pane tilts in for easy cleaning.

"You did a wonderful job, Sid."

He put a hand to his chest. "It gets me right here to think these town houses will be standing long after I'm gone."

As Arlee Sparlow said at the last closing, if you get your foot out of a bear trap in one piece, ma'am, what do you have to complain about? We now had $112,620 in our money market at Southland. I never thought I'd live to see so much in the bank.

Crabbe sent us another letter. He couldn't stop gushing about Sid's success. He said Southland was raising our Ready Credit to $25,000 and our MasterCard limit to $5,000.

Everyone thought Sid was brilliant. Even Bernstein made a point of congratulating him after the memorial concert for Arthur Godfrey at the Cabaret. The highlight of the evening was Bernstein's ukulele solo.

"From now on, will you have more faith in me?" Sid asked on the way home. "Promise?"

All right, I promised. After making a fool of myself twice, I mistrusted my own judgment. No wonder I didn't put up more of a stink when Arlee Sparlow cast out his next bright idea and Sid swallowed it hook, line, and sinker.

CHAPTER 14

THE ARMS OF VENUS

With the boys' room still in mint condition almost two and a half years after our arrival in Florida, Sid decided to convert it into an office to contemplate the next move on the Monopoly board. I didn't object too strenuously. I was still furious with Dewey for declining all invitations to visit, and with Zoot for slipping in and out of our lives like a cat burglar.

Maybe the boys weren't wearing out their room, but Sid made up for it. He was worse than the Collyer brothers. There were piles of old newspapers all over—on the floor, the chairs, the night tables, the twin beds. After a few weeks of picking up after him, I felt like Alice when the Red Queen told her you had to run as fast as you could to stay in the same place.

A foot-high heap of paperwork covered Sid's knee-hole desk—actually, my father's desk. He had built it from pine, his favorite wood. He made the most beautiful stuff out of pine: May's baby cradle, my mother's dresser, my rocking horse.

Rutgers Slip—that's where my father worked as a coffin-maker. He used to take me to watch on school holidays. I'd sit on the sawhorse, surrounded by sawdust, as he chiseled and sanded. His hands were as rough as sandpaper, but he was the most gentle man.

I have this picture in my mind. Every few minutes, he stops to caress the grain of the board he's working on as if it's warm human flesh. He sees me looking at him and holds the wood out to me, a piece of fine pine.

"Take it, Sheyneh. Here, look at the grain. Touch it, smell it. With wood like that, you want to do something good."

Well, Sid would hole up in his office for hours at a time. In spite of my best efforts, it looked like New York when Mayor Lindsay had the garbage strike. Now don't get me wrong. I was still happy to see him taking an interest in life. But in the immortal words of Bette Davis, what a dump! I could have used the Venus de Milo's missing pair of arms. I read somewhere that the difference between a good housewife and a bad one is only an hour a day. That's nonsense. There weren't enough hours in the day if you lived with a slob.

Meanwhile, Zoot may have considered our Chalet no-man's land, but he hadn't broken off diplomatic relations. He'd call us from New York whenever he ran short of money—collect, of course. I think he needed another hundred for his rent that May after trading in the Yanagasawa to buy a new saxophone—actually, an old one this time, a beat-up Conn. It was a Chu Berry, an older model from when Conn was making a top-of-the-line horn.

"Why do you keep trying to push water uphill?" Sid

asked him. "Let me call Guerrini about getting you a job in the school system. We were very close when he was a shop teacher."

"Hey, that was cool for you, but jazz is what I do. My day will come. As Eubie Blake said, if you hang around long enough, they get to you."

If we didn't hear from Zoot for a few weeks, it meant he had a gig and we'd have to call him. That was the case the next month when he was working on Avenue A in the East Village with a drummer and a very hip pianist who couldn't read a note but knew all the charts by heart.

"We laid down a lot of music," Zoot said. "We were only supposed to do two sets, but the people wouldn't let us go. They were clapping until their palms were sore."

"I hope you got paid extra for all that work," Sid said.

"Loosen up, will you? You don't punch a time clock if you dig what you're doing."

As for Dewey, he quit his job at *The Hollywood Reporter* in May and flew to New York to see Cindy Adams. She was looking for a new legman in Hollywood, but that didn't work out. Of course he made no effort to get together with Goofy, as he called his brother. Not that Zoot would have wanted it. As far as he was concerned, Dewey could spend all his time in Disneyland.

Well, Dewey went to work for *Variety* later in May, doing the industry gossip. He had lunch with Melnick at the Polo Lounge and Gladys Begelman stopped by the table, but all she wanted to talk about was Cliff Robertson, not her husband. He also had an item about a Hollywood agent named Swifty Lazar. Dewey wrote that this fellow looked like a bare knee with a pair of glasses on it, but Swifty—his real name was Irving—didn't think that was so funny.

"He calls me the next day to say he's really hurt. How could you do this to me, Dewey? I consider you one of the family. Whoa! I didn't know what to say. Me? I'm one of the family? Do me a favor. What am I, the brother-in-law?"

Fred Allen had it right. To a newspaperman, a human being is an item with the skin wrapped around it. Naturally, the newspaperman in question had boss trouble at *Variety*, too. This time it was a little editor with a Charlie Chaplin mustache and a Napoleon complex. It was sometime in June that the ax fell again. Dewey was bloodied but unbowed as he gave Sid and me the postmortem.

"Let him keep his Mickey Mouse job. I don't need a pipsqueak in a swivel chair telling me what to do. I'm supposed to be too tough on the moguls. Me? I belong to the *res ipsa loquitur* school of journalism—the thing speaks for itself. I call a spade a spade."

I wasn't really worried about Dewey. Fleur was the one who kept their checkbook balanced and she always had something squirreled away for a winter day. Not that it was snowing yet in Southern California. Fleur was doing quite well, thank you.

She'd just finished redecorating the house of a retired clothing manufacturer in Holmby Hills. He wanted an underground grotto with a heart-shaped pool like Jayne Mansfield's. She got a ninety-year-old fig tree for the living room—a bonsai from Kyoto. Oh, and a Picasso and two Warhols for the master bedroom, the soup cans.

Fleur got quite a bundle from this job, but Dewey made a big joke of it. To hear him talk, she barely earned enough to meet the payments on the Mercedes she needed to impress her rich clients. I think he was un-comfortable about her success. I don't know what he had to complain about. Fleur was very good to him.

To celebrate her latest coup, she got him a cashmere sports jacket at the Ralph Lauren outlet in Tijuana. She was good at sniffing out a bargain. I'm no impulse buyer myself, but she could have taught me a thing or two.

Fleur called later that month. I hardly ever heard from Lady Astor herself, but Dewey must have twisted her arm. This was on June 18, 1983, the day Sally Ride went up into space—the first woman. I made scalloped potatoes for my brunch. I got it from Heloise: three lay-ers of sliced potatoes between three of grated cheese. I had just stuck the casserole dish in the oven when the phone rang.

Fleur gave me a status report on the high cost of hous-ing in Mecca. She and Dewey had saved over fifty thou-sand in seven different banks around the country, but that still wasn't enough for a down payment. Every week, the price of a house was getting more out of reach. Three quarters of a million would now buy you two bedrooms and one and a half baths, if you were very lucky. She couldn't stop talking about the unfairness of it all.

"The more you save, the more you fall behind. If you do nothing but live in your own home in Southern Cal-ifornia, you'll make lots of money. But how do you get a foot in the door?"

Money and real estate were all she wanted to talk about. I tried to interest her in my favorite subject, but Fleur was a tough customer. She cut me off before I could get five words out.

"As far as I'm concerned, Selma, babies come in only two models—the Herbert Hoover and the J. Fred Muggs. I still haven't figured out which one is funnier looking."

CHAPTER 15

FAT-BACK GRAVY

The butcher, the baker, the candlestick-maker, the whole world loved Arlee Sparlow. He made friends with the caddies on the fairway and the bankers in the clubhouse. Up and down the Space Coast, he couldn't pass someone by without a shake of the hand and a pat on the back.

I don't know what it was that bothered me. Maybe he was just too nice. He was too eager to help you out of the goodness of his heart. Nobody could be that nice. Well, who was I to argue with success? Everything he'd promised so far had come true.

Arlee's latest brainstorm was mortgages. I got the whole spiel that June. Who needed the headache of owning the property? Real estate might be a cash cow, but mortgages were—if you'll excuse me, ma'am—the teats. He was a real operator. He had an answer to every question.

"Why, you could talk the hind leg off a donkey, ma'am. But let me assure you there's nothing for you to trouble yourself about if all the proper safeguards are in place."

We were standing by the window at Reliable Realty, looking out at the parking lot. Two brown pelicans flew over the cars on their way to the Banana River. I could see Arlee's toothy grin in the glass as he put an arm around my shoulders. Oh, to be up there with the pelicans!

"You can trust in the common sense of a good old Southern boy, ma'am. I wasn't born with a silver spoon in my mouth. I grew up on biscuits and grits and fatback gravy."

I hate to admit it, but I sometimes found myself liking Mr. Sparlow, even if I suspected it was all a false front, like the town in a cowboy movie.

As Arlee explained it, the banks were suffering from hardening of the arteries. They treated every borrower with the same rigid formula. Your down payment had to be this percent of that and your income had to be that percent of this, no exceptions to the rule. As a result, a lot of creditworthy people fell through the cracks and would pay almost anything for a mortgage.

"The mortgage business isn't only a big boys' game, ma'am. There's room for everybody. Let the banks, the large operators, milk the cow; we'll do just fine skimming off the cream."

You could get a return of seventeen percent or more on a mortgage at that time, which was over twice what you'd earn on a CD at the bank. Of course, the CD was insured by the FDIC, but Arlee insisted a mortgage was as good as money in the bank if you had a comfortable cushion. That is, the difference between the amount of the mortgage and the value of the property.

The way it worked, Arlee was the mortgage broker—the middleman. He got the two sides together and did all the paperwork. He'd collect the monthly payment from the mortgagor, then turn it over to the mortgagee, keeping two percent for himself, the handling fee.

"What I'm doing is conducting asset-liability management, ma'am. I've got this portfolio of supplies on the one hand and this portfolio of markets on the other. I package the product and service it to meet what the market is demanding."

Well, we signed the papers at the end of June. It was an otherwise unremarkable day. No hurricane or tropical storm, not a cloud in the sky to indicate Sid and I had crossed our Rubicon.

In the beginning, I tried to keep up with everything. I went with Sid to see the properties. I read through each new package that Arlee got us—the package of legal papers that accompanied the mortgage. The first one came to $12,500 for a warehouse in Melbourne. Then there was a mortgage on a little cottage in Coco owned by a couple with two children. He was a draftsman for McDonnell Douglas in Titusville and she was at home with the baby. This one was for $15,000. I think they wanted the money to add on a family room and a second bath.

Next was a house on the river. The owner, a tree surgeon on Merritt Island, was moving across the state, over by the Waltzing Waters. It was $25,000, but for only six months, until he could sell the old place. He needed cash right away for the down payment on the new one.

"Isn't that a lot?" I asked Sid.

"The equity's there, Bubbie. It's worth a hundred and twenty-five thousand, according to Arlee. I even double-checked with a fellow at the Century 21 on Merritt Island. The house may be too old-fashioned for some people, but riverfront property is valuable."

I was worried about the big numbers, though I had to admit Sid was being careful. He went around and checked out everything Arlee recommended. He spoke to the appraiser and called the people who owned the property. In a few cases, he went door to door and interviewed the neighbors. He even turned down a package that Arlee was pushing on him.

"I don't care what kind of garbage the appraiser came up with. I told Arlee to go out and find me something else, a property worth what it's appraised for."

In the meantime, I redecorated our Chalet Luxe. It cost me only $2,478, but I did most of the work myself. I put the La-Z-Boy over by the picture window, which faced south and had good morning light, not that you needed more light in Florida. Sid had wanted Naugahyde, but I insisted on tapestry, $51 a yard for wild roses. I read somewhere that Bing Crosby had the same model. It was a Louis, but I can't tell you which. You'd have to ask Fleur. My daughter-in-law would have had a stroke if she'd seen Annette's recliner. It was a Contour Cuddler big enough to hold two people at the same time— with slipcovers in metallic-flecked Vinelle.

The spinet from Yonkers was in the corner next to the La-Z-Boy. It was a cherrywood Baldwin with club feet, a Queen Anne. We gave both boys a chance to take piano lessons, but Dewey was a thumper and Zoot wouldn't look at anything except the saxophone—well, the clarinet, too, for a while. I had the sheet music for Beethoven's four mandolin pieces on the piano, open to the Adagio in E flat, my favorite. I think he wrote them for his friend Wenzel.

My mandolin was on the piano, next to an old photo of The Three Musketeers at Times Square. It was taken just before Rose met Sol. I'm in a muskrat coat and Rose a leopard-trimmed jacket. Kitty is wearing her sable wrap. We're behind a wooden bar with a shot glass and bottles of whiskey. In front of us is a sign: Souvenir From Times Sq., New York.

Rose had the same photo in her living room and Kitty carried a smaller one around in her wallet. We were so sophisticated, but what did we know? Kitty was dancing at Radio City, and even she didn't know anything. It was a make-believe bar, a prop for tourists to pose behind. In fact, mere alcohol didn't thrill us at all. Kitty and I drank on occasion, but Rose wouldn't take a sip. We may have had our disagreements, but we were such good friends. You never saw better friends. I'll tell you how close we were. How close are three coats of paint?

CHAPTER 16

ALFONSE AND GASTON

On the bamboo étagère just outside Sid's office there was a *Beeton's Book of Household Management*. You know, the one about the evils of the untidy home. Rose had given it to me as a wedding present, along with a soup tureen and ladle that were far more appreciated. Isabella Beeton must have been turning over in her grave.

For every pile of junk I'd get off the floor of Sid's office that July, two new piles would appear the next day. I couldn't help thinking of the time the mounted police had a parade on Pitkin Avenue when I was a girl. There were three schlemiels with buckets and shovels who brought up the rear and picked up after the horses. I knew just how they felt.

"How can you work like this?" I snapped at Mr. Trump one morning. "Do you want to get us condemned by the Board of Health?"

"If you're so worried about the health inspectors, Selma, you might spend a little less time complaining and a little more time cleaning."

Oh, yeah? And he didn't even pay me the respect of looking up from his Sun Bank calculator. I think he was comparing the returns on two new packages, a car wash in Palm Bay versus a professional building in Titusville. Well, I was used to insults, but not to injury.

What happened was I'd been trying to clear some junk off one of the twin beds later in the day while Sid was searching for a file on the other. We both finished at the same time, but there was room for only one of us to turn. We were each waiting for the other: You go first; no, you go first. I finally put an end to this game of Alfonse and Gaston, took the first step myself, and of all the stupid things slipped on an old newspaper clipping.

The accident was a little nothing, but I knew I had trouble from the way my foot hurt, the left one. I let out a shout that would have done Tosca proud.

"Are you okay, Bubbie?"

"No, I'm not okay. Can't you hear me crying bloody murder?"

Sid helped me to my feet—or, rather, to my one good foot—and offered a few words of sympathy, but he didn't really think it was serious. He gave me a pat on the head, tsk-tsked a few times, then returned to that junk pile on his desk.

"My foot never hurt like this before," I said. "I want somebody to see it."

"Don't work yourself up over nothing, Bubbie. It's just a sprain. Soak it in hot water and you'll feel better."

"Why don't you soak your head? All you think of is that wheeling and dealing."

I should have insisted he get off his behind and drive

me to the emergency room. Instead, I followed Dr. Kildare's advice and soaked my foot for an hour after lunch. Not that it did the least good. If anything, I felt worse. There was a stabbing pain each time I put any weight on it.

Sid drove off to the Titusville property about four o'clock, leaving me alone with a bottle of Extra Strength Bufferin. I tried to prepare something for supper, but I could barely stand up.

I finally called Kitty to come for me. She and Leo were still driving their old Buick, a '55 Roadmaster with a V8 and a double-barrel carburetor. Naturally, Kitty gave me a good talking-to on the way to Citrus Memorial—it was in Indian Harbour Beach, just down A1A from Satellite Beach.

"How the hell could you wait so long, Selma? If the grand pooh-bah wouldn't take you, you should have called me at once."

From the way I was bouncing around on the velour seat covers, Kitty must have been going double the speed limit. Well, at least we were safe. The car was built like a tank. Leo once told me the fender alone weighed a hundred and thirty-five pounds.

Kitty made a jerky stop at Palmetto Avenue and my foot pressed against the floorboard. Oh, my God! I felt like a centipede, with all one hundred feet in excruciating pain. I knew for sure then; it had to be a fracture.

I let out a yelp when the intern examined me, a young woman with the delicacy of a Veg-O-Matic. The radiologist took X-rays and it showed up right away, a crack at the bottom of the left foot, one of the metatarsals.

The orthopedic man, Poole, came right over from his home on Riverside Drive and took care of it.

I was able to get around on crutches after that, but the sharp edge of the cast would scrape against my skin like a knife. Of course, a knife can cut two ways. In bed, I'd kick Sid with the cast whenever I turned over in my sleep. It served him right for his stubbornness.

You didn't have to be Dick Tracy to figure out I'd need help with the housework. Rose came by once a day, mincing around from room to room as she dusted my furniture with a chamois cloth and wiped out the nicks with Tibet almond stick, but I didn't like taking advantage of her. She did so much for me.

It was early August when Rose came over with a jar of her homemade apple sauce. She'd throw together apples and plums, cored and pitted but with the skin still on. Later, she strained out the skin. I loved it, and there were practically no calories.

When Rose wasn't cooing over me, she was carrying on about osteoporosis in the older woman, the disease where your bones wear out and turn brittle. Florence Nightingale wanted me to have the doctor examine the X-ray one more time for any signs of calcium loss.

"If you have bone deterioration, it's comparable to putting yourself through extreme shock each time you leave home," Rose said. "I'm taking estrogen supplements to be safe. I also drink Tums liquid. It's a good source of calcium."

A few days later, Kitty came over with a potted African violet—I had her put it on the window sill in the little bathroom. A neighbor had given it to her, Nettie somebody, not realizing Kitty hated plants. The only one she had was a crown of thorns from the Welcome Wagon, but it would have been long dead if not for me. I'd sneak into the guest bathroom and give the plant a pick-me-up whenever I visited. It reminded me of Kitty. The white flowers were very pretty, but the thorns would stick you if you didn't watch out.

"Why the long face?" she said. "At our age, an ache is good news. If you get up in the morning and nothing hurts, you must be dead."

I tried to smile, but Kitty soon had something to say that really did cheer me up. Her cleaning woman—Birdella Goodwillie, if you recall—had a half-day free. I jumped at the chance, figuratively speaking.

I got Birdella on Tuesday mornings, starting the second week in August. In the old days, I'd have called her a colored girl, but I'm more sensitive about such things now. Anyway, she wasn't a girl. She was a grown woman who'd raised four children—a very grown woman, actually, as large around as Ethel Waters and then some.

Birdella was a good worker, but Sid wouldn't let her set foot in his junk-strewn office unless he was there to supervise. That made it difficult because the two of them kept bumping into each other. If Birdella dared straighten up while he was away, Sid would explode.

"I can't turn my back on you for a minute. How am I supposed to find anything after Hurricane Birdella has been here?"

"Listen here, Mr. Waxler. I don't like a mouthy man. What was your mother thinking of when she taught you manners? That's no way to talk to a respectable lady."

"Just stay out of my office unless you have my permission."

"This is not holy ground. When Moses was at the Burning Bush, somebody higher than you told him to pull off thy shoes for the ground you stand on is holy."

Birdella wasn't afraid of Sid—or work, either. In an hour, she'd do what it took me two to accomplish when I had both good feet. I couldn't get over how fast she went through that house. Maybe Rose would have been a bit more careful, adding Dr. Bronner's Pure-Castile Soap to the laundry, but not many people were so fastidious.

As for mortgages, Sid was still being careful. He turned down two others that August, but he asked for something else to replace them. One good thing to come of my accident was that I didn't have to accompany him to Reliable Realty until the cast was removed after Labor Day.

Poole, the orthopedic man, said I could have my internist in Melbourne Beach take it off. Ramsool would only charge me for an office visit instead of a hospital procedure. He got his medical degree from Punjab University, but he did his residency in Baton Rouge.

I was tickled to get the cast off—literally. The buzzing from Ramsool's power saw made me laugh so hard that Lu Ann, his nurse, had to hold me down. Later, she gave me an elastic tube to put my foot through. It was easier to get around after that. I used an aluminum walker at first, then a four-legged cane, then the single-legged one, and finally nothing but my own two feet.

To my surprise, Sid didn't object when I suggested

keeping Birdella. No matter how much he carried on about her, he must have enjoyed the arguments. When he wasn't questioning her housekeeping, it was her religious beliefs.

"Look at all the craziness in the world, Birdella. If God isn't dead, he's on his death bed."

"Watch your mouth, Mr. Waxler. There's a right and there's a wrong. If you go to the IRS, they have a book with a record of you. In heaven, there's also a book where your life is written down. That book will be opened for you one day."

CHAPTER 17

MONEY TREES

Nathanson took us to the local beach that September for Rosh Hashana, the Jewish New Year. He was Conservative like Kleinman, our old rabbi in Yonkers. We were supposed to celebrate the New Year by throwing bread on the water—casting out our sins, you know.

To show that it was Satellite Beach, the Jaycees had put up a fiberglass globe with an orbiting aluminum satellite next to a dune covered with sea oats and sea grapes. We were all wearing beach outfits, even the rabbi, though he threw a black robe over his cabana suit before the service began. The bright sun made his face look even more liverish than usual.

We stood there with our hands full of stale bread, everyone except for Sol. He'd gobbled up most of his while Nathanson wasn't looking. He was in the surf, looking like a beached white whale. The rabbi spotted his empty hands just as Sol was swallowing the last bite.

"Please, everybody, don't eat your sins," Nathanson said.

"I didn't have time for breakfast," Sol said, crumbs flying. "Doesn't the Bible tell us we should eat and drink, for tomorrow we shall die?"

"If you have a complaint, send a letter to the boss upstairs. In Hebrew, please."

We got together later that day—The Friends—for the early-bird special at Golden Chopsticks. Sid had wanted to make a pig of himself at Oinkers, but Rose couldn't eat anything there. She didn't keep kosher anymore, but she wouldn't touch pork—not even if she were stretched on the rack and Torquemada offered to loosen the screws.

There was an excellent early bird at Golden Chopsticks: only four ninety-five for anything on the dinner menu, even the Buddhist Delight house special, if Mr. Moon seated you before six.

"Why don't you use your chopsticks, Sid?"

"They slow me down, Bubbie."

"What's the hurry?"

"I don't want the water chestnuts to cool off."

Leo was a fast eater, too. He'd finished before anyone else and was squirming in his seat, waiting for the rest of us to catch up.

"Here, try one of my shrimp, Leo," I said.

"No thanks, Selma."

"I thought you liked them."

"I do, but shrimps don't like me. They give me hives."

Sol was making faces at his Buddhist Delight as he waved for our waiter.

"Here, what's this, Yu Wa?"

"A mushroom."

"No, this is a canned mushroom."

"It is?"

"I know a canned mushroom when I see one."

To distract Sol, I refilled his cup. I love the tea you get in Chinese restaurants. It's supposed to be good for cancer, something to do with the free radicals.

Leo was polishing off Kitty's leftover beef and broccoli when she poked him in the ribs.

"Look at that woman in the hot-pink bolero."

"Where?" he said. "Which one?"

"The bleached blonde. She's got nothing on under it."

All three men swiveled around.

"What's a bolero?" said Leo.

"A goddamn jacket, dummkopf."

The men turned back to their food.

Sol lit up a cigar as we ate our fortune cookies and lychee nuts, but Mr. Moon made him put it out. Now Sol was glaring across the room at him like Winston Churchill when the photographer took away his cigar.

Sid waited until dessert to bother Leo and Sol about mortgages. I started to open my mouth, then read my fortune cookie: The grass must bend when the wind blows across it. I may not be superstitious, but I know when somebody's trying to tell me something.

"It's not too late to get into mortgages," Sid said. "They're practically giving them away."

"They could be selling elephants two for a quarter," Leo said. "That's a great bargain, but what do I need with elephants?"

"Mortgages are like money trees planted all over town—you only have to pluck the fruit."

"I don't want more paper," Sol said. "I was nuts to take paper for my dry cleaner's. I was too greedy. If I had it to do over, I'd take ten percent less and be free of the aggravation."

"Don't you miss the old business?" Leo asked, trying to steer the conversation in a different direction. "Not even a little?"

"I wouldn't go back one day and relive it. That place cost me every hair on my head. Now is better. It's time to enjoy. You don't live forever."

Kitty and Rose were trying to outdo each other with war stories about their children. You know, a game of one-upmanship, like that Charlie Chaplin movie where the two dictators are sitting next to each other in the barbershop, each trying to crank up his chair higher and higher.

After two divorces and God only knows how many affairs, Kitty's daughter was now reduced to using dating services. Myra had met one fellow who was interested in her, a smart redhead from Smith Barney, but he was too smart for his own good. I think the SEC got him with Boesky or one of those other inside traders.

Rose was a little luckier. Zach had finally settled down with Chloris in Santa Fe, where they had a pottery factory. But any resemblance to Ward and June Cleaver was coincidental. I think they tied the knot in 1981, ten or twelve years after meeting at a Jefferson Airplane concert in San Francisco. Chloris's father was a Chippewa medicine man named Standing Elk, but her mother was Jewish, a Teitelbaum.

Becky, Rose's youngest, was settling down too, in a

manner of speaking. She had her own exterminating company in Oakland—Bugsy Moskowitz, Licensed to Kill. She'd met a nice girl in 1982, an entomologist at Berkeley, which meant the two had a lot in common. It was a brave new world, as Shakespeare noticed.

Becky was always different, and not just because she was such a tomboy. There were always tomboys, but what kind of girl would collect dead bugs? Or what kind of boy, either? She had dozens of them mounted on plywood in the basement, seventy-five dragonflies on one board alone. Dewey once had a live caterpillar in a bottle. He watched it go from the pupa to the butterfly, but that was different. He let it fly away.

It was a few months after the dinner at Golden Chopsticks that Arlee came over to our place with an armful of new packages and laid them down on the coffee table in the living room.

"It's time to break open the piggy bank," he said. "Look at these goodies, my friends. You have to be well capitalized in this market, but the opportunities are tremendous. Lord, it's like being a mosquito in a nudist colony. The only question is where to strike first."

Sid couldn't have been happier. Like Will Rogers, he never met a mortgage he didn't like. We'd already invested $79,942 so far and the rest of our savings, $36,251, was in the money market at Southland, just waiting to be used.

I tried to take an interest in the new investments—I remember one of them was for a pitch-and-putt off US 1 near Sharpes—but you had to be a Philadelphia lawyer to understand all the whereases, heretofores, and aforesaids.

On the way out, Arlee insisted on wasting Birdella's time with a lot of small talk, as he did with everyone who crossed his path.

"I don't like that man," she told Sid after she'd managed to push Dale Carnegie out the front door. "I never trust a man who has shiny skin from eating too much rich food."

"Is there anything in the world that isn't your business, Birdella?"

"I speak my mind and I speak it clearly, as the Bible commands us. If the trumpet gives an uncertain sound, who shall prepare himself to the battle?"

To be honest, Birdella had a little too much old-time religion for me. Now, I also believed in God, but not in the people who claimed to have a hot line to heaven. It was enough for me to go to services on the High Holy Days and do good deeds the rest of the year. I had True Sisters for that—the United Order of True Sisters—the oldest ladies' charity in America.

We had a nice group of girls in Melbourne—the Brevard Lodge. *The Orbiter* wanted to write up our special Monday breakfasts for cancer patients and their families at Cape Canaveral Hospital, but we declined to take credit. Good deeds should be on the QT—that's rule number one for True Sisters. If you talk too much, you'll embarrass the people you want to help.

We had to hop to it that first month of 1984 because we could only use the hospital kitchen for an hour at a time. I think the kitchen staff was renovating the old equipment, replacing the vats and paddles with new stainless steel ones.

We got the eggs wholesale from a dealer in Orlando, thirty dozen to the carton. I did the scrambling, and Rose made the oatmeal for patients on chemo or radiation who couldn't eat eggs. There were also intravenous feedings for anyone too sick to hold down solid food. But the nurses took care of that.

Rose once tried to do the scrambling, but she was a slowpoke. I could crack a whole carton of eggs in fifteen minutes.

CHAPTER 18

ANNIVERSARY WALTZ

I had a few people over for dinner the next month to celebrate Kitty and Leo's wedding anniversary. This was the day before their forty-fourth—Valentine's Day, in fact—but they were leaving for a second honeymoon the next morning, a cruise to the Bahamas on the *Royale*.

I made sesame green beans to go with the flank steak marinade. You sauté the beans in sesame oil, then add sesame seeds and lemon juice. Rose brought along a wild-rice side dish that she got from *Prevention*. Kitty baked the dessert, a German chocolate cake decorated with golden lace filigrees. She was very good at desserts, though you couldn't tell by looking at Leo. I don't know where he put it. After all these years, he was still as bony as a stick of macaroni.

I got my mandolin from the case on the piano and played "The Anniversary Waltz." Kitty and Leo made an odd couple on the dance floor. Leo was a head taller than Kitty. He had two left feet, but she was a good leader. Do you know the movie where Fred Astaire dances with the coat rack? Well, that was Kitty waltzing with Leo, if you get the picture.

After the dance, we toasted the anniversary couple with sparkling wine—all of us except Rose, who got her kicks from Welch's grape juice. Kitty and Leo then regaled us with reminiscences about their great romance.

"Leo, the year we met, it was '35, wasn't it?"

"No, '34, don't you remember?"

"Are you sure it wasn't '35? I think we saw Katharine Hepburn."

"I can see it quite clearly, Kitty. We went to the Brooklyn Paramount at Flatbush and DeKalb. Rosa Río was at the twin organs. It wasn't Hepburn, it was Miriam Hopkins. *All of Me.* You liked that skimpy dress she had on."

I have no doubt Leo was right. He had a memory like an elephant. Not Kitty, especially after she turned sixty. If you asked her anything to do with a number, it was all gone.

"I noticed right away how shapely Kitty was," Leo said. He poked Sol in the ribs. "She's still gorgeous, isn't she?"

Kitty gave me a wink. "He's a charmer, Selma. He can charm the pants off you."

She was wearing her Lilly Pulitzer capri pants and tropical blouse, the one with palm fronds, flamingos, and papayas. Kitty wasn't exactly an American Beauty Rose. She had a funny face. Funny peculiar, not funny ha-ha. You know, Buster Brown bangs and a lot of teeth, like Imogene Coca. But she could be a real glamour puss if she put her mind to it. Whenever she walked into the room, all heads turned. So maybe she was a clothes horse, but why shouldn't she be? She knew what looked good on her, and Leo could afford it.

"You should have seen the way she chased me," Leo said. "I wasn't ready, but a girl expects a fellow to settle down."

"Don't listen to that crap," Kitty broke in. "Believe me, he wasn't the only guy in my life."

"She wouldn't give me a moment's peace until I bought her a ring."

"That's absolute bull. Don't pay attention to him."

Kitty was smiling. She held up her hand so we could all admire her engagement ring, like Queen Elizabeth showing off the Koh-i-Noor. It was a night to remember, until Sid brought us down to earth.

"What's the most important thing in a marriage, Bubbie?"

"Love?"

"Nope."

"Romance?"

"No, it's the ring. Love and romance may wax or wane, but the ring is the symbol of commitment."

"I didn't realize you were such a romantic, Sid. Harry Winston should hire you to do a commercial."

Now everybody got into a discussion about love versus commitment. All of us were talking across the dining table—I carried on three different arguments at once.

It was at this point that Sol tapped his champagne glass with a fork, interrupting us for an important announcement. Young Garfinkle—the fellow who'd bought Lady DuBarry—was finally ready to make the last payment. Sol was purring louder than a cat in the fish market. He'd take the plane to New York in three days to get his certified check and sign the receipt of payment.

"I thought he was having trouble making a go of it," Sid said.

"He's doing better. The economy is picking up and Garfinkle now considers Reagan the Messiah. Reagan had nothing to do with it. The boy's finally learning how to wipe his behind. But what do I care? I'll soon be free of the albatross and that's all that matters."

"I still miss my business," Leo said. "Everybody undercutting everybody else, all the hungry piranhas eying you from down the street. That was the life!"

"How about the aggravation? I don't know why anyone wants to own a business. Is there something a little soft in the head? No, thanks. I'm seventy-one. It's time to stop."

Rose tried to serve Sol more wild rice, but he waved her off. He was sick of healthy food. He wanted to celebrate the first day of the rest of his life by getting his teeth into more red meat.

"I'll have another slice of flank steak, Selma. Make it a thick one, this is an occasion."

"What did the doctor tell you? " Rose said. "Your cholesterol is over two seventy-five."

"Ramsool can eat wild rice."

"At least let me slice you an extra-lean piece off the end. Selma, the carving knife, please."

"Extra-lean means extra-no-taste. I'll have that piece over there, Selma, the fatty one."

"Sol, your blood pressure. The systolic was one sixty-five the last time."

"And some gravy, too."

Rose sighed and gave in. She didn't even complain when Sol asked for a third helping and a fourth—more fatty slices.

He was a contented man, like Bernstein the day before his renal treatment. I felt good, too. I liked to see a man enjoy his food. What is it they say? A smiling face is half the meal.

Unfortunately, Sid now began pestering Sol about putting the final $75,000 payment for Lady DuBarry into a mortgage. Arlee Sparlow had one for fifteen and three-quarters percent on ten acres of commercial land just up the road from the Alligator Farm on US 1.

"Why keep your money in a mutual fund? You might as well be driving a Model T."

"I need more paper like I need more chins."

"If everybody thought that way, we'd still be using leeches instead of penicillin."

Suddenly, Sol got up from the table, his face drained of color. He stood there shakily, trying to catch his breath. He was panting as he put his hands on the table to steady himself, rattling the coffee cups and dessert plates.

"What's wrong?" I asked.

"I'm fine, Selma, maybe a little indigestion."

"I hope it wasn't something you ate."

"No, the meal was just fine, thank you. Now, please excuse me."

Sol hurried off to the guest bathroom. We could hear him splashing water on his face. Sid and Leo got up and followed him down the hall. Soon everybody was crowding into the little toilet. Rose was starting to panic. To tell you the truth, she looked worse than Sol.

"What is it? The chest? The heart? The sinuses? I told you not to stop taking those stress pills. Why did you have to eat that fatty meat? You never listen to me!"

"It's nothing, Rose—an upset stomach. What's everybody doing in here? Can't a man go to the bathroom by himself? I want all of you out of here now. Out, out!"

The color was coming back to Sol's face. He wasn't exactly the picture of health, but he was looking more his old self—red as beet soup and sputtering at everyone like Captain Bligh.

CHAPTER 19

SENTIMENTAL JOURNEY

I was sitting on the piano bench with my mandolin a few days after the anniversary dinner, practicing the solo from "Sentimental Journey" for the next Pelican Pluckers concert. I had to break in a new pick, which may have accounted for the trouble I was having with my tremolos.

I'd finally gotten the hang of it about an hour after breakfast when Rose burst in without knocking—Rose, who was always so careful to observe the niceties. I almost dropped my mandolin when I saw the look on her face.

"My God," I said, rushing over. "What's wrong?"

Her face was gray, her eyes blank. I led her to the sofa. As soon as I took her hands in mine, she began making odd little whimpering noises.

"Rose? Rose, what happened?"

"I want to be dead, Selma. Just let me lie down and die."

At this point she lost whatever self-control she still had and started shrieking and clawing at her hair. Oh, no, I thought. I took her in my arms and held her close until the tears came.

"Don't move, dear." I stroked her hair as I stood up. "Stay there while I put on the kettle."

I ran to the kitchen and made a pot of Earl Grey, but Rose took only one sip, then threw her arms around me. Sobbing and shivering, she struggled to get out a few words at a time.

Yes, Sol was gone. It happened on the way to La Guardia, not more than ten minutes after the lawyers had given him the certified check in Manhattan. The cabbie got off the Grand Central and drove to Elmhurst General, but it was too late. A coronary thrombosis.

"I want to crawl under the bed and hide," Rose cried. "I can't go on without him. Dear God, what will I do? You won't leave me, will you, Selma?"

"Now, now, I'm not going anywhere, darling."

"I don't know how to fill the gas tank or turn on the garage light. I don't remember how to balance a checkbook. Sol does everything. My God, I haven't even told the children."

The police wanted Rose to identify Sol at the morgue on First Avenue. Of course, I offered to fly up with her. There was nobody else. Kitty and Leo were on their cruise and Rose's two children were thousands of miles away. Sid had to see Arlee about refinancing the mortgage for Sunny Simonize, the car wash, but he'd join us in New York the next morning.

Until then, I was on my own with Rose. She was so helpless, poor thing. I tried to comfort her and make the plane reservations at the same time.

"Why him, Selma? He worked so hard all his life. I always knew that store would kill him. All those years of aggravation. What was he working for?"

"Oh, Rose, I'm so sorry. Who can understand?"

Poor Rose! She couldn't even pack for herself. It was February in New York, and I had to search around to find her winter things—the ones for real winter—in the guest room closet. I threw a bunch of them into a suitcase, then brought her back to my place. I didn't want to leave her alone at her house. It was depressing there at the best of times, full of gloomy old furniture that only Queen Victoria could have appreciated. Everything was her fault, of course.

"I knew he was eating himself to death, but I did nothing," she said as I packed my bag. "I was an accomplice. I might as well have killed him with my own hands."

"You did whatever you could, dear."

"I should have nagged him from morning until night. I should have gotten him up in the middle of the night and nagged him some more. Life is such a cruel hoax."

I was the one who notified the family and friends. I found Zach at his workshop in Santa Fe, but Becky was out on a job—a wasps' nest in a dormitory at Mills College. I left a message with her girlfriend, the entomologist.

Zach was going to get a flight to New York later in the day, switching planes in Chicago. He'd nearly given Sol a stroke when he dropped out of MIT, joined a Zen Buddhist monastery in the Catskills, and called himself Junpol Zachary. Sol wouldn't speak to him for two years. He had no son. But all was forgiven when Zach and Chloris were finally married, even if it was a Reform ceremony where the rabbi waved a crystal and did their charts with Cabalistic astrology.

As for Becky, she called to say she'd take the red eye and arrive the following morning. This was cutting it close. In Jewish law, you're supposed to be buried within three days, which doesn't leave much time for complications. But Becky had promised to finish a house by the Bay Bridge. The termites were eating everything. They even ate the label and half the cork from a bottle of zinfandel, but the wine itself was all right.

I had a private talk with Sid about the arrangements before he drove Rose and me to Melbourne airport to catch the noon flight. We'd used Gutterman's when my mother passed away, the one on Flatbush Avenue in Brooklyn, but Sid wasn't happy with them.

"They're too high, Bubbie. I have a better idea. Do you remember Gurey?"

"Who?"

"Abe Gurewitz, the guidance counselor at Gompers."

"Was he the fellow with the big ears?"

"No, you're thinking of Guerrini, the shop teacher who's now the principal. We called him Dumbo. Gurey is the guy with flat feet and a crooked smile. His son, Leonard, is with Duberman & Daughter in Kew Gardens. He married the daughter. Why don't you give the boy a call before leaving Florida? Just mention Gurey. It helps to know someone."

Sid also got me the phone number of the fellow from the burial society who had to get the cemetery to open the grave. All three of our families had plots in the Garden of Isaiah. My father made the original arrangements through the Flatbush Relief Society. He was the recording secretary. Little did he know that he'd be the first one buried in the cemetery—the first grownup, anyhow. Malka—my sister, May—was already there.

We had twenty plots in all—eight of them for me and mine, the rest for the families of my two friends. We were still little girls, but my father had made sure there'd be room for husbands and children when the time came. We had three rows. The first, where we buried the grandparents, was full. Now, Sol would join May in the next one. The last row, the one farthest from the footpath, was for the grandchildren, the children of our generation.

We flew Delta to La Guardia, one of those older Boeings where you can't straighten your legs. Poor Rose was wearing her ranch mink, but she was shivering worse than the girls at the World's Fair. I put my arm around her and pulled her close, trying to give her some of my warmth.

"He denied himself for so many years, Selma, but he expected to enjoy his labors one day. He was going to travel and see all the places he should have seen when he was a young man. The young don't realize they're not forever."

As the plane circled Long Island Sound, I turned up the shawl collar of her coat. Underneath, she was wearing the same maroon chemise she had on when the call came from New York. I should have made her change, but there were too many things on my mind.

CHAPTER 20

WHEN THE FILM BREAKS

The cabbie, an ox of a fellow from the Ukraine, wanted to take the midtown tunnel, but I insisted on the Fifty-ninth Street bridge so there wouldn't be a toll. The morgue was at Thirtieth and First, the building with the turquoise bricks in front, like the tiles of the Econo Lodge in Florida.

The guard in the lobby was eating eggplant Parmesan at his desk. He didn't acknowledge our presence until he'd scooped the last of the tomato sauce off his takeout plate. Then he scratched his W. C. Fields nose while he searched for Rose's name on the list.

We waited on a tufted imitation-leather couch for someone to come get us. No matter where I sat, one of the buttons poked me in the behind. There was an un-opened box of Scotties by the magazine rack and something on the wall in Latin about life and death. Rose had just made shreds of the last tissue in the box when we were called.

The Interview Room was just off the lobby. There was a black-and-white photo of Einstein in a polyvinyl frame on the desk. I once heard that Einstein's brain was pickled in a bottle somewhere, but I'm not sure if that's true. Rose had so many questions to answer. It was like doing your income tax. I don't know why passing away should be so complicated, especially when it's natural causes. Imagine what it must be like if there's some funny business.

It was a stuffy room with barely enough space to cross your knees. I felt more cramped than on the plane. It didn't help that the interviewer took up two-thirds of the place, her flabby arms shaking like Jell-O molds each time she handed Rose a form. Miss Bumpus—she was officially called a technician—wore a cloying perfume that made it even more suffocating.

Rose was breaking down in tears every minute. She couldn't even remember the date Sol was born. She kept changing her mind until I made it 1913. I did all the paperwork for her. The only thing Rose had to do was sign on the dotted line, which wasn't even dotted.

"I'm so sorry to put you through this," Miss Bumpus told Rose as she led us out of the room to a stairwell.

"Be prepared," she whispered in my ear as we descended the depths. "You'll have to be strong for her. We don't use makeup or other cosmetic enhancements."

I don't intend to go down those dreadful steps again, at least not while I'm alive, and preferably not after that, either. No amount of Lysol could have washed away the stench. Not from the deceased, but from the friends and relatives who got sick after identifying them.

There was an open door at the bottom. Just inside was a table on wheels, the gurney, waiting for us like in the movies. There was a white sheet on top, a disposable plastic one.

As Miss Bumpus put on her latex gloves, I got a glimpse of the room through the doorway. There were dust-coated fluorescent lights hanging from the ceiling. The walls were aquamarine or maybe turquoise like the bricks outside. I didn't see any refrigerator drawers.

Miss Bumpus pulled back a corner of the sheet. Rose let out a gasp and her face lost whatever blood was still left. She stood there frozen like when the film breaks during a movie. I touched her cheek, but she didn't respond. Her skin was damp and sticky to my finger tips. I remember thinking her eyes looked lifeless, and then I saw Sol's.

It was Sol all right and yet it wasn't. Something was gone, the soul or spirit, the life force, whatever you call it. Of course, he hadn't been to the funeral parlor, which makes a difference.

"Is this your husband?" Miss Bumpus said, touching Rose on the shoulder.

Rose was staring at Sol's face.

"Mrs. Moskowitz, we need your help."

"It's Sol," I broke in. "I'll swear to it."

"I'm sorry, Mrs. Waxler, but I have to ask her."

Rose made a nothing of a noise, not even a whimper.

"All you have to do is nod," Miss Bumpus said.

It must have taken only a minute or two, but the minute hand slows down when your world is coming apart at the speed of light. Finally, Rose nodded, then turned from the gurney.

"Selma? Where are you?"

"I'm right here, Rose."

"I'm sorry," Miss Bumpus said.

Of course she was sorry. I wouldn't have had her job for all the tea in China. She took Rose and me by the elbows and led us back up the stairs.

I began to say something to Rose on the sidewalk outside, but I couldn't put the subject before the predicate and make a sentence. Instead, I put the two suitcases down and wrapped an arm around her. She leaned on me as I waved for a taxi to take us to Herald Square.

We had to get the F train near Macy's, around the corner from where I worked at Ansonia. Do you know Leonardo called feet an engineering miracle? That's what Mr. Wolfowitz used to tell the customers. The things we remember!

Rose and I got off the train at the Union Turnpike station in Queens. The next stop was Duberman & Daughter, the funeral home in Kew Gardens. Leonard—Gurey's boy—was waiting for us. He was a Thomashefsky type who tiptoed around with talcum powder on his face and a lace handkerchief in his breast pocket. He had a poor excuse for a mustache. I could have drawn a better one with an eyebrow pencil.

My hands were sore from carrying the suitcases, but he let me leave them behind the reception desk before he took us down in the elevator. He had a lopsided smile like his father's, but I couldn't tell about the feet. Is it possible to tiptoe if you have flat feet?

He showed us to a couch in the Consultation Room.

It could have been an insurance office: popcorn ceiling, recessed lighting, Danish modern furniture, wall-to-wall carpeting. Rose's home looked more like a funeral parlor.

"I realize this is a hard time for you," Leonard said, offering Rose a tissue. "I'm here to make it easier. If you don't feel up to it, you can leave all the bothersome details in my hands."

Rose looked from him to me, shook her head helplessly, then buried her face in the tissue.

"We'd like to have the arrangements as simple as possible," I said. "I'm sure Sol would want us to keep the frills to a minimum."

"Everyone wants it simple, but some things can be too simple," Leonard said. "The coffin, for instance. You don't want it to come apart on the way to the cemetery. Speaking from experience, I'd recommend a sturdy steel model."

"I thought Jewish coffins had to be made out of wood," I said. "If there's any metal, it won't turn into ashes and dust."

"That's only for the Orthodox. Mrs. Moskowitz isn't observant, is she?"

"No, but a simple wood coffin will do just fine."

"I was hoping to spare the bereaved," Leonard said, standing up. "Why don't you let me show you our floor models?"

He held out a hand to each of us. His palms were clammy, like what's-his-name, the creepy one in *David Copperfield*.

"We carry only the highest quality merchandise," he said, leading us down the carpeted hallway to a room at the end. "Boxspring mattresses, hand-stitched pillows, fine lace coverlets."

The sign over the entrance said Coffin Corner in English, but the letters were made to look like Hebrew. Leonard held open the door and switched on the lights.

"Every model has the *Good Housekeeping* seal, Mrs. Moskowitz. I don't want to twist your arm, but Hygrade has an indestructible-steel line that can't be beat for cost and quality."

"I'm sure Rose would prefer a simple wooden one," I said.

"Steel is more durable," he insisted, taking us over to one strongbox. "Here we have a sturdy model that's fully lined in velvet. Look at that lace pillow. You can order it in foam or down. The lining comes with or without flounce. I don't know why you're so set on wood."

"I'll have you know my father, may he rest in peace, used to make the most beautiful pine coffins. You should have seen them. He called pine the carpenter's wood."

"I agree, wood is beautiful, but I'd still recommend the Hygrade 211. It's solid steel with a velvet interior— or silk crêpe, if you'd prefer. Nothing beats steel for durability. It's under a thousand—only nine ninety-nine, in fact—and worth every penny."

"How much is a wood one?"

"Whatever you say. I don't want you to feel this is a high-pressure organization. We're not selling used cars. If all you care about is the bottom line, we have one here in cloth-covered flakeboard. Unfortunately, it's non-protective and the hardware is nickel-plated."

There was also a low-cost pine model for three twenty-nine, the Wedge, but the thing looked as if it were knocked together out of orange crates. We finally compromised on the Hygrade LS11 at seven ninety-nine, a pine model with a Star of David carved on the cover.

"That's an excellent selection for the dollar-conscious client, ladies. No cornices or railings to jack up the price, and you have your choice of a rubbed-wax or polyure-thane finish."

That wasn't the end of it. There was another two hundred for getting Sol from the morgue to the funeral home. It seemed a lot, but you couldn't just call a taxi. Duberman got seven seventy-five for arranging things and five and a quarter more for the incidentals—hearse, rabbi, death certificates, opening the grave, tips for the diggers, tolls—subtotal A, subtotal B, etc.

My father would have liked that coffin, though he might have objected to the carving. He preferred to em-phasize the natural beauty of the wood rather than the talent of the carpenter.

God only knows what I would have done without Rose the night he died in 1937. The doctors at Beth Is-rael said apoplexy, which was what you called a stroke in those days. I remember the nurse gave my mother string and brown paper for his clothes. I was no good and Rose had to help her tie the knot.

On the train home to Brooklyn, my mother sat between Rose and me, clutching the package in her lap and talking to herself about the holes in my father's shoes. Rose leaned over and gave her a hug, dear old Rose. "We have so little time," Mama said. "As soon as the seed sprouts, God steps on it."

CHAPTER 21

HAPPY ROCKEFELLER

The people you meet in New York! There, the crazy ones are normal. On the way from the funeral home in Queens to Zoot's apartment on the Upper West Side, a bum on the train insulted me just because I wouldn't give him a ten-dollar bill.

He looked me up and down, then shook his head. "Pregnant?" he said. "And at your age?"

All right, so I was bundled up in my winter coat, which didn't show off my figure to its best, but that was no excuse. Well, the craziness of strangers shouldn't keep you awake nights when you have craziness enough in your own family.

Zoot lived in a brownstone a few blocks from the Seventy-ninth Street stop on the Seventh Avenue local. My arms were coming out of their sockets by the time I climbed the five flights to his apartment. I could smell the litter box before the door swung open. One of Zoot's girlfriends had left her black kitten when she dumped him for a drummer with Tito Puente. Zoot named her Billie—for the singer.

Well, at least I didn't smell pot, thank God. I don't know what gets into me when I'm around my children. The next thing you know, I was acting like a mother again.

"Don't you ever empty that cat box, Zoot?"

"How's it shaking, Mama?"

"How do you think?"

"Bummer, I guess."

"Are those cockroaches I see in the cat bowl?"

Zoot's red beard was down to his ankles, especially when he wasn't standing up straight. He had on his usual patched-up overalls, but he was walking around in bare feet this time, not in those ugly Earth Shoes. He had his hands in his pockets and shifted his weight from one foot to the other like Li'l Abner. The only thing missing was a piece of straw in his teeth.

Rose came up behind me, huffing and puffing from the stairs. She put her hands on Zoot's shoulders to steady herself. He gave her a sad look and she began sobbing all over him. Poor Zoot! He didn't know what to do with his eyes; he didn't know what to do with his hands; he didn't know what to do with his mouth.

"Why did it have to be Sol?" Rose cried. "Life is such a bitter pill, Zoot."

Zoot patted Rose on the back as if he were burping a baby.

"You must be totally wiped out," he said. "I remember when I was a kid and Uncle Sol used to throw me up in the air. He had big hands, as big as Chu Berry's. He was a trip and a half."

"Thank you, Zoot. Sol would appreciate that."

Zoot was such a sweet boy, but he could be forgetful. I had to remind him to take in the luggage for us. He put the two pieces on the sofa in his living room. I also had to remind him to clear away a place in the hall closet for us to hang our things.

I don't want to spend another night like that. Zoot took the sofa while Rose and I shared his lumpy bed. I thought sharing a bed with a snorer like Sid was bad, but Rose was something else again. She slept like a baby— each hour, she woke up and cried. She blamed herself for everything. Lady Macbeth's hands were covered in blood.

The next morning, I had such an aching back and a pounding headache, you wouldn't believe. The last thing I needed was a pain in the behind, which is what I got when Sid flew up on Eastern and met us at Zoot's. He made a big stink about the arrangements. He wasn't satisfied with anything I'd done.

"How could you throw all that money away, Bubbie? I never heard of anybody spending twenty-five hundred on a funeral. Who do you think you are, Happy Rockefeller?"

"It's only twenty-two ninety-nine. And Rose is paying, not us."

"You should have gone somewhere else."

"I did what you told me to do. Gurey's boy will take care of you—that's what you said."

"Well, he really took care of you. I should have handled this myself."

"Nobody's stopping you." I got Zoot's phone from the hook and gave it to him. "Here, let's see how much better the big shot from Florida can do."

Sid gave me a smirk as he took the receiver, dialed Queens, and started in on Leonard: What are you doing to me? I was very close to Gurey at Gompers. Is this any way to treat a friend of the family? All of a sudden, Sid wasn't smiling anymore.

"No, I didn't say that, Lenny. I don't want to go anywhere else. I appreciate that. You won't charge me a penny if I take the remains? No, that's not what I want. But twenty-five hundred is high. Well, twenty-two ninety-nine. It still seems high. You mean to say you can't do a little better? Gurey would appreciate it. Well, if you can't, you can't. Yes, I'm happy, thank you."

Actually, Sid did save Rose a few dollars by arranging for a single service—a graveside instead of one at the funeral home and another at the cemetery. That meant she wouldn't have to pay the rabbi twice. I asked Rose if it was all right, but she didn't want to know about the details.

It began snowing as soon as we crossed the Triborough on the way to the funeral—the weatherman had predicted three inches on Long Island. There were five of us in the jalopy from Rent-a-Wreck. Rose was up front next to Sid. I was in back with Zoot and Garfinkle, the new owner of Lady DuBarry, who'd closed for the day out of respect.

Rose's brother, Mort, flew up from West Palm. He used to have a place off Seventh Avenue, notions and trimmings. He was very tight with a buck. He even sold his plots at the Garden of Isaiah to get cheaper ones at Menorah Gardens in West Palm. Sol's younger sister, the cranky one, was too sick to leave her nursing home in Boynton Beach. The older one passed away the year before in Albuquerque, the cervix.

There were a couple of people from Kimball Terrace in Yonkers—Hy Zucker, the chiropractor down the street, and Essie Sussman, a real character before her laryngectomy. But the rest of the old crowd were occupied elsewhere: the retirement village, the nursing home, the hereafter.

"Where is everybody?" Rose asked as we gathered by the plots. "We used to know a million people. I thought you were going to call them, Selma."

Rose seemed so tiny. In twenty-four hours, she'd shriveled on the vine.

"You know how these things are," I said. "The older you get, the smaller the crowd."

Actually, the turnout wasn't so bad, especially considering the clumps of snow coming down. There were a dozen of us, not counting the rabbi. Becky had arrived from Oakland with her friend, Nellie, a very pretty girl, and so well turned out. Nellie was wearing a camel's hair coat over a cashmere sweater set and a pleated plaid skirt. She had a very tasteful strand of pearls, too.

This was another example of opposites attracting. Becky was always the tomboy type. I'd be surprised if she had a skirt to her name, let alone pearls. She used to beat Zoot at arm-wrestling on Kimball Terrace. From the looks of her, she could do the same now.

"I'm so sorry," I said, giving Becky a squeeze on the biceps. "Sol was such a dear friend."

"Thanks for looking after Mom, Selma. I don't know what she'd have done without you."

I never know what to say on such occasions. Or, rather, I do know, but it's so inadequate, like the message on a sympathy card.

I was hoping Becky didn't feel guilty about what she'd put Sol through. He almost had a heart attack the day she came home from Sarah Lawrence with her hair cropped short and slicked back. She was all in black except for the red-and-white Commie Dyke Slut button on her leather jacket. Of course, Becky had outgrown most of that nonsense by now, but she was as allergic as ever to pumps or pantyhose.

"I see you're still buying your clothes from the L. L. Bean catalogue," I said. "You used to have such lovely knees. It wouldn't hurt if you showed them once in a while."

"You haven't changed, Selma. You're still minding everybody else's business. I wouldn't be surprised if there's a serious feminist lurking beneath that Donna Reed facade."

Becky leaned over and gave me a peck on the cheek.

"Let me introduce you to my friend. You two have a lot in common. Nellie is also trying to reform me. Be nice to her, Selma. She's only been out to her family for a month now. Oh, look, she's blushing. I've embarrassed her."

Nellie was fidgeting with her pearls. She was very sweet. Smart, too. She was doing research at Berkeley on the goat-moth caterpillar and had just published a paper about the virgin reproduction of aphids. They made a very nice couple.

Kitty and Leo were on the high seas, so the Seligmans

were represented by Myra. She was taking a break from the hardware stores to pay her respects, though she was paying most of her attention to Zoot.

Myra was quite attractive, even if she insisted on hiding behind eyeglasses the size of satellite dishes. Somehow, she always managed to get Zoot's goat. The argument this time was over which female vocalist was the greatest, Ella or Billie.

"Nobody has a voice like Ella's," Myra was saying. "I have all the Deccas and Verves."

"She's got the instrument, but she doesn't make you laugh or cry."

"What! Ella can lift you up to heaven."

"Okay, she's got the chops, but let's not get carried away. Billie has the heart and soul. It takes more than singing the notes to make a great singer. You also have to sing the lyrics. If you don't know that, you don't know the first thing about jazz."

"I don't need you to teach me about jazz. What makes you such a big expert?"

"Will you two keep your voices down?" I hissed.

I was wrapped like a mummy in my alpaca coat, but I knelt down and picked up three pebbles—a pitted one for my father, one worn smooth for my mother, and a tiny pearl-like one for May. You leave them on the gravestone to show someone was there.

Rose was standing next to her parents' plots with Zach. He was about Dewey's age, but his white beard made him look older. I could hear him doing his best to comfort Rose.

"Take a deep breath and listen to yourself for a minute," he said. "I mean really stop and listen. It's a haiku sort of thing—the essence of simplicity—like a snowflake falling."

"Don't waste your time on me, Zachary. I'm as good as gone, only no one has gotten around to burying me."

Chloris couldn't make it. She was visiting her father's tribe in North Dakota. She always attended synagogue in Santa Fe on the High Holy Days, but she returned to the Chippewas once a year for their services—the sun dance, the sweat lodge, the purification ritual.

Zach wanted Rose to come with him to the East Village after the funeral and try his Relaxman. From what I could gather, this was something like a kaleidoscope, but with earphones and goggles. It was supposed to synchronize the brain waves. He was staying on St. Mark's Place with some of his old hippie friends.

Well, the funeral was about what you might have expected. Lescher, the rabbi, led us in the mourner's kaddish and two psalms. He was very patient with Rose when she broke down during the widow's prayer at the part that goes help me, oh God, to bear this burden bravely.

Lescher asked the children to say a few words. Becky tried to speak, but she choked up. Zach was able to say something, but it was all about himself, how his faith was a neo-pagan Buddhist Hindu kind of Jewish New Age thing.

In his eulogy, the rabbi got in most of the stuff I'd given him. The only thing he forgot was Sol's honorable mention from the Neighborhood Cleaners Association. He was very highly thought of in his field. *The Bronx Home News* once called him the Sultan of Stain. Anyone can clean and press, he told the reporter, but spotting is an art.

CHAPTER 22

ULYSSES AND THE SIRENS

Kitty returned from her anniversary cruise while Rose was still sitting shiva, the seven days of mourning. Kitty and I, her oldest and dearest friends, would pass the hours with Rose on the old velvet sofa in her living room. We were there for her, but we didn't intrude upon her grief. That's the Jewish way of handling loss. The mourner goes through a period of weeping and lamentation. You're allowed to beat your breast while your friends maintain a respectful distance.

You could never relax in Rose's home, even on happy occasions, and not just because of the ugly furniture. Even worse was the suffocating air. To keep out the germs and whatever else she imagined could be carried in, she kept the place sealed tighter than King Tut's tomb.

The only cheerful touch in this mausoleum was Snow White and the Seven Dwarfs, a set of hand-painted figurines on the upper shelf of Rose's china closet. Sol had gotten them for her on their honeymoon in the Poconos. The Bluebird of Happiness was perched on Snow White's finger.

Rose was still blaming herself for everything. If only she'd done this or not done that, Sol would still be there enjoying his retirement. I could understand how she felt. Even I had a guilty conscience about those fatty slices of flank steak.

Becky flew down to Florida after the funeral and spent a few days with her mother. Zach could stay only one night. He had to return home to see Chloris do the sun dance for a New Age group in Santa Fe that prayed to Mother Earth and Father Sky.

I helped tidy up after the children were gone. Rose was particular, even in her grief. Wilbert's lemon oil on this, Murphy's soap there, Clorox on the counters, Old Dutch in the tub, Spic and Span on the kitchen floor. You had to use a string mop, not the sponge—the sponge left streaks.

"I just walk from one empty room to another," Rose sighed. "The only company I have is my reflection in the mirror. Wait, Selma! What are you doing?"

I was about to mop the tile floor in the guest toilet. "Not Spic and Span," she said. "That's for the kitchen. I use Top Job in the bathrooms."

It was a difficult time. Rose would make a little progress, then a fellow selling monuments or cemetery plots would call and everything would begin all over again. Not that I'm complaining. I could never repay Rose for all she'd done for me over the years.

As you can see, I had my mind on other things, which may explain why I let Sid wheel and deal to his heart's content. Not that I had reason to worry. Things were going along very nicely as spring arrived in Satellite

Beach. The monthly checks came in like clockwork. If an interest payment was late, Sid would get a five percent penalty. As soon as the check arrived, he'd put it in the bank to save up for another package.

When a mortgage was paid off, Arlee would write a check and Sid would hand it back before the ink had dried. Give me another. It went on like that month after month. The money came in, the money went out. I never saw any of it, but every day Sid would remind me how rich we were getting. I didn't need to be rich. Well, no matter. If it made Sid happy, that was enough.

By June, we had $116,567 invested in mortgages and only $356 left in our money market at Southland. Anyone else would have been content to stop now, but not Sid. My God, what happened next! I didn't find out until I opened one of our bank statements by mistake. Sid had begun borrowing from Ready Credit—our $25,000 line of credit at Southland—and was putting this into mortgages, too. It made me sick inside.

"How could you do this without telling me, Sid? I don't want to be in debt to anyone."

"We can't sit on our hands, Bubbie. If you don't want to be left behind in today's economy, you have to take a few risks. I know what I'm doing. We can make two and a half percent more from the mortgages than we have to pay Southland in interest. You don't have to be concerned."

Well, I was concerned. It was like Ulysses and the Sirens. All Arlee had to do was call about a new package and Sid would forget everything else. He was up at dawn each day and off to see the latest property before I had a chance to clear away the breakfast dishes. Some days, he didn't return home until suppertime.

Thank God he was still being careful. He made sure each property matched the description in the papers. He spoke to the appraiser and the borrower. He called up the credit references.

Some of the other investors weren't so careful. Annette was very concerned about Rocky. He was becoming too trusting—naïve, in her opinion.

"We Italians say the eye of the owner makes the horse fat," Annette said when I went in to get my bangs trimmed that July. "Rocky would rather be the horse and wear blinders."

"Sid listens to me, but he does just the opposite. If you say day, he says night. Do you think that's short enough, Annette?"

"I could take off a little more. You're easy to do, Selma. So many of my clients have unrealistic expectations. They come to me and pull out a picture. They don't want to hear they can't wear something like that. How's it now?"

Rocky wasn't the only gullible one. Arlee had a lot of trusting people begging to invest with him, everyone from Bernstein to Mo Bialer. Of course, Bernstein had money to throw around, or at least his wife did. The Bernsteins had just put a pool in the backyard of their Château. It was in the shape of a mandolin—pear shaped, with a neck to swim laps in and a Jacuzzi for the pegbox. Bernstein invited all of Pluckers to a swimming party the last week of July. I did laps in the neck, but the Jacuzzi tickled my toes.

Even Wanda Schlachman's husband invested a few thousand in a package. That is, her second husband, Bucky, a retired periodontist. He was barely old enough to collect Social Security, but who was I to criticize Wanda for marrying someone ten years younger? I should look so good at her age.

If Bucky's shenanigans worried Wanda, she didn't show it at Healthercise that month. She had on Day-Glo yellow shorts over a black bodysuit. She was on a golden oldies kick. You know, "Runaround Sue," "Long Tall Sally," doo-wah diddy, diddy dum, diddy doo.

"Come on, girls, let's do the twist," she said as she put on a Chubby Checker tape. "Side to side, side to side. Twist, one, two. And a twist and a twist. That's the way. Work on that tummy. Twist it one. Twist, two, three. Now tighten that toches. Come on, let's twist."

I needed my Healthercise. After a few minutes of Wanda's contortions, Arlee Sparlow was a distant memory. Next came kicking-in-place exercises. I was a good kicker, as good as anyone in class except Kitty. She never said it in so many words, but I always suspected Kitty would have preferred to be a Rockette instead of a ballet girl. Of course, she was too short for that. Rockettes had to be five-five or more, and kick six inches over their heads.

"Now let's work on the heinies, ladies. Tuck in the tummies, squeeze the cheeks. Tuck, tuck, squeeze, squeeze. And a tuck and a tuck. And a squeeze and a squeeze. Lettie, your wig's slipping."

Wanda ended each Healthercise by having us growl like the M-G-M lion. I should have been growling at Sid instead. By the end of July, he'd already borrowed over fifteen thousand from Ready Credit. Then in August he borrowed $5,112 more to come up with enough for a mortgage on a family-practice building in Coco. Sid looked through the papers, but this time he didn't bother checking out the property itself.

"I spent more time picking the fabric for our sofa than you did looking at that deal, Sid. I don't want you to accept anything unless you go out and look at it yourself."

"I don't have time, Bubbie. We're on the express train, not the local."

By summer's end, Sid had borrowed all he could from Ready Credit. Oh, excuse me, I'm forgetting the escape clause. Whenever I raised the slightest objection, Sid would pat me on the head and tell me not to worry. Everything was guaranteed in writing, thank you.

"If we're unhappy with a package, Arlee will take it back for whatever we paid, no questions asked. How can we lose?"

"Why should he do that? Why should anybody be so nice?"

"Show me something, Bubbie, one thing bad that's happened to us since we met him."

"You sound like the fellow who's falling out of the Empire State Building and he's still on the way down. Nothing has happened yet."

"I don't need this, Selma. Talk to me when you have something intelligent to contribute."

That really struck a nerve. I was as capable as anybody of adding one and one and coming up with two. I could have done anything with my life. Miss Cowper wanted me to go to college. Instead, I stayed home and took care of an ungrateful husband and two ungrateful children.

One thing for certain, I didn't have to be a house-wife—not that I'm ashamed of it. I knew all about book-keeping from Ansonia. I was able to do a lot of other things, too. But Sid didn't like the idea of paying for help to come in. Yes, I could have worked. I had plenty of opportunities. Now he was treating me like the first monkey that came down from the tree.

CHAPTER 23

TRIBAL RITES

Wisdom may come with experience, but Dewey never got the word. He left King Features that fall—a personality clash, needless to say—and was back at *The Hollywood Reporter*. The lady who owned the place may have been a major ego-basher, but he needed the job and she had the checkbook. I wouldn't be surprised if Fleur had something to do with his return. She kept a watchful eye on the piggy bank when Dewey was unemployed.

Anyway, Dewey called us from his old desk in the news room the day after Rosh Hashanah. I was on the wall phone in the kitchen and Sid was on the line in Trump Castle.

Dewey didn't sound happy to be working there again, but he was stoical about it. "If I wanted a job without stress," he said, "I'd be the Good Humor man in Honduras."

Once again, we invited him to visit. I tried to point out a few of the Space Coast's many attractions, but he called me the poster girl for the Satellite Beach Chamber of Commerce. Sid made a joke about splitting the difference and meeting in Chicago. Like Queen Victoria, Dewey wasn't amused. Of course, he'd have visited us a dozen times if we were living in Palm Beach, especially if all expenses were paid.

When a few billionaires from Florida invited the Hollywood moguls and their hangers-on to a free weekend at the Breakers in October, Dewey came fast enough. As usual, everyone had an ulterior motive, or so he said. The local yokels wanted the Hollywood people to make movies in Florida. But the moguls wanted Florida money to make movies in Hollywood.

The big spenders who arranged all this were very generous. One flew the moguls over in his own plane, a Lear Jet with ostrich-leather seat covers and two Italian marble toilets. There were so many limos leaving the airport in West Palm that it looked like a funeral procession. All the invitees, including the Fourth Estate, had suites facing the sea.

Even the wives were invited—the spouses, more accurately, but I don't think there were any husbands tagging along. Of course, Fleur wouldn't have missed a free trip to Palm Beach with three blue-ribbon meals a day, plus high tea with scones and clotted cream, even if it meant a month of Lean Cuisine afterward.

"All of Hollywood is here," Dewey called to tell us while Fleur unpacked their bags. "Big, big players—Begelman, Freddy Fields, Marvin Davis, the guys with the bucks and the Armani suits. Forget about all those movie stars running around like kids in sneakers, blue jeans, and T-shirts. The most dangerous guy in Hollywood is the one in a suit."

Dewey phoned again after the cocktail party on Friday evening. There was a string quartet playing a medley of the classics. The waiters carried trays of hot hors d'oeuvres and chilled Dom Pérignon. They had a fish carved out of ice on the buffet table under the Venetian chandelier. The mouth was stuffed with Russian caviar and the scales were slices of Scottish smoked salmon.

"These jerks from Florida don't have a clue," Dewey was saying. "They think they know all about films because they watch them, but they know less than zero about the tribal rites of Hollywood—what's real and what's voodoo."

Sid was out with Arlee—they were meeting over coffee at Wendy's—so I had the phone to myself this time. Dewey seemed to be enjoying himself at the Breakers. It made him feel like a big shot to be around these people. He couldn't stop talking. You could put the phone down, take a shower, come back, pick it up again, and he'd still be talking.

"It's mind-boggling. Everybody's selling, but no one's buying. Florida is touting Hollywood, and Hollywood is touting Florida. I'm up to my eyeballs in bullshit. I love it."

In other words, he was in his milieu. He loved mingling with the moguls to get tidbits for his column. At one point, he was speaking to Marvin Davis while all the other big shots were coming up and whispering deals in this Davis person's ear.

"I'm asking myself is this *The Twilight Zone* or what? I'm talking to the guy, and he's carrying on a dozen conversations at the same time. What am I? A floor lamp? Then I realize he's got all these deals in his head at the same time. The man's a genius."

Dewey was going on in this vein when Sid returned home and joined me in the living room. Without asking, he grabbed the receiver from my hand.

"How much are you getting on your savings, Dewey? What did you say? You don't know? It's not your department?"

I tried to get the phone back, but Sid kept me at arm's length.

"Well, you tell Fleur to call me if she doesn't want to be eaten alive by inflation. How'd she like to make fifteen percent? I know something good that's coming along."

By the time I got to the extension in the kitchen, the call was over. Sid had been wasting his breath on Dewey, of course. Fleur was the one in charge of the pocketbook. But I was still furious. He wasn't satisfied with getting us and our friends involved. Now he wanted to sacrifice Dewey. And Zoot would be the next burnt offering, if a gig paid more than the price of a subway token.

We heard from Dewey again after the champagne brunch the next day. He was very opinionated, which may be why he got into an argument with Melnick or Fields over whether the kiss should come before the hug or vice versa. I tried to ask him when the stork should come, but he didn't want to talk about that.

As for Fleur, I was busy wiping the countertops that night when she phoned, so I had Sid pick up the extension in the office. When I returned to the kitchen phone ten minutes later, my fashionable daughter-in-law was going on about how the Florida wives had more money than they knew what to do with and no taste to do it with.

"Everyone is trussed up like a Thanksgiving turkey," she said. "I haven't seen so many foundation garments since the fifties."

I liked Fleur, even if she was a little too quick to judge people. She acted like a poor little rich girl, which wasn't so far from the truth. She was a member of a very wealthy family on her mother's side, the Philadelphia Skinners, but they treated her badly. I think they were angry with her mother for marrying into the Truitts, who were quite comfortable, though not rolling in money like the Skinner side of the family.

Anyway, I was talking to Fleur when Dewey got on and monopolized the conversation. You'd think the whole world wanted to hear what Swifty Lazar had to say about the outfits on the mariachi band. Finally, my chance came and I invited them to visit us before going back to L.A. Was that a conversation stopper! Well, I hadn't expected a positive answer. It was miracle enough that they condescended to let Sid and me travel to the Breakers on Sunday and pay our respects.

CHAPTER 24

GEORGETTE KLINGER

I t took two and a half hours for us to drive down A1A to Palm Beach. Sid grumbled all the way about having to cancel a big meeting with Arlee Sparlow, something to do with a mobile-home park off Dog Track Road. We could have saved an hour by taking I-95, but I preferred the more scenic route. Not that we saw much of the sea, thanks to all the high-rise hotels and condos grinning at us from the beach like false teeth.

We had a few minutes to stroll around the Breakers before Dewey and Fleur came down. Cecil B. De Mille would have been right at home in this place, from the Venetian chandelier to the Flemish tapestries. We were outside by the water fountain, the one where the cupids are wrestling the alligators, when the younger generation caught up with us.

Dewey was wearing white sneakers, blue jeans, and a silk sports jacket that must have cost him a month's gossip. Fleur was dressed nicely, too, in a simple linen suit. It looked like nothing, but I knew better. With something like that, the more you spend, the less you get.

We had a car and chauffeur for the day, thanks to the billionaires. I could get used to a stretch limo. It was nice to straighten my legs for a change, not like in our Corolla. Hubert, the driver, dropped Fleur and me off on Worth Avenue. Dewey and Sid were going on to the Palm Beach Polo and Country Club. It wasn't the polo season yet, but they wanted to look around while the tycoons and moguls met behind closed doors in a villa next to the polo fields.

I would have been content to sit around the Breakers and eat all day, but Fleur wanted us to share things, which was why we were going to Georgette Klinger for a Day of Beauty. It was like Glamour Girl Day at the House of Aloha, only more so. And don't ask. I don't want to think how much it cost, even if we weren't paying. The billionaires had gotten them to open on Sunday so the wives would have something to do while their husbands were meeting at the polo club.

What a place! I was tugged from room to room, rubbed and scrubbed from top to bottom—a scalp treatment, a pedicure, and everything else in between. It was like an old jalopy getting the works at Sunny Simonize.

I was embarrassed by the massage. I didn't particularly like being poked in one personal spot after another by an Amazon who'd just escaped from the German opera. Her name was Hildy. Instead of a breastplate and horned helmet, she was wearing a nurse's uniform, which only made me more nervous, even if it was a pink one.

"Don't fight me, Mrs. Waxler."

"Who's fighting? I'm just trying to get comfortable."

"I'm finding a lot of tension here. If you want to be comfortable, you have to concentrate on relaxing."

"How can I relax if you're kneading me like a ball of dough?"

"Please turn your head to the side. No, the other side. That's more comfortable, isn't it?"

"Not particularly."

"Of course it is."

"How do you know if I'm comfortable or not?"

"I can read your body like an open book, Mrs. Waxler, and it's not a pleasant story."

Well, the massage may have been a disappointment, but the body treatment made up for it. I was wrapped like puff pastry in towels soaked with peppermint. At first, the mint made me sneeze, but then my body went rubbery and I experienced the most extraordinary sensation. The girl had to wake me for lunch with Fleur.

All we got to nibble on was rabbit food: a wilted leaf of iceberg lettuce, a few soggy tomato slices, two carrot sticks, and herbal iced tea to wash it down.

"I thought we were supposed to be basking in the lap of luxury," I said as we sipped our tea. "For what they must be charging, we should be getting a decent meal."

"Will you lower your voice?" Fleur shushed me. "I want you to smile and stop kvetching."

"I'm not kvetching, and you should learn how to pronounce the word if you're going to use it. Listen to me—kvetch. One syllable, not two."

My socialite daughter-in-law was trying to be blasé about all the other wives, but I could see her peeking out the corner of her eye at one of them, somebody who used to be on television.

"Isn't that what's-her-name?" I asked

"Yes, Selma, and don't stare."

"Me? I'm not the one who's staring. I'm just curious."

Fleur picked up a *Vogue* from the next table, flipped through a few pictures, then put it back without reading anything. She took a sip of tea. From the way she was playing with her sprig of mint, I could see she had something on her mind. She put the glass down and cleared her throat. Was it good news, finally? You know me, the perennial optimist.

"That husband of yours," she said. "I never suspected. Who would have thought a man like Sid, somebody from his background, would have such hidden depths?"

"My Sid? Are we talking about the same person? Hidden depths, no less."

"You don't have to make a joke of it. When we talked last night, I found him so informative about the mortgage business. I could hardly tear myself away from the phone."

"No! Not you, too. Tell me I'm not hearing this, Fleur."

"You don't give him enough credit, Selma. I didn't realize you could get such a good return on your money in Florida. And he was so sweet. Mortgages have been pretty darn good to me, Fleur, and now I'd like to share my good fortune with somebody else."

Her words sent chills up and down my spine. If Brünhilde thought my muscles were balled up before, she should have felt them now.

"How dare he try to drag you and Dewey into this! Promise me you won't listen."

"Keep your voice down, Selma. I wasn't born yesterday. I've crunched the numbers and it makes perfect sense. I appreciate Sid even if you don't."

God help us, Mr. Trump had talked her into investing in a mortgage on a 7-Eleven a few miles from us.

The interest was almost twice what she could get on a CD in Oklahoma City—and guaranteed, too.

"This is our window of opportunity," Fleur said.

"You shouldn't be too greedy. Why not leave your money in the bank like other people?"

"We can't afford to play it safe."

Now, where had I heard that before?

"Don't look at me like that, Selma. We'll never save enough for a house that way. Every month, the cost goes up ten or twenty thousand. What you can get for seven-fifty now is a piece of trash. For a million, you still have to do a lot of work."

"Don't do this, Fleur. I'm warning you. Sid's a retired schoolteacher, not Daddy Warbucks."

"He warned me you'd say something like that. He said you were a naysayer."

Before I could reply, I was led away for Part Two of the overhaul. How about this for a coincidence? Robin, my beautician—excuse me, aesthetician—at Georgette Klinger, was formerly of Tip to Toe at Moonwalk Mall. Not only that, she knew Theresa quite well, the manicurist and cosmetologist at the House of Aloha.

I didn't realize, but Theresa had been married once before. The Bishop of Orlando gave her an annulment because her husband, the first one, didn't want children. Theresa had two now, a two-year-old boy and a baby girl born with six toes—I forget what that's called.

As Frieda, the stylist, was blow-drying me, I could hear Fleur two seats over. Her hairdresser, Rudy, was trying to talk her into letting her hair grow out.

"You have such a pretty face," he said. "With more hair to work with, you'll have so much more flexibility."

"I have enough decisions, Rudy. It used to be fun going out in the evening, but now it's a responsibility. No matter how many functions there are, you have to look good all night."

I once complimented Fleur on how gorgeous she looked. I expected a simple thank you in return. Instead, I got a lecture on the burdens of looking beautiful: If you only knew how much work it takes, Selma. Of course I knew. Where did she get off?

Well, I tried again to warn her about the mortgages when we went for manicures—we were at adjacent tables—but she turned away from me and held out her hands to the manicurist.

"Look at these," she said. "They're a wreck. Show me what you can do with them."

Oh, I'm forgetting. Fleur and I picked the same color. I don't remember the number—the colors had numbers in this place—but it was like Max Factor's Wine and Roses, though a shade lighter. It didn't dawn on us until we saw each other's nails on the way out.

CHAPTER 25

A GLITCH IN THE GITALONG

Arlee was collecting for Reagan around this time— you know, the fall of 1984—and he was asking everybody he met to contribute. He even asked Kitty when he saw us coming out of Save-a-Lot at Spaceport Plaza a few weeks before the election.

"You know what they say, ma'am, those who give will get."

"Right now, I'm voting for the man in the moon," Kitty said. "Reagan's a fascist and Mondale's a nothing. When I get to the polls, I'll go eeny-meeny-miney-moe."

She was lying, of course. If you held that do-gooder's feet to the fire, she wouldn't vote for a Republican. She was very opinionated about politics. I'm just the opposite. For me, there's too much politics in politics. If I had my way, everyone would get a lie-detector test every four years and the one who wanted to be President the least would have to take the job.

As for our financial situation, things were still looking good in spite of the butterflies in my stomach. Southland was certainly happy to have the Waxlers as customers. Crabbe took us to lunch at the Villa Romana in November and said the bank was raising our Ready Credit limit to $50,000. He even ordered a bottle of Asti Spumante for a toast. Best of all, he talked Sid out of two mortgages Arlee was trying to unload.

"Eli Potts wants to borrow on his used-car lot," Sid said. "He's anxious to pick up the vacant lot next door on A1A."

"I wouldn't lend a penny to that lowlife, Sid. You can scrape the bottom of the barrel with a fine-tooth comb and never come up with a bigger liar."

"But I'm only getting eight and a half percent at Southland. Arlee says there's somebody in Sherwood Park—a fellow named Weems—who'll pay sixteen to refinance his mobile home."

"I wouldn't bet my dog on that old cracker, either. Trotter—Trotter Weems—likes to play the hounds and drink his Southern Comfort."

Arlee didn't get up to greet us when we went to see him a couple of months later. He had one leg up on the desk and an aluminum cane hanging from the antlers, next to his white jacket and Panama hat. He straightened his tie and apologized for not being able to reach his jacket. I didn't want to be nosy, but curiosity got the better of me. The thing he had was gout, the disease that causes crystals in the toes.

"The doctor swears it's just a glitch in the gitalong," he said. "Well, if that's the case, why in hell do I feel like a one-legged man in an ass-kicking contest? If you'll pardon me, ma'am."

It was supposed to be from eating too much rich food. His doctor wanted him to eliminate meat and butter, fatty desserts, that sort of thing—a diet of mostly vegetables. If you'll remember, Birdella had warned us about his shiny skin.

Well, Sid went on a binge in January, but it had nothing to do with rich food. As he gobbled up mortgages over the next two months, I was the one getting the indigestion. By March, he'd borrowed all but a few thousand of the fifty available to us from Ready Credit. There was only one thing that worried him. The more cash he had, the more heavily it weighed on him. I never saw a man so anxious to get rid of his money.

Nothing else mattered. If something had to be done at home, he was too busy. He'd do it tomorrow—and tomorrow and tomorrow. If it was important, I'd get Leo to come over. I think he began doing his home-repair column for *The Orbiter* around this time. It ran each week over the notice for Overeaters Anonymous. Leo wrote about everything, but I could follow only the easier stuff, like how to raise the water level of the toilet by bending the metal rod in the tank.

It really burned me up when Sid began putting my household money into his mortgages in the spring of 1985. He kept after me until I let him take a few hundred. And that was just the beginning. Whenever I had a little extra, he'd be there with his hand out, ready to take it, too.

I needed that money. I used it for a lot of other things, not just the household expenses. I gave donations—UJA, True Sisters, Hadassah. In April, I was collecting to fix the CAT scan at Cape Canaveral Hospital, but he wouldn't let me make my own contribution. He wanted this money, too, money that should have gone for a good cause.

By now, we had $181,265 invested with Arlee Sparlow. Mr. Trump would throw that number in my face if I raised any objection to handing over my household money. He'd talk about how rich we were getting, but I couldn't help dwelling on the $49,747 we owed Ready Credit.

Things went from bad to worse that spring. Now he wanted me to hand over my inheritance, the money my mother scrimped and saved to leave me. It was still in East New York Savings, her old branch on Pitkin and St. John's, more than four thousand. I hadn't touched a penny of it since she'd passed away. I wanted to leave it for my children one day.

CHAPTER 26

A GOOD NAME

One day my mother got too old to work. She'd been doing embroidery for a seamstress on Madison Avenue. She sewed the most beautiful stuff. Once she did a silver bird of paradise on a pink organza gown—I can't tell you how beautiful it was.

But the time came when she couldn't see well enough for delicate hand work anymore and the arthritis made it hard for her to sew except on a machine. This was in the fifties, not long after the Rosenbergs were executed. Someone put an anonymous note in our mailbox on Kimball Terrace: All you Jews belong in the electric chair. It was probably that drunk three doors up, Wormley.

My mother had just turned sixty-five, like me when I moved to Florida with Sid. She had to leave the seamstress, but she found a job at a dress shop down the block. I think she boned strapless bodices so they wouldn't bunch up, but that lasted only a month.

Then she worked for a men's shirtmaker on Seventh Avenue, sewing Prince of Wales collars. After a few months, she had to give this up, too. She wanted to work, but she couldn't. For a woman like her, it was a terrible thing.

"The hardest work in life is to be idle, Selma. I don't want to sit at home with empty hands. I could weight hems. I could do shoulder darts. You never see shoulder darts anymore."

In those days, Social Security was a pittance. She tried to earn a little extra by sewing bridal gowns at home, but that didn't last long, either. I wanted her to come live with us in Yonkers. Do you know what she said? Better not to live than to be dependent on your children.

She wouldn't budge from Livonia Avenue, not even after the last of her friends moved out in the sixties. There were only two Jews and one Italian family left on her block. Perlmutter's candy store had become a bodega, and Gorelick's, the fish store on the corner, was now the Ebenezer Faith Mission.

We had other responsibilities—Dewey would be going to college soon and Zoot a few years later—but we gave her $75 a month to help out. I'd keep her occupied while Sid went to the kitchen table and slipped it under the Shabbat candelabra. She never took money gracefully.

"You should think about your own children," she told me. "When a mother helps a daughter, everyone is happy, but when a daughter helps a mother, the whole world cries."

The old neighborhood had been going downhill for years. By the seventies, even the policemen were afraid to walk their beats. I feared for my life when I visited, not to mention hers. My mother wasn't blind to all this, but she wasn't a worrier, either.

"We all have to die, Selma. If we worry too much, we won't have time to live."

"But Mama–"

"I have bars on the windows. I mind my own business. Why should anyone bother me?"

Let me tell you what kind of person this was. She arrived on Ellis Island with $70 sewn in her underwear and didn't spend a penny of it until my sister came along. I got that from my father; she wouldn't talk of such things. She still had $35 left when May came down with influenza, but all of that went to Dr. Amos and the funeral home.

They deloused her on Ellis Island and she never forgot the smell. It was like kerosene in the hair. After the physical, she had apple pie and milk. She couldn't get over it. She never ate like that in the old country—or the new one, either, from then on. She'd have only boiled potatoes and carrots during the hard times so I could have a piece of chicken. She lived by two little words, shem tov—in Hebrew, a good name. If you had a good name, nothing else was important.

Even later, when she was on Social Security, she managed to save a little and buy me presents. A scarf from Loehmann's, a Whitman's Sampler. I still have a teacup she gave me. It was from a set of four, but there was only one left when we got to Florida. I kept it in the china closet next to a Wedgwood teapot the girls from Ansonia had given me as a wedding present.

I used to drive from Yonkers to Brooklyn on weekends

to check on her, and she needed checking on. Once she looked like those hungry Armenians in *Life* magazine. I don't know what she was living on. I made sure the refrigerator was full before I left, and insisted she come to Kimball Terrace for dinner the next weekend.

I cooked a pot roast and potato pancakes. I used whole-wheat flour and two tablespoons of wheat germ in the pancakes. It's healthier that way. For dessert, I made a Polish apple cake with cinnamon, like the ones she used to bake for us on the holidays.

I was the hostess. I was supposed to provide the meal. But when Sid chauffeured her from Brooklyn, Perle Mesta arrived with two shopping bags stuffed with lox and sable, potato salad, pickled herring, cream cheese with chives, and a charlotte russe for each of us. I invited her and she brought the dinner.

Another time, I was visiting her in Brooklyn and mentioned that I had an aching back. Sid had been hogging even more of the blanket than usual, so I got a chill.

"I have a heating pad I never use, Selma. Let me get it for you."

"I already have a heating pad, Mama."

"This one is better. I want you to have it."

"But I don't need another heating pad."

A few months later, Zoot was visiting her—he had a gig in Sheepshead Bay—and she gave him a package for me. He was living on the Upper West Side by now, which meant he had to schlep it all the way up to me in Yonkers.

It was so sad when I opened the wrapping. The heating pad was in no condition to use—the cord was fraying and the plug was bent out of shape—but it was the thought that counted.

She was in her late seventies when she developed old-age emphysema. She'd never been sick as a young woman, never needed surgery, but then one day she fainted in the street. An elderly black man helped her up, a total stranger. Next time it happened by the dairy cooler in Dos Hermanos, the grocería on Pitkin. A policeman had to take her home. -

One evening Gustavo, the super in her building, phoned—he'd heard her crying for help from inside the apartment—and I drove over with the keys. We found her on the living-room floor, trying to get up by grabbing for the window bars. I gave him a spare key just in case, but that was only a temporary measure. I knew something would have to be done.

It was sometime in 1973—Haldeman and Erlichman, all that news we had then—when I spoke to my mother about going into a nursing home.

"I won't go," she said. "You go to a home if you want."

That was the first thing I got from her. So I let it alone and a few more months went by. I finally got her to come live with us on Kimball Terrace, but it was too late.

One night in Yonkers, she was in the tub and I was giving her a bath. She couldn't stand up and I couldn't pull her out. She was nothing but skin and bones, yet I didn't have the strength in my arms to get her up. What I finally did was let the water drain out of the bathtub. Then I got right in there with her and lifted her out. Sid was angry with me when he heard about it.

"Why didn't you wake me, Bubbie? I would have helped."

He'd been sleeping in the next room, but what could he have done? A woman from the old country would never let a man see her like that. It made me wonder as I got older. Who'd be there for me when the time came? Was I supposed to depend on the boys? They were too busy thinking of themselves. Or Fleur? Tell me another one.

I didn't want to put her in a nursing home. I felt terrible about it, but I simply couldn't cope with her on Kimball Terrace. Even my mother now realized she was too sick for that.

We talked again and she said all right it was time. But she wouldn't go where I wanted. There was a lovely place in Riverdale, the Hebrew Home for the Aged, only ten minutes by car from us. There were nineteen acres on the Hudson. It was beautiful—Canada geese on the lawn, oak trees, a view of the Palisades across the river.

"I don't want to live in the country," she said. "If you like the country so much, you go to the country."

This place was in the Bronx, but for her it was still the country.

"The Polish peasants used to say it's good wherever you aren't, Selma, but that's not the way I think. If I have to go in a home, I want it to be the home around the corner."

In other words, Shalom Gardens, a broken-down nursing home a block from her tenement. It was a dump, but the trouble I had getting her in there! These people made me fill out two inches of questionnaires before they were satisfied.

My mother was eighty-one when she went into the home. I used to be scared to death when I visited her. I still tremble from thinking of the characters out on the street. I'd try to park my car as close to the gate as possible. You didn't want a long walk in that neighborhood.

The food there was awful, not that my mother complained. I tried it once. Ugh! It was kosher, so you couldn't mix meat and dairy. Instead of a cheeseburger, you got cheese on a patty made from soybeans or some other non-meat product.

At least she had a few friends there. Mrs. Mossman, Rose's mother, was at the place too. And Mrs. Perlmutter, the wife of the fellow from the candy store. All the husbands were gone.

Even at the home, my mother managed to save her pennies and buy presents for the rest of us. She always had a piece of candy for the boys when they came to visit—a lemon drop, a butterscotch. She crocheted a drawstring handbag for me that I still use. It's ivory lace so you have to be careful. I don't know where she got the material.

As so often happens in a nursing home, she went downhill fast. She was there only a year and a half. September 12, 1974—that's the date she passed away. A few weeks before, she handed me the bankbook. I don't know where she'd kept it, probably under her mattress.

"Here, Selma, this is for you. Spend it wisely."

My mouth fell open. She had over three thousand dollars in East New York Savings. A drib here, a drab there, all those years she'd been depositing money into a savings account for me. If I had known, I would never have let her do it, which was why she made it in trust for me.

I shouldn't have been surprised. As the Bible tells us, there's nothing new under the sun. I don't know what more to say about my mother, except that each year when I light the yarzeit candle for her, I say two little words: shem tov.

CHAPTER 27

BLOOD MONEY

The Good News Family Worship Center gave Arlee Sparlow its Good Samaritan award in June for his adult-education classes on the Space Coast. *The Orbiter* put the story on page one, next to a press release from NASA about using smart robots to search for minerals on the Moon.

You couldn't miss Good News, the Plexiglas church between Bob's Jiffy Lube and Sunny Simonize on A1A. The steeple was actually an electronic bulletin board. The Bible reading curled around like the news at Times Square: Render therefore unto Caesar the things which are Caesar's; and unto God the things that are God's— Matthew 22:21.

As for the things which are Caesar's, Sid was still putting money we didn't have into investments we didn't need. After wringing all he could from Ready Credit that summer, he borrowed five thousand from Visa and five thousand from MasterCard for more mortgages. Every night, we went to bed another day older and deeper in debt.

Come fall, I was giving Sid so much of my household money that I didn't have enough to make my annual contribution to True Sisters. We did such good things. Once a month, we prepared a spaghetti dinner for the needy in Melbourne. We cooked twenty-five hundred meatballs for the three sittings. On Thanksgiving, we had a lovely meal for the alcoholics at CITA—Christ Is the Answer—the rescue mission on US 1. There were nine turkeys. We washed them, stuffed them, roasted them. Rocky let us use his ovens, but we had to clean up.

Do you think Mr. Trump appreciated my good work? All he cared about was the next mortgage. He was in such a hurry to get rid of more money the Monday after Thanksgiving that I hardly had a chance to powder my nose.

"Let's get a move on, Selma," he shouted. "Arlee's waiting with the papers for us to sign."

"I feel like one of the Wallendas," I said, searching for my purse in the living room. "Someday we're going to fall off this tightrope and break our necks."

"Can we please go, Selma? Why do you always have to keep me waiting?"

God only knows which was worse, signing those papers or getting my kiss on the hand. Do you remember the line from Bette Davis? After you kissed me, I always used to wipe my mouth. Well, whenever Mr. Sparlow kissed me, I wanted to wipe my hand.

He was becoming bigger and bigger. They interviewed him on *Eyewitness News*. There was something about him in *Florida Today*. He had two full pages in *The Orbiter* one week, right after Leo's home-repair column and the notice for Overeaters. All the smart men were hurrying to invest with him. It was like in the Honda commercial: I'll take it! I'll take it!

Sid borrowed five thousand from Checking Plus at the beginning of December, but even that wasn't enough. Now he wanted to put a $55,000 mortgage on the Chalet—our own home, for heaven's sake!—and invest that money, too. I get such a headache thinking about it. Even Crabbe was against this. He felt Sid was into Southland for enough already—about $65,000, if you added up the Ready Credit, Checking Plus, Visa, and MasterCard.

Sid went from bank to bank until he found one willing to give us a mortgage—Beachview Savings, a little hidey-hole a block from the Snake-a-Torium in Palm Bay. The loan officers were actually in Fort Lauderdale. They spoke to you by intercom, then faxed the papers for you to sign.

Just the thought of going into more debt was giving me stomach acid, but Sid had an answer to all my questions. We could get six and a half percent more from one of Arlee's mortgages than we'd have to pay in interest on our own. He kept shoving the faxes into my hands.

"You have to borrow money to make money, Bubbie."

"You were singing a different tune when we moved down here. You didn't want us to be tied down with a mortgage, remember?"

"Times change, and you have to change with them."

He wore me down again. It was Christmas week when we went to Beachview to fax back the signed papers. There were three wooden wise men on the lawn of the

VFW hall as we drove down Tropicana to South Patrick. I didn't need wise men to tell me this was a mistake.

I can't even say that mortgage on our home was the end of it. Before my signature had a chance to dry, Sid started in on me again about my inheritance. It was up to $4,751 now.

"My mother denied herself for that money, Sid. It should stay in the bank where it belongs."

"The bank pays you nothing. You might as well hide it under the mattress."

He gave me the Henry James treatment, one turn of the screw after another. I couldn't believe what he dredged up as we were going to bed one night—the tiny paycheck I got fifty years before at Ansonia.

"What do you know about making money, Selma? You never made anything but chicken feed. You go feed the chickens and let me take care of the money matters."

How was I supposed to sleep after his insults? I raised his two children. I wiped up after him. I was at his beck and call at all hours. If he'd stayed home instead of me, I could have done anything. My teachers considered me college material. I was Mr. Wolfowitz's favorite. And now he was belittling me and demeaning my mother's memory.

"This is blood money, Sid. My mother never went to a doctor. She lived like a hermit, saving her nickels and dimes. That's what this is—a lifetime of nickels and dimes. I'll be the one to decide how it's spent, even if that means throwing the money out the window."

Oh, what's the use? In the end, I let him have this money, too. It was just before Christmas '85 and a month until our fifth anniversary in Florida. My mother must have been turning in her grave..

On paper, we looked like rich people. We now had $255,734 invested in mortgages. We owed $65,000 to Southland and $55,000 to Beachview, but that would still leave us with more than $135,000 if we cashed in and paid off our debts. So why, I asked myself, didn't I feel rich?

CHAPTER 28

TWO TACOS SHORT

With Sol gone, Rose was a sitting duck, I'm sorry to say. How did somebody who once kept a ledger for a living know so little about financial affairs now? She couldn't even work the money machine at Southland.

What happened was we took her to the Villa Romana for dinner a few days after Christmas. The holiday lights were still up on the Titan in front of Patrick Air Force Base and a plastic Santa Claus was straddling the rocket like Dr. Strangelove.

Sid and I ordered fettuccine Alfredo. Rose had the shrimp and broccoli rigatoni. We shared a small pizza— meatball and mushroom—for the appetizer. Rocky was always pushing pasta and pizza because he could get the orders out like lightning. He was about to leave our table when my diplomat of a husband let drop that he'd been to the Pizza Hut around the corner from Francine's Haute Ecole of Ballet.

"You'll ruin your stomach," Rocky said. "You don't want to buy a pie in a place with a scale for ingredients. There, it's all portion control. Here, we have a free hand."

Rocky had decided to wait on us personally so he could have a word with Sid about a new package Arlee was pushing on him. He had five already and was considering number six, a mortgage on a convenience store—the Pic-Pac on Wickham Road near Sherwood Park.

"Arlee considers the owner as dependable as a Swiss watch," Rocky said. "The neighborhood's growing, too. But Annette wants to kill me. She's prejudiced against Arlee."

I was listening to Rocky with one ear and Rose with the other. She was telling me about a problem with her cilia, the little hairs inside the respiratory tract. For such small things, she was saying, the cilia could be big troublemakers.

"They're supposed to move around at four thousand rpm's and sweep out all the pollution you breathe in, but mine don't work right. I think the problem is immotile cilia syndrome. Not the complete syndrome, God forbid. My cilia still move, but some aren't going in the right direction."

The pizza was terrific—that is to say, the bite or two I had before Rose began describing the cilia inside her throat in graphic detail. By going forth and back instead of back and forth, they were brushing her food up and out of the digestive tract.

"Actually, it doesn't matter which way they brush because the mucus in my throat is so thick the cilia are matted down. That's why I can't feel a thing when I choke on my food."

No doubt the main course was excellent, too, but Sid

managed to ruin what appetite I had left after Rose's anatomy lesson. Mr. Trump had finished with Rocky and was now offering to fill the financial vacuum in Rose's life.

"Sol wouldn't want you to leave that last payment for Lady DuBarry in the bank, Rose. What are you getting—seven percent, seven and a quarter? At that rate, you'll be eaten alive by inflation. If I put in a word, my friend Arlee will get you in on something good."

Rose was out of her depth. She bent over her food and tried to disappear. I kicked Sid under the table and got a look.

"Why can't I just leave it in the bank?" Rose finally said. "They know me there and Sol wouldn't want me to take risks."

"Nothing's a sure thing, Rose. But I can assure you Sol wouldn't want inflation to nibble away at his hard-earned money."

"Don't listen to him, Rose."

"Stay out of this, Selma."

"Put your hands over your ears, Rose."

Rose was uncomfortable about being caught in the middle. She was picking at her food and sighing, separating the shrimp, broccoli, and rigatoni into three different piles.

"How do I know what's the right thing?" she said. "I relied on Sol for so much. He was the man of the house. Maybe Sid is right, Selma."

I couldn't believe my ears. What's wrong with some women, especially the women of my generation? She even had the nerve to lecture me about arguing with Sid.

"If you want a happy marriage, Selma, you have to cooperate with your husband. You can't be angry all the time."

Rose can thank her lucky stars about one thing. Sid got his hands on just the last $75,000 payment from Garfinkle. The first two installments, $150,000 plus dividends and appreciation, were still safe where Sol had left them, in his Windsor Fund. There was also another $50,000 plus in a five-year CD at First Federal—that's what Sol used to call their security blanket.

I considered asking Leo to speak to Rose—maybe she'd listen to another man. But now Leo was showing symptoms of the same virus. Think of it, Leo of all people, such a sensible man. I was starting to wonder. Was everybody on the Space Coast as nutty as a Snickers bar except me?

Leo had taken to visiting Sid now instead of the local hardware stores. He even stopped writing his column in *The Orbiter* so he could spend more time with my financier husband. He'd come in like a whirling dervish, wanting to know all about Arlee and the latest mortgages. I'd stand out in the hall, my ear to the office door, fuming at what I could hear going on.

"I'm comfortable, Sid. I get a check from Myra once a month and put it all back in the business. But I'm used to action. I miss the old days when everybody was cutting your price."

"An experienced businessman like you can put that money to better use than somebody who's wet behind the ears like Myra."

"I taught her everything she knows and now she

doesn't want me interfering. Me! I was the heart, the soul, the legs of that business. Without me, there's no business."

Kitty wasn't about to let Leo throw their money away on some harebrained scheme. She came over one morning just before New Year's and put an end to it. I wanted to cheer as she grabbed Leo by the elbow and dragged him from the office.

"You're two tacos short of a combination plate," she told Sid on the way out. "I wouldn't trust Arlee Sparlow if his tongue were notarized by all nine justices on the Supreme Court."

Kitty wasn't the only smart one. Birdella also told Sid where to get off. He had the gall to ask her to put a few thousand into a small package with Loretta Liebowitz's husband—a rundown warehouse in Coco.

"No, sir, not now, not ever, and don't you give me the sad face. The answer is still no. When I get two nickels to rub together, I put them in the savings bank."

"That money should be working for you, not for your banker. You might as well hide it in the cookie jar at home."

"Stop following me around, Mr. Waxler. I can't breathe. How do I clean this office if you're stuck to me? My, my, we certainly have thrown our papers about in here, haven't we? Oh, boy, these rubber bands thought they could hide from Birdella."

Sid even tried to put Zoot's head into the noose when we called to wish him a happy New Year. Zoot had been in Hoboken the night before for a gig with a pianist named Wah-Wah and a bass player who did this Chinese thing where you push your energy down into the liver.

After being lectured by Sid about a career in the school system, Zoot let slip that he'd put away a few hundred in Greater New York Savings—enough to get himself another horn with a trade-in on his Conn. This one was going to be a King Super 20.

"What do you need with another saxophone, Zoot? It's time to start thinking of the future. I could get you seventeen and a half percent plus two points on your savings."

"Hey, that may sound cool to you, but it's not the tune I want to play."

It was a few weeks later that Sid took me to Reliable Realty for the last time. I gritted my teeth as he received a $22,575 check for a mortgage that was paid off, then handed it right back to Mr. Sparlow for another one. It was like going from the *Hindenburg* to the *Titanic*.

As usual, I got my kiss on the hand, like the mafia gives the next victim. Sid got a lot of double talk when he asked his good friend Arlee about something on TV—Irving R. Levine had reported a glut of mortgages on the Space Coast.

"Good Lord, I wouldn't say glut, just a substandard inventory of markets," Arlee said, showing us to the door. "The trick in this business is knowing your inventory of supplies. Now, if you'll pardon me, good buddy, I have to hurry off to see a property in Coco Beach."

I never saw such a busy man. Arlee didn't have a few seconds to sit and talk with us, but he wasn't too busy to grab our check and push us out the door.

"Why is he in such a rush?" I asked Sid on the way home. "Did you see how he wouldn't look you in the eye when he waved goodbye?"

"You're imagining things, Bubbie. Now stop distracting me or I'll have an accident."

Well, what more can I say? If this were a horror movie, we'd be coming to the place where the phone goes dead and the lights go out.

CHAPTER 29

MAJOR MALFUNCTION

To begin the beguine, it was a bitter morning for a space brunch. Icicles were hanging from the jalousie windows in my Florida room and the louvers were frosted over. I turned up the baseboard heating, but a few extra BTU's would make no difference in a room without insulation.

As The Friends began arriving, I tried to bury all my forebodings about Arlee Sparlow. For the time being, I didn't have Walter Mitty around to remind me. He was in his office, shuffling papers and dreaming of the millions he'd be making.

I seated the early birds, Kitty and Leo, at the folding card table I used for my brunches. Kitty had brought a bottle of French champagne to toast the start of our sixth year in Florida. It was near the end of January 1986, two days after the actual anniversary, but who was counting?

As soon as Rose made her appearance, I switched on the TV in the living room and turned up the volume. The Motorola was swiveled around on its Lazy Susan turntable, so we'd have two views of the space shuttle going up—one through the jalousies and the other on television.

"Sid, come taste the chicken Newburg before it cools off," I said, knocking on the office door when his absence was noticed. "I added sweet sherry to the sauce the way you like."

"In a minute, Bubbie. I have to finish the comps on a new package. That mortgage on the time share in Sun Manor is coming due and I want to put it into the Mr. Tux on Merritt Island."

I use margarine instead of butter in Newburg sauce. It's healthier that way. I got the recipe from a *Woman's Day* at the House of Aloha, an ad for Blue Bonnet. It's supposed to make eight servings, but not very large ones.

A few minutes later, I excused myself and knocked on Sid's door again. When he didn't respond, I turned the knob and looked in. He was at his desk, scribbling on a legal pad.

"Sid, will you please put that away and join us? They'll be starting the countdown soon. Come on, I need you to help me open the jalousies."

"In another minute, Bubbie. I have to do one calculation over. I didn't realize you could get a free limo for the night if your wedding party ordered six rentals from Mr. Tux."

Leo opened the jalousies for me. I had on a wool cardigan, but the chill cut right through me. Not that you could tell it was cold from looking at Kitty. She had on a nothing little thing that was cut up to there and down to here. Leo must have noticed me staring at her.

"Kitty always liked to show her figure," he said. "Even her wedding dress was sexy."

"If you have a good figure, you should show it," Kitty said. "Leo, remember how I used to lend that dress out to all the other ballet girls to get married in?"

The *Challenger* was just going up. The white trail across the sky was now visible through the louvers. On TV, a group of schoolchildren were looking at the sky. Their teacher was up there. We could finally hear the roar outside—light travels faster than sound, you know.

"It was a nice piece of goods," Leo was saying as I served him a slice of applesauce nut bread for dessert. "I think it cost one twenty-nine at Altman's."

"No, it was one nineteen on Grand Street," Kitty said. "You must remember, Leo."

Suddenly, no one was talking. We could see a puff of white through the windows and the shuttle was veering around jerkily in the sky. I gripped the edge of the card table.

I don't know when, but Sid had joined us. Maybe he sensed something, or maybe he'd finished his calculation. We were all standing next to the chaise longue now, looking from the TV to the sky, then back to the TV, waiting.

Finally, official word came from the Cape. A major malfunction. The *Challenger* was breaking apart above us with all seven people aboard. That poor girl! The teacher from New Hampshire, she wasn't even a real astronaut. What must they be going through up there? And the families on the ground.

"I'm going to be sick," Rose said, hurrying out of the

Florida room. A few seconds later, I could hear her flushing in the hall bathroom where Sol had gone before he passed away.

"Christ, I need a drink," Kitty said.

She poured herself a glass of champagne. She was finishing her second when Rose got back from the toilet, still looking sick to her stomach. Leo stood and started to thank me for the wonderful brunch. He was getting a little too effusive when Kitty frowned and he stopped. Leo put an arm around Kitty and gave her a squeeze. He put his other arm around Rose.

"Come on, Rose, we'll take you home."

Sid and I stood wordlessly, staring at the door after our guests had gone. He took my hand and started to say something, then shook his head and returned to his office in silence. I peeked in a few times, but he was only staring at the wall.

I was still in a state of shock hours later. I hadn't even bothered to turn off the TV. The afternoon was almost over before I remembered to wrap the leftover applesauce nut bread in foil so it wouldn't go stale. I was just putting it into the freezer when I heard something on the news.

My heart was pounding in my chest by the time I got to the living room. There was Arlee Sparlow on *Live at Five*. The sheriff's deputies were closing the doors of Reliable Realty and taking him off in handcuffs.

"Sid! Come here, he's on TV. Hurry! The police have him. They've got Arlee."

I didn't realize Sid could move so fast in his bedroom slippers. It turned out this was a videotape from earlier in the day. Arlee had actually been arrested just before the shuttle took off.

There it was, staring us in the face. A crowd of people were banging on the door of Reliable Realty and getting no answer. I recognized one of them—Bernstein, my conductor. He looked like a wild man, his hair flying off in every direction.

"I don't believe any of this," he was saying. "It must be a mistake."

Sid sat slumped in the La-Z-Boy, hypnotized.

There was another video. Arlee's head was buried in the collar of his white jacket as a policeman led him from the patrol car to the county jail in Sharpes. The next report was from the Circuit Court, the little branch by the sheriff's office in Melbourne.

The judge—an old fool named Ewell—didn't know which end was up. Arlee always had something on the tip of his tongue. This time he'd promised to help them clean up the mess. That was the string attached when the judge let him go on $100,000 bail.

Sid ran to the phone in his office. He was in such a state that he forgot to shut the door. From the way he wore out the redial button, I'll bet Arlee had taken the receiver off the hook.

I knew it was a waste of time, but Sid made me get into the Toyota with him and drive to the Gold Coast. There was a gate across Arlee's driveway, so we had to park down the street on Wickapecko Boulevard and walk back up Riverside to Waccabuc.

Two couples were there before us and three more arrived a few minutes after we squeezed around the gate to reach Arlee's door. The only people I recognized were Rocky and Annette. She was saying something about the *Andrea Doria* going down and all the lifeboats were gone.

Nobody answered the bell. Arlee was the man who wasn't there. Actually, he was probably under the bed hiding from the lynch mob. Sid gave up after fifteen minutes. We didn't talk on the way home. God only knows what he was thinking.

I put a meatloaf in the oven for supper. I was the only one who touched it and I didn't have much appetite. Sid's mouth was occupied elsewhere. The phone never stopped ringing. He and the others were back and forth with one another all evening long.

Like Bernstein, Sid couldn't accept that Arlee was a crook. He wouldn't let go of his illusions. He reminded me of a marathon dancer on his last legs, hanging on to his partner as all the other couples dropped around them.

At midnight, I offered to reheat a slice of meatloaf, but he waved me away. His gills were two shades of green. I was getting worried.

"You have to eat something, Sid. How about a cup of decaf and a piece of applesauce nut bread? I'll defrost it for you in the micro."

"I know what you're thinking, Bubbie, but you're mistaken. This will turn out okay. Just wait and see. Maybe Arlee had a bad break, but he intends to put back whatever he borrowed."

"Why are you still defending him?"

"Maybe he took a few shortcuts. He could have been careless, but he's not a bad man."

"You'd trust him if he were running around with a dead body in a sack over his shoulder."

"So he got a little sloppy toward the end. Give him a chance and he'll straighten it all out."

Oh, sure, and while he's at it he'll straighten out the Hunchback of Notre Dame. It was two in the morning when I finally said goodnight and went to sleep—or what passed for sleep. I had the bed to myself all night.

Sid was snoring at his desk when I got up to make breakfast. I was still groggy, which might have accounted for the dumb idea that came into my head. Maybe it was all a bad dream—the *Challenger*, everything. I took a deep breath, opened the front door, and got the paper.

Disaster! There it was on page one of *Florida Today*. And inside the paper, on the business pages, was the other one, my Disaster. The extent of it was starting to sink in. I propped the paper on the kitchen counter as I put an extra spoonful of coffee into the percolator.

After what had happened to those young people up in space, especially the poor teacher, I was ashamed to find myself thinking of our own misfortunes. Well, the world may be full of troubles, but you feel your own most of all, as the saying goes.

I was pouring myself a second cup when Sid shuffled into the kitchen in his leather slippers. I handed him— well, threw him, I'm sorry to say—the business section, which was turned to the page about Arlee.

"Well, are you satisfied now? What do you have to say for yourself?"

Sid went white, his lips trembling. He looked as if he were about to have a stroke.

"I don't want to hear another word," he said. "If I have a heart attack, will that make you happy? Do you want me to die like Sol? You've said enough already."

I tried to apologize, but Sid turned away and walked to the La-Z-Boy. He sat down with *Florida Today* lying open on his lap. He stared at it for ten minutes, then threw the paper on the floor as if it were radioactive.

CHAPTER 30

THE EMPEROR'S CLOTHES

I won't give you an organ recital, but the next few days were miserable. I was the one who had to talk to the wives, the real injured parties, while Sid hid in the office, concocting one excuse after another for his friend Arlee.

"Don't jump to conclusions, Bubbie. Let's get all the facts first. You can't put a man in the electric chair, pull the switch, and then say oops I made a mistake."

I guess he was talking about himself, too. But what was I supposed to tell the Greek Furies when they hounded me—my friends, people he encouraged to put their savings into mortgages? Maybe it wasn't the electric chair, but I was in a hot seat of my own.

Rose was hysterical. She must have phoned fifty times that first week: God help me! Is it true? What will I do? Then there were all the others. Annette, Mrs. Bernstein, Loretta Liebowitz, Mo Bialer's wife, Muriel. Everybody was having conniptions.

"Will you speak to them, Sid?"

"You handle it, Bubbie."

"I don't know what to say."

"Just tell them it'll be all right."

I defrosted a large slice of the applesauce nut bread for Rose a week after the Disaster. It was eleven-thirty in the morning when I arrived at the Hacienda, but she was still in her nightgown, a posy print that she'd bought with me at Burdine's.

She cut the slice in half and made tea in her pear-shaped pot. Neither of us had much appetite. I don't know how long we sat silently at her drop-leaf dinette table, picking at our plates.

One of the spaghetti straps had slipped off Rose's shoulder. It was obvious her mind was elsewhere. I dropped a crumb on the tile floor and she didn't even notice.

I took a sip of tea and tried to collect my thoughts. It was herbal—chamomile, not red zinger, the one she usually made.

"I don't know what to tell you, Rose."

"Sid promised me. He said it was as safe as money in the bank."

"He told me to tell you it will all work out."

"Do you believe that, Selma?"

"I'd like to believe it, dear. Let's leave it at that."

She offered to refresh my tea, but it was too watery for my liking. I didn't realize at the time, but Rose was already tightening her belt. She'd used only one tea bag for the whole pot, as if that would make a difference in her financial condition. Rose was so worried about the Disaster that she forgot to unwrap her latest New England Journal of Medicine. It was still with the rest of her unopened mail on the commode table by the front door.

"Should I call somebody, Selma? A lawyer? A CPA? What would Sol want me to do?"

"The question is what do you want. You have to follow your own judgment."

"I always had Sol to tell me what to do. He liked to lead, and not just on the dance floor."

"Come on, stop rewriting history. You could lead Sol around by the nose if you had to."

"I never told him what to do. I just helped him make up his mind."

"Well, it's time to make up your own mind."

"You don't understand, Selma. I still wake up in the middle of the night and hear his voice. When the phone rings, I expect a policeman to be on the line and tell me it's all a mistake."

"Oh, Rose."

Her daughter, Becky, flew in from Oakland a few days later and banged so hard on our front door that she broke the knocker. I tried to head her off, but Becky brushed right past me, throwing open door after door until she found Sid's office. He was at the desk, his head buried in legal papers.

"Dammit, Sid!" she shouted. "How could you do this to my mother? She trusted you. I ought to wring your neck. What the hell did you think you were doing?"

Sid must have been half asleep, otherwise he wouldn't have stood up and tried to push Becky out of the office. That was a mistake. She was a big girl and she pushed him right back, but I'm sure she didn't expect him to fall and land on his tail bone.

It was a miracle Sid didn't break something. Fortunately, he landed on a mound of legal documents lying on the floor.

"Please, Becky," I said. "You won't accomplish anything by breaking his neck and giving me a heart attack. We lost our money, too."

"And you, Selma, why didn't you do something?"

She wasn't really mad at me. She eventually calmed down after waving her fists in Sid's face for five minutes more, shouting all sorts of things I won't mention.

Every day there was something else to worry about. More calls, more problems, another person to calm down. Eventually, somebody came down from the State Comptroller's office in Tallahassee to speak with all the victims, a young man named Purdy. We met with him just before Lincoln's Birthday at the VFW hall on Tropicana Trail. Purdy was only in his thirties, but he had a worried, pinched face that gave you an idea what he'd look like when he was eighty.

"We're in a war against white-collar crime," he said, opening a bulging briefcase. "My job is to come by after the crook is arrested and clean up the mess he's left behind."

He had everybody's undivided attention. It came out that Arlee had made copies of the packages and sold the same one again and again. If possession was nine points of the law and you had to share a package with two other people, how many points did that leave you with? Not even the lawyers could agree on this without going back and looking at their law books.

We learned a few days later from Dunaway, our lawyer, that all these identical packages weren't really identical. Ipso facto under the law, the person who got the mortgage first had a first mortgage, the next person had the second mortgage, and so on down the line. The last one in was left holding the bag when the money ran out.

Worst of all, there weren't even any properties to go along with some of the mortgages—the emperor had no clothes. Did I mention the bait-and-tackle shop in Coco that Sid had never bothered to check out? Well, this one didn't even exist.

No wonder I was neglecting my appearance. Whoever said beauty is a gift of God didn't know anything. You have to feel beautiful to look beautiful. And I wasn't feeling very good when I ran into Annette at Spaceport Plaza a few weeks after Purdy spoke to us.

"Mother of Mary, you got more hair in your eyes than a sheepdog," she said.

"I never have time anymore, what with …"

"Yeah, yeah. Listen, honey, I've got twenty minutes until my next hair appointment. I can do something about those bangs if you come on over."

As usual, we wasted the first ten minutes commiserating about our brilliant husbands.

"I'll strangle Rocky," Annette said.

"You can practice on Sid."

"I was counting on that money to redo this place."

"So you're hurting too?"

"Does a pig have a curly tail? Hey, listen to me. You don't want to hear my troubles."

She put on a smile for my benefit and did a little hot-cha-cha.

"How about wearing your hair up again? You could use the oomph."

"I don't know, Annette. I never know where I want it. If it's up, I want it down; if it's down, I want it up. Maybe I should just leave it on my dressing table."

Too bad I couldn't have left my financial problems there that spring. The next drip of the Chinese water torture involved a mortgage Sid had with Bernstein. The property, a rundown mobile home in Sherwood Park, was owned by none other than Trotter Weems. This time Bernstein was first in line and insisted on getting back everything he'd put in, including interest up until the last day. By the time Sid's turn came, nothing was left.

Well, Bernstein may have gotten his money back on this mortgage, but it wasn't enough to save him from going into bankruptcy. In the end, he lost almost everything except for his Château on Society Hill. And the bank was trying to foreclose on that, mandolin-shaped pool and all.

CHAPTER 31

RESPIRATORY MAN

D o you know that old song from Tin Pan Alley? After forty, it's patch, patch, patch. Well, my dear, patches aren't enough after seventy. For some of us, the machinery breaks down once too often and the spare parts are out of stock.

I still had the plumbing of a ten-year-old, as Ramsool delicately put it, but Rose wasn't so fortunate. She'd become tight-fisted right after the Disaster, pinching pennies on her utility bills, and this would have unhappy consequences.

It looked as if she'd get back only a few thousand from the seventy-five she invested with Arlee. It was in one big mortgage—a waterfront condo near Cape Canaveral. Bigelow, a banker from Titusville, was ahead of her and he wanted to squeeze out every drop he had in this lemon.

It was a big loss, but Rose still had her Windsor Fund, the CD, and Social Security. She also owned her home free and clear—if only I could say as much. In other words, there was no good reason for her to lower her thermostat to sixty-five. It was still winter, after all, and winter is winter, even in Florida.

"Be reasonable," I'd tell her. "A few more dollars a month won't break you."

"It's a matter of principle. Why should I pay for those three-martini lunches at Florida Power?"

Of all the winters to get principles, this was the wrong one. The thermometer kept falling below freezing and the orange growers were having fits. They normally start picking in the fall, but if I remember the oranges were greener than usual and still on the branches when the cold struck.

I had to wear an extra sweater whenever I dropped in on Rose. I forgot once and my elbow stiffened up. I needed to get a cortisone shot from Ramsool. You should have seen the needle Lu Ann came in with. It was big enough for a race horse.

Until the soreness went away, Sid helped me on with my pantyhose. He was stubborn about this, too. He insisted on doing both legs together instead of one at a time. It was supposed to be more efficient that way. It was so efficient he ruined two pairs of Hanes in three days.

Well, I didn't intend to have another cortisone shot, if I could help it. To be on the safe side, I'd turn up the thermostat to seventy as soon as I arrived at Rose's. If she wanted to live in an ice box, that was her business. I wasn't going to suffer along with her.

"What are you doing, Selma? You act like the majority stockholder in Florida Power."

"It's freezing in here. Do you want to catch your death?"

"I'm quite comfortable."

No, she wasn't. She was cheap.

One morning, Rose awoke with a terrible cough. She was hacking away when I came by to take her to the Washington's Birthday sales at Gemini Landing, the mall on Merritt Island. She needed new bath towels and Dollar Bill's was selling Fieldcrest for sixty off—irregulars, but you couldn't tell.

As soon as I heard her, I knew something was wrong. I wanted to drive her right over to Ramsool, but she wouldn't spend the money. Rose? I didn't believe my ears. Was this the Rose who'd never pass up an opportunity to see a doctor?

"Don't give me that," I argued. "You have Medicare."

"They only reimburse you eighty percent."

"But you have Medigap for the rest of it"

"It's the principle of the thing, Selma. Let's wait a few days."

It was March before she finally agreed to see Ramsool. He had an excellent reputation on the Space Coast, but do you know what that man gave her? Cough syrup! She could have gone on her own to the Cold Care aisle at Save-a-Lot for that.

Rose continued hacking away over the next few weeks. She saw Ramsool twice more, but got only refills for her cough medicine. On the third visit, he prescribed a syrup with codeine, but that was all. He never once gave her an antibiotic to knock the thing out of her system.

It wasn't until Rose began wheezing at a Gray Panthers rally in Moonwalk Mall—we were protesting the Medicare surtax—that Ramsool sent her to his friend

Soukary, the respiratory man at Cape Canaveral Hospital. Soukary could see right away what was wrong.

Asthma—after all these years, to come down with a thing like that. Soukary was young, but very smart—another Iranian, like Hooshman. He explained the problem, the two types of asthma, allergic and intrinsic. Children get the allergic from all the junk in the air they breathe. The intrinsic comes later in life. In Rose's case, it began as bronchitis, which then became chronic and developed into asthma as the bronchial tubes suffered permanent damage.

Soukary was supposed to be the best man in his field. From what he charged, he must have been. He wanted $175 the first visit, but Medicare approved only a third of that. All he did was listen to her chest and write out two prescriptions. He put her on one prednisone a day and Proventil as required, her inhaler.

Rose wasn't supposed to exert herself for six weeks, so Kitty and I did everything for her. We even washed the dishes by hand. Rose had a wonderful dishwasher, a brand-new GE installed before the Disaster, but she didn't want to subsidize the power company. The tags were still tied to the top rack, the one for tumblers and highball glasses.

CHAPTER 32

THE HOPE DIAMOND

Sid still hadn't gotten up the courage to tell Dewey and Fleur about the Disaster. He was living in dread that something would show up in the Los Angeles papers. Maybe he was hoping for a miracle, like Moses and the parting of the sea, to save him from having to tell them.

Unfortunately, there was more than Sid's feelings at stake. Dewey and Fleur had put over forty-five thousand, most of their savings, into that mortgage on the 7-Eleven. Now Sid was trying to sort it out on his own, but things weren't looking good. Three or four other people were ahead of them: the ants were crowding around the sugar bowl and no sugar was left.

It would have come out already, Sid or no Sid, except this mortgage was a two-year balloon, which meant you didn't get any principal or interest until the one lump-sum payment at the end. In other words, there was no good reason for Dewey or Fleur to be suspicious—at least not until one of the moguls said something to Dewey that April.

I think Freddie Fields told Marvin Davis, or vice

versa, and then whoever it was told Dewey that the mortgage market in Florida was all smoke and mirrors. That was all Dewey had to hear. He couldn't wait to get to his phone at *The Hollywood Reporter* (yes, he was back at the old plantation again) and call us.

"The word out here is that it's plain wacko to have a mortgage in Florida," he started in before giving us a chance to say hello. "One of these days, adios, all the appreciation in the real estate will disappear and the guy with the mortgage is left holding a piece of worthless paper."

Sid was on the office phone and I was on the extension in the kitchen. I tried to tell Dewey the truth, but Sid interrupted and told me to keep out of it.

"Calm down, Dewey," he said. "Why should some Hollywood big shot give a damn about you? I'm your father. I have your best interests at heart."

"You swore to Fleur and me that this was a sure thing. Go for it, baby."

"You can rest assured, but you have to be patient. A diamond isn't made in one day."

"Well, this better not be the Hope diamond. It looks good, but you get a lot of bad luck."

Sid wasn't lying to Dewey, mind you. He was lying to himself. He still thought that somehow it would all work out. Maybe a few mortgages were sick, but they were still breathing.

"Dewey and Fleur have a right to know," I said when we got off the phone.

"Why worry them? You can't expect everything to go according to Hoyle in this business."

Well, Sid must have pacified Dewey because mortgages never came up when Walter Winchell phoned a couple of weeks later to let us know he was now with *TV Guide*. He'd lost his job at *The Hollywood Reporter* over an item about Begelman. One of the studios complained. Of course, the first thing he did at *TV Guide* was write another nasty story about Begelman.

"Everybody's talking about it," he said. "I bet Begelman's shitting a brick. I've made him shit so many bricks, he must have a square asshole by now."

Don't blame me for Dewey's barnyard language. But you can blame me for keeping him in the dark. It was wrong not to tell him that his money was being piddled away. And it was even worse for me to participate in the deception when Fleur called that spring.

She wasn't a Nervous Nellie like Dewey. Au contraire. She was absolutely confident in her own judgment, not to mention Sid's. As a matter of fact, she now wanted him to get her in on one more deal—another one, for heaven's sake!

"We'll have twenty thousand to spare in a few weeks," she said. "I'm finishing a house in Holmby Hills, five bedrooms and a maid's. It'll be abstract, more abstract than surreal, very Kandinsky. So, what can you do for me, Sid?"

He didn't know what to say. He was stammering in front of the speakerphone until I spoke up. Of course, it was easy for me to sidetrack Fleur before she could connect the dots. All I had to do was mention the ticking clock and stand as far back as I could get.

"Let me spell it out for you again, Selma. We are

not—n-o-t—planning a family. I have the maternal instinct of a cantaloupe."

Zoot called around this time too—collect, of course—and tried to borrow money, of all things. He needed only a few hundred, but it might as well have been a few hundred thousand. He didn't know the well was dry. It was a saxophone, of course, a vintage Selmer Mark VI to replace the King Super 20. Please be honest, I whispered to Sid, tell him the truth. But he was too embarrassed.

Zoot had found this instrument at Manny's, the music store near Times Square where we'd gotten him his first tenor, a student Conn. The fellow in the horn department was cool and let Zoot borrow it for a gig on the Upper West Side, a hip little club called Augie's.

"The whole room got off on me. We were doing this post be-bop thing and there was an invisible connection. Everyone was plugged in and it was like we all had the same headset on."

"Another saxophone?" Sid said. "You were just as gung-ho about the last one."

"Man, in this business, your sound is your signature. The Super 20 is a good instrument, but the Mark VI is a great one. The metal is lighter and the sound is heavier."

"I'm sorry, Zoot, I can't help you. Everything is tied up now."

Well, the Disaster had a silver lining as far as Zoot was concerned. Sid was so busy trying to untangle our finances that he didn't have time to bother his younger son about becoming a teacher.

Rube Goldberg couldn't have imagined a more complicated situation. Sid was on the phone all day. Our bill from Southern Bell was $125 in February and $129 in March. It would have been over two hundred in April if he'd made one more call to Purdy's office in Tallahassee.

The things Arlee threw our money away on! There was a restaurant at the end of Citrus Lane on Merritt Island, the Polaris Lounge. It was too high for us, but Millie Bernstein used to speak favorably of their swordfish steaks when she could still afford them. Well, Arlee owned sixty percent of it, and poured over a million dollars of his ill-gotten gains into this one place alone.

Then there were the options and the futures and the options on futures—pork bellies, hogs, pig iron. He also had a quarter-million in an orange grove to the west of us, but he lost everything in the last freeze. And it didn't stop there.

He was a gambler, too. He liked to play at the tables in Atlantic City. If he won at craps, he'd lose it at blackjack or roulette and vice versa. A reporter from *Florida Today* found out Arlee would bet ten thousand on a single roll of the dice. He made eighty-five thousand one morning at Caesar's, but he lost it all that afternoon at Harrah's.

Now even Sid could see that some of our investments were worthless, but he was still predicting we'd make money in the end. If we couldn't save a mortgage, we'd get the money back by writing it off on our taxes. A complete loss this year and carryover losses after that.

Speaking of losses, he'd leave important papers scattered all over his office, which meant he could never find anything. I'll give you one guess who got blamed. Selma threw this out; Selma threw that out. He treated me like a maid. Actually, he treated Birdella better. He wouldn't dare say some of the things to her that he did to me.

Birdella understood. I unburdened myself to her the last week of April. She was spraying the bathroom walls with Tilex and scrubbing the mildew from the grout with an old fingernail brush.

"All I get from Sid is do this and do that," I said. "My mother used to say if you want a helping hand, you should look at the end of your arm."

"The Lord made him, so there must be a use for him," Birdella said. "But some people wouldn't work if you got them a job in a bakery eating the holes out of donuts."

CHAPTER 33

VANITY FAIR

Needless to say, those April showers didn't bring any flowers that May. No matter where I went—Aquacise, True Sisters, Healthercise, House of Aloha—the conversation always came around to Arlee Sparlow and the latest complication. I couldn't even escape it at Bob's Jiffy Lube. I was there for a new oil filter when Mrs. Bernstein pulled up next to me in her station wagon, the old heap the creditors let her keep.

This was a few days after Chernobyl, but the only meltdown Millie wanted to talk about was her own. The Bernsteins were now living in a Sandpiper, one of the rental bungalows on South Patrick, just about as far from Society Hill as you could get at Pelican Pond. He had one half of it and she had the other. They weren't speaking, and there were invisible territory lines that the other couldn't cross. Even the freezer was divided into equal parts.

As for the mortgage mess, everything was happening and nothing was happening. Read this, sign that, don't sign that, take a deep breath, wait twenty-four hours, sleep on it, count to ten. Everybody was moving around and nobody was going anywhere, like the Mad Hatter's tea party.

Dewey was also going in circles. He lost his job at *TV Guide* sometime in May. As usual, he had a fight with the boss, but this time it didn't concern his work. What happened was he got quoted in *Vanity Fair*, a snide remark about Reagan he'd made to the person sitting next to him at a benefit in Beverly Hills. I don't know, maybe his boss at *TV Guide* was a Republican.

Anyway, the editors at *Vanity Fair* must have felt bad because they gave Dewey a chance to fly to Palm Beach and write up Mar-a-Lago for them. This was the last week in May, a few months after Donald Trump had bought the place from what's-her-name's estate—Post Toasties.

Fleur had wanted to go, too, but she changed her mind when she learned how cheap *Vanity Fair* was going to be about Dewey's expense account. He got only a room at the Palm Beach Hilton, not a whole suite at the Breakers, and he couldn't take his wife along for free.

I think the Trumps were still redecorating, but they agreed to let Dewey in anyway. This was when the Trumps were still billing and cooing, and Donald hadn't dumped Ivana for that younger one—Marla, who turned out to be such a rotten actress.

Anyway, Dewey had the estate to himself for three hours. I don't know where the Trumps were, maybe raking in the chips at one of their casinos. The manager gave him an electric golf cart to roam around the grounds. It would have been handy inside the house, too.

There were a hundred and twelve rooms, counting the servants' quarters and three A-bomb shelters. Imagine being the housekeeper there. Of course, this was when Trump was still Trump. Actually, he may be Trump again, for all I know, but what does that mean? The bigger you are in the end, the more the worms have to eat.

"It costs a million bucks a year just to keep the place going," Dewey said, calling from the hotel after his visit. "There's enough gold in the ceiling to pay off Guatemala's national debt."

He always did have a good eye for detail. Anyway, he was going to spend the night in Palm Beach, then fly back to California the next morning. I didn't expect to hear from him until he got home and let us know the date his piece would appear in *Vanity Fair*.

So, I was putting away the supper dishes a few hours after he called and feeling lucky I had only two bedrooms and a bath and a half to care for. I was about to stretch out on the couch when the pounding on the front door began. As usual, Sid was buried in the office and didn't hear a thing.

"I'm coming," I shouted. "Hold your horses."

You can imagine my shock at finding Dewey on the doorstep—about 7.5 on the Richter scale. He had his right hand in a fist—Sid still hadn't fixed the knocker—and was about to bang the door again. He was clutching a copy of *Florida Today* in his other hand.

"Welcome, stranger." I held out my arms. "What a wonderful surprise."

It was then that I saw the look on his face. I'd never seen him so angry.

"How could you let him do this to me?" Dewey was waving the paper in my face. "I'm not a child playing with blocks. This is my life we're talking about. What's Fleur going to say?"

The light bulb finally came on over my head. There'd been something in the paper that morning about Arlee Sparlow, a new complication. My God!

"Oh, Dewey." I reached out to touch him, but he shrank from my hand.

"When were we supposed to find out? On the way to bankruptcy court?"

"Come inside, Dewey. You don't know how sorry I am, dear. Sid! Sid, it's Dewey!"

He was still breathing fire when we got to his father's office. Sid was sitting at the desk, eyes shut and chin on hand—*The Thinker*.

"How the hell could you do this to us?" Dewey shouted, barging into the room.

Sid turned white when he saw Dewey standing over him.

"I see you know," Sid said. "I'm sorry you had to find out about it like this."

"It's all about ego, isn't it? You had to be the big man."

"You may not believe me, but I was always acting in your best interests."

"Damn right I don't believe you. This isn't some TV sitcom. What do I tell Fleur?"

"Calm down, Dewey. The situation isn't as bleak as it looks."

I couldn't listen to any more nonsense. Now he was

promising a miracle, something coming from out of no-where, like Venus on the half shell.

"Tell him the truth," I said.

Sid looked at me as if I'd slapped him in the face.

"I want my son to know the truth, no matter how embarrassing it may be to his father."

Dewey looked from Sid to me and from me to Sid. He was drenched in perspiration, and his chest was heaving.

"Fleur was supposed to have the bullshit detector," he said. "But all you had to do was hold up a hoop and say jump and she jumped right through it."

He made a fist and raised it as if to strike Sid. I opened my mouth to say something, but then Dewey banged his fist on the desk.

"I really bought it," he said. "I should have bought the Brooklyn Bridge while I was at it."

Dewey turned to me. I tried to take his hand, but he didn't want his own mother touching him. Without another word he stormed out, leaving Sid and me to stare at each other in silence. No matter how old you get, you can always learn something. Now I knew what a deafening silence was supposed to mean.

Sid didn't move for more than an hour after Dewey left. He just sat there at the desk, worn out and waiting for something to happen. I brought him a cup of decaf, but he shook his head. I left him staring at the wall and drank the coffee myself.

Fleur called as we were going to bed. I could see Sid knew who it was without being told. After the beseeching look he gave me, I didn't have the heart to put him on the line. Fleur turned all her bitterness on me.

"I'll never forgive you, Selma. You stood by silently, the dutiful wife, and let your husband tear our hearts out."

"You have a short memory. I warned you plenty, but you didn't want to hear the truth."

"Don't you dare throw that up to me. And another thing—about my goddamn biological clock—I've already had three abortions: a suction and two D and C's. And I'll have three more, if I need to. Now stay the hell out of my life."

Was she telling the truth, or just trying to hurt me? Either way, it was a terrible thing for somebody to say to her mother-in-law. And that wasn't the worst of it, not by a long shot. I'm beginning to sound like Homer talking about the Trojan War.

CHAPTER 34

THE BLUEBIRD OF HAPPINESS

I thought history was supposed to repeat itself twice, first as tragedy and then as comedy. For Rose, it was one tragedy after the other. No sooner had her asthma been diagnosed than she tripped over the hula-girl floor lamp at Annette's and broke her left wrist.

You wouldn't believe all the calls Rose got from the lawyers. She had no intention of suing Annette, but these mouthpieces wouldn't leave her be: This is a dream case, Mrs. Moskowitz. It's a gold mine, ma'am. Summer was the slow season in Florida, Arlee Sparlow or no Arlee Sparlow.

The broken bone wasn't the last of it. The X-ray revealed osteo, where the bones wear out, and showed she already had holes in hers. What bothered her even worse was she'd lost her Pucci pin at the hospital. That brought it all back, Sol's passing away and her self-reproaches.

"I'll never forget the sight of him in that place, Selma. You try to think of more pleasant things, then you turn on the TV and there's Quincy with a scalpel in his hand."

"Oh, Rose!"

"Why can't the election people get anything right? I've written to them three times now, but they're still sending him a registration card."

I may have been furious with Sid, but I dreaded the idea of him lying like that on the table under a disposable sheet. Or me wringing my hands and crying mea culpa to my friends.

To save the rest of her bone tissue, Rose had to take estrogen and increase her intake of Tums Liquid—she was up to three glasses a day in June. She was still economizing, however, and switched to Kmart liquid. It had everything Tums did and was ninety-five cents less.

The osteo wasn't the end of it, either. Whenever she ate something now, she had to go right to the toilet. Ramsool said there was a leak in her plumbing, but he didn't know which pipe was broken. So he sent her to a stomach man in Indialantic—Kushner, a Jewish doctor this time.

Kushner did a colonoscopy. The bill was supposed to be only one twenty-five, but he jacked it up to one seventy-five by adding extras. He promised her the procedure wouldn't hurt, but it hurt plenty. And it was disgusting, too, though I won't go into particulars.

He found a polyp, a big one like Reagan's, though the biopsy was benign in Rose's case. He removed it, but that didn't solve her stomach problems. Now he was ready to give her an endoscopy, where the hose goes down your throat and into the stomach.

Rose was leaking like a newborn baby by early July, but she didn't feel up to another test. Kushner had his receptionist, Shirleen, keep after her, but Rose wanted to try Kaopectate first. She took three tablespoons at a time. I used to give it to the boys. It was terrible stuff.

Everything was going wrong for Rose that summer. One day she banged into the china closet and knocked over Snow White and the Seven Dwarfs. The Bluebird of Happiness broke off Snow White's finger, which set her to sobbing again.

Kitty and I tried to cheer Rose up by taking her out to eat—Pancho Villa's, Golden Chopsticks, Mo Bialer's, everywhere except Oinkers—but she didn't have an appetite. Usually, she just picked at her meal, separating the food groups on her plate.

As if all this weren't enough, Rose's chest began bothering her in July. Usually it was a stabbing pain, but once she woke up in the middle of the night and couldn't breathe. She felt as if an elephant were standing on her.

Ramsool couldn't decide whether the pain was from Rose's stomach or heart, so he sent her to his friend Hong in Titusville, a cardiologist from Taiwan. Hong wanted to do a catheterization, but Rose was more afraid of the test than whatever might be bothering her. He finally talked her into going to Citrus Memorial in July for magnetic resonance imaging.

The MRI discovered a slipped disk in her lumbar region, but the picture of the cardiovascular system was unclear. To make matters worse, the radiologist charged $853 and he wouldn't accept Medicare. This meant Rose was responsible—an out-and-out fraud in her opinion.

If she didn't have chest pains or inconvenient bowel movements, her asthma would act up. Soukary increased her prednisone, but that inflamed the stomach lining and she had to cut back.

Nobody could give her a simple diagnosis. It was on the one hand this and on the other hand that. When she wasn't taking tests, she was twiddling her thumbs in doctors' waiting rooms.

Once Rose demanded an explanation after Kushner kept her waiting for over an hour. Oh, the emergency calls, he told her, blah, blah, blah, excuses, excuses, excuses, and with a straight face, too. Shirleen whispered in Rose's ear on the way out: Don't believe a word; he was playing golf at Turtle Creek with Ramsool.

Well, Rose did have the endoscopy after all, but there were only a couple of benign tumors. She had the catherization, too—everything looked fine. Then, just as she was letting her guard down, boom! A routine chest X-ray discovered it.

The bad news came at the end of July during Rose's annual checkup. She broke it to Kitty and me in the Roadmaster on the way home from the House of Aloha.

"Ramsool says it's cancer—the lungs."

"Oh, my God, no," I said.

"Don't ask how. I never smoked a day in my life."

"I bet they screwed up," Kitty said. "Ramsool doesn't know shit from Shinola."

"I only wish, but I had a second opinion. I start chemo day after tomorrow."

I didn't want to think about losing somebody I'd known longer than I could remember. I never said a word to Rose, certainly, but I couldn't help thinking. With a husband like Sol, you didn't have to be a smoker.

Rose had always been such a hypochondriac. But now that she was really ill, she acted as if everything were all right. We shouldn't worry; she was in good hands. Still, no amount of acting could hide the fear in her eyes.

Her oncologist, Butcher, had an excellent reputation. With a name like that, you'd better be good. Ramsool said there wasn't a better cancer man in central Florida. Lettie Buxbaum from Healthercise—she was his patient, too—couldn't say enough about him.

Rose spent two days in the hospital for each treatment. The chemicals knocked her out so badly that she couldn't do anything for a week afterward. And which hospital do you think it was? Yes, Cape Canaveral, where we had our brunches for the cancer patients.

Like a rose in the garden, she lost her bloom over the next few weeks. And not just her bloom. By the middle of August, she'd lost ten pounds from her behind and there was nothing left to sit on. Her hair was coming out in clumps. I patted her on the head one day and got a handful.

Butcher said it was all to be expected. He told Rose that on average she had an excellent chance of survival. Now what was that supposed to mean? A person with one foot in a bucket of boiling water and the other in a bucket of ice water is comfortable, on the average.

You can't imagine what they charged for all this. Every two to four weeks, Rose had chemo. The bill was $1,493 each time before Medicare shaved it down to $850. There were so many other things. The pathologist wanted $215 for each tissue exam, but Medicare said it was worth only $58.

During the last half of August, Rose hardly left home, except to see the doctor. She didn't want people asking how she was. She hadn't even told Becky and Zach what was going on.

"They should know," I said, driving her to the hospital. "It's wrong to keep it from them."

"They have enough on their minds without worrying about me."

With summer ending, Rose's condition got worse. Most of the time, she wanted to be left alone. When she did see anyone, she didn't sound so brave anymore.

"Why am I knocking myself out, Selma? I'll be in the plot near Sol before the year is over."

"You can't give up, dear. You have to be patient and give the chemo a chance."

"The only thing I have left is patience. Why is it that the young have all the time in the world but none of the patience? We old people have the patience but none of the time."

Rose had chemo again in September—four days this time, twice as long as usual. It helped, whatever they did. She gained back a few pounds and had some color in her cheeks. As Kitty and I took her home from the hospital, I tried not to get my hopes up too high.

"Well, how the hell are you?" Kitty asked. She didn't believe in beating around the bush.

"A little better, thank God. I still have to go in once a month for chemo, but the doctor said I was doing so well he was lowering the dose."

"So he's optimistic," I said. "That's good news."

"The chest is clean. I'm feeling stronger. I'm so glad to be able to tell you this."

I crossed my fingers and said a little prayer. I once asked Nathanson if it was OK for Jews to cross their fingers, but he didn't know.

CHAPTER 35

THE DIVINE COMEDY

Kitty, God bless her, was still going strong, but she didn't have a bed of roses to lie on either, only the thorns. Let me back up a few months now. This was June, not long after Rose tripped over that lamp in the House of Aloha. I'd just finished putting away the breakfast dishes one morning when the phone rang. Kitty started in before I could even say hello.

"Selma, I can't get Leo to stop laughing. Everything I say is a big joke. I'm tearing my hair out and he's acting like a laughing hyena."

"What do you think is going on?"

"Christ, how am I supposed to know? He was watching TV—Reagan in Berlin, tear the wall down, yackety-yak—when all of a sudden he starts acting like it's Milton Berle on the screen."

I could hear Leo cackling in the background.

"Don't you think you should call the doctor, Kitty?"

"I don't know what I should do. He won't budge from the sofa. How do I get him to go anywhere?"

This didn't sound like Kitty. She was always the decisive one.

"Hold on," I said, "I'll be right over."

"Oh, Selma."

"Just give me a minute to change into something."

Leo was sitting on the sofa in his pajamas and giggling to himself when I got there. I tried not to stare, but it was like when you're in the shopping mall and someone is being wheeled away on a stretcher. You know you shouldn't stare but you can't help yourself.

"Look at him," Kitty said. "He's enjoying himself. At least somebody finds this a laughing matter."

Well, we got to work right away. I dialed the doctor—Ramsool was their internist, too—while Kitty went to get Leo something to wear. It took the two of us to pull off the pajamas and get him into his street clothes. Then each of us grabbed an arm. It was like trying to hold up an overcooked noodle.

Once we got him in the car he sounded almost normal, talking a blue streak about how the new Black & Decker jigsaw had more bells and whistles than the Skilsaw. But he was laughing again by the time we got to the doctor's office. You could hear him from the waiting room during the examination. He was having a terrific time, everything was hilarious.

Ramsool was frowning when he finally came out and invited Kitty and me into his office. The nurse was helping Leo get dressed in the examining room next door.

"I'm sorry I have to ask you this, Mrs. Seligman. I

didn't smell anything on his breath, but we need to know if he's been drinking."

"Drinking? Jesus, you got to be kidding."

"Maybe he got into the liquor cabinet when you weren't looking."

"And maybe I'm the Queen of Rumania. Leo's not a secret drinker. Not on your life. Forget about it."

"Well, sometimes even the spouse doesn't know, but let's move on. How about his Lasix? How many tablets did he take this morning?"

"He took the usual—two of the water pills with breakfast."

"Has he fallen recently? Any blows to the head?"

"No, nothing. But if this keeps up any longer, I'll give him a blow to the head."

Ramsool went down his checklist, bing, bing, bing. But everything was negative.

"Enough already," Kitty said. "I want to know what the hell is happening here."

"I must be candid with you, Mrs. Seligman. We'll have to wait for the lab reports to rule out some other things, but I have a strong suspicion. I don't think this will be good news."

I could see from the look on Kitty's face that Ramsool didn't need to say the word. I used to think it took years for such an advanced case to develop, but I soon learned differently. You couldn't be certain without a brain autopsy, God forbid, but Leo's symptoms pointed to Alzheimer's.

There was nothing for us to do now but take him home and wait for the test results. We didn't have to wait long. Everything was negative, and all those negatives didn't make a positive.

Kitty was a wreck, of course, as bad as Rose when Sol passed away. May you never know what that poor woman suffered. I remember speaking to her the week after she got the test results.

"He's going down so fast, Selma. One day, I'll clutch at something and wonder to myself if this is the bottom. But, no, the next day I can see he hasn't reached it yet—it's still downhill."

Soon, Leo didn't find life so funny. He began to suspect Kitty of the most dreadful things.

"He acts like I'm Lizzie Borden. I'm trying to poison him. Not that the thought hasn't crossed my mind. Jesus, he even accused me of fooling around—me, the last person in the world. I'm planning to collect on the life insurance and run off with my lover."

At the end of June, Leo knocked the bedroom phone off the hook while Kitty was in the kitchen making rice pudding. It was a small thing, but Leo was having a fit by the time Kitty put the casserole dish into the oven and looked in on him.

"Oh, my God!" he said, staring down at the phone on the floor and up at her in panic. "What am I going to do? Kitty must have been trying to call. My God, what'll she think?"

"Calm down, Leo, it's all right. I'm Kitty. You recognize me, don't you?"

"You're not Kitty. Get out of here, whoever you are, and stop trying to drive me crazy."

A few days later, Kitty had an even worse story for me.

While she was putting the trash out, Leo lay down in the bathtub and slit his right wrist with a razor blade. It was just a nick. She patched him up with a Band-Aid, but it aged her ten years.

"He was afraid I'd deserted him, Selma. He doesn't understand. I'm there all the time. I undress him; I wash him; I wipe him. He has a bell in his room and never stops ringing for me."

She needed a break. I offered to stay with Leo while she and Rose went to the Fourth of July sales at Gemini Landing. The Satellite High band was doing Sousa marches.

"If you want to help, Selma, get me a cup of hemlock to drink."

"That's not funny, Kitty."

She may have been down in the dumps, but she wasn't ready to give up. She got the name of every specialist in Florida from the Alzheimer's Hot Line. They tried all the experimental drugs on him. No luck—no good luck, anyway.

"He has a five-minute memory," Kitty said when I dropped in at the end of July. "You ask him during dessert what he had for the appetizer and he can't remember."

We were on the settee in her living room, over by the cactus hat stand. All of a sudden, she began punching a throw pillow, then hurled it across the room, just missing her bird's-eye maple chiffonier. She balled her fists and held them to her head as the tears came.

"I was lying in bed last night and holding Leo in my arms. Every few seconds, he'd twitch or jerk or shudder. It was like a car running down."

Soon, Leo was getting lost around the house. Kitty had to Scotch-tape signs and arrows all over so he could find his way. In a few weeks, he couldn't read the signs and she had to put up pictures. I came over with an armful of old magazines and we cut out ads for socks, undershirts, shorts, and so on. That worked for a time, then he didn't recognize pictures.

Even when Leo came out of it for a while, the recovery would be less than miraculous. Somehow he managed to remember our phone number one morning and wouldn't stop calling Sid. I think Kitty was in the bathtub.

"He's driving me crazy, Bubbie. He wants us to open a hardware store together and he won't take no for an answer. He won't even take maybe. If I hang up, he rings right back."

"Be nice. He's a sick man."

"I tried to put him off. Leo, I'm working on it. But he wants to do it now. All right, I say, I'll order the inventory as soon as I get off the phone. You won't forget, Sid? No, I won't forget, goodbye. Then he's calling me back a second later. Is it done, Sid?"

Kitty had to buy a lock for the phone, but now Leo began getting up in the middle of the night and turning on the TV. I remember looking in on them one day on my way to True Sisters.

"Did you have a good night's sleep, Leo?" I asked.

"Yes."

"No, dear, you didn't," Kitty said. "He was up at four again, watching a Sergeant Bilko rerun. I hid the remote, but he found it."

A week or so after this, I brought Leo a bouquet from Bloomer Girls. I thought he might enjoy the smell of flowers. This time, Kitty was treating him like an infant: Come, come, say hello to Selma; look at the pretty flowers; say thank you, Leo. She must have noticed me staring.

"I'm sorry, Selma. I realize he's not a child. He contributed to society and deserves to be treated like an adult, but he has the brain of an amoeba."

Kitty had to feed him like an infant, but he was a picky eater and would spit out almost everything she put into his mouth.

"He's so skinny, he'll disappear," she said. "Shrimps disagree with him, but he won't eat anything but shrimp cocktail, even if it means having hives all over his body. Everything else on the plate, he leaves for me to finish."

Kitty stood up and patted her hips. She was still wearing her housecoat. In the old days, you'd never catch her that way with company in the house.

"Jesus, look at the saddle bags."

Kitty needed a change of scenery. I offered to audition for Pelican Players in August if she'd try out, too. We could get Birdella to stay with Leo.

"They're doing *Cactus Flower*," I said.

"Oh, sure, Selma. I'll be the cactus and you be the flower."

"Stop being sarcastic about everything."

"Oh, Selma. I don't know what to do."

The scariest thing was they didn't have a cure. A doctor from Germany, Alois Alzheimer, discovered it in 1907. I read that in *Modern Maturity* at one of the nursing homes we checked out in August. Kitty had gotten a list from the hot line. She was reluctant, but what else could she do?

The first one we saw, Clearview, was in a seedy stucco building near an iffy section of Palm Bay. Scrubbs, the director, was dressed like a golf pro in flamingo pink and heliotrope. His voice was just as loud, but that might have been from talking all day to people who were hard of hearing. In any case, he smiled too much and was too helpful—another Arlee Sparlow.

"We have three categories here," he said, opening an alligator-skin binder on his desk. "At the top of the mobility scale are the go-go's, the ones who can get around on their own. Next we have the go-slows, who may need a helping hand on occasion. Finally there are the no-go's, the ones who need a jump start just to get out of bed in the morning."

I think it was at this point that the big jerk gave Kitty and me the once-over, put his elbows on the desk, and smiled at us like all get-out, if you know what I mean.

"I can't promise anything until our medical doctor does the physicals, but you two young ladies look like excellent go-go candidates to me."

He was flipping through the looseleaf pages of the binder, oblivious of our shock.

"You're in luck. I have two adjacent singles facing the front lawn. Or would you like to share? There's a bright double in back next to Mrs. Eisner. Goldie's one of our go-go's, too."

I was speechless; not Kitty. "For Christ's sake, clean the wax out of your ears and listen. It's not for us, you jackass, and even if it were, we wouldn't be caught dead in a dive like this."

I don't know how many homes we visited that month—ten or twelve, maybe more. The best of the lot were bad and the rest were, well, you don't want to know. Clearview and Scrubbs were par for the course. Kitty was at her wits' end by the last week of August.

"Let's stop the wild goose chase, Selma, or I'll end up murdering one of these morons."

"You can't give up. Sooner or later, we'll find something. Now, just try and relax. Do as it says on the mayonnaise jar: Keep cool but don't freeze."

Bingo! It was a few days later that we found one right under our noses—Silvercrest, the last name on the list, naturally. It was in Indian Harbour Beach, just over the Satellite Beach line. We knew right away, this one was different.

The main attraction was Dr. Bidwell, the owner. God how I embarrassed myself. Maybe I was a sexist in spite of my sex or maybe I couldn't see beyond the color of her skin. Actually, do you know what I think? She had too nice a smile to be a doctor, which was why I mistook her for a nurse. I felt myself turn bright red when she corrected me.

"I'm so sorry, doctor. I can't apologize enough."

"I've already forgotten. As a black woman in the medical profession, I'd have a bleeding ulcer if I let a thing like that bother me. My grandfather gave me a piece of advice when I was a girl: If you have two strikes against you, that just means you have to hit the third one."

She was so kind and understanding that I fell in love

with her on the spot. She was an internist specializing in geriatrics, and such a good-hearted person. She gave Kitty the biggest hug when she heard about her life with Leo.

"I know what you're going through. My granny had Alzheimer's. I felt so helpless—I guess that's why I went into geriatrics. I still feel helpless sometimes. We doctors want to fix everything, but in a case like this we can only make things more comfortable."

Dr. Bidwell took Kitty's hands and looked into her eyes. That was all it took for my tough old friend to start sobbing like a baby. The doctor waited for Kitty to collect herself, then led us through the lounge to a terrace overlooking the ocean. She pulled three beach chairs together.

"I don't want to give you false hope," she said. "It's a cruel disease, but that doesn't mean you should throw your hands up. There's life to be lived at every stage, even the most advanced."

Leo entered Silvercrest a few weeks later. Kitty and I helped him settle in. He got a cozy room facing the sea, with hibiscus curtains at the window and a wicker rocking chair by the bed. Skippy Holzer, the one who gave up his seat for me at Pluckers, was down the hall. I hummed something from Mendelssohn as we passed his room on the way out. A light came on in Skippy's eyes. He popped out his upper plate and gave us a toothless grin. Dr. Bidwell smiled at me.

"You have to find a key to unlock the personality," she said in the lobby. "A photo, a song, a smell. What you have to do is look for the little bit of human spirit still there."

I went over to Kitty's that evening with poor Rose. Actually, Rose was having a good day. There was even some color in her cheeks. The Three Musketeers were together on the settee in Kitty's living room. Nobody knew what to say, but I imagine we were all thinking the same thing. It was both a blessing and a heartache to have Leo at Silvercrest. Kitty finally broke the silence.

"What the hell should we do now?" she said. "Sit shiva or open a bottle of champagne?"

CHAPTER 36

ASK AND YE SHALL RECEIVE!

In the words of Ann Landers, trouble is the great equalizer. Sid and I may have been in good health that summer, but our financial condition couldn't have been any greener around the gills. Everyone had a hand out—the lawyers, the bankers, the accountants. A few of our mortgages were going to be good, knock on wood, but we couldn't touch them yet to pay off our debts. Everything was in limbo while the lawyers tried to settle the civil case in Titusville.

The stream of income from our investments was now down to a dribble. It was like when you turn off the faucet and all that's left is a slow drip. We still had our Social Security and Sid's pension, but that wasn't enough to keep up with the bills. If we paid our home loan at Beachview Savings one month, we wouldn't have enough to pay Ready Credit or Checking Plus at Southland, let alone Visa or MasterCard.

The legal fees were killing us too. Dunaway was supposed to be giving us a break, but his first bill was for over a thousand and his legal secretary charged fifty an hour every time she wrote us a letter. All the other law-yers wanted to get in on it, too. Bray & Bray promised us the moon if we'd declare bankruptcy—chapter seven, eleven, or thirteen, I forget which—but we had to pay four thousand up front before they'd take the case.

Sid tried to increase our Ready Credit another five thousand so we could pay the legal fees, but Crabbe didn't think we were such good risks now that the onion was peeling apart. Sid even tried to borrow more on our home from Beachview, but the loan officers weren't interested.

Each week there was a new problem. Yes, we got stuck with that mortgage on Eli Potts's car lot. Six others were in on it with us, and everybody was fighting over the as-sets—the jalopies, the furniture, the two palm trees, even the sign out front: You Can Rely on Eli. It was like when the Eskimos kill a whale and use every single part—the teeth, tail, bones, blubber, oil, whatever.

In spite of these setbacks, Sid was still promising he'd restore everything to the status quo ante. I knew better. When a sweater shrinks, it doesn't get any bigger the next time you wash it.

At night, he'd toss around in bed by the hour, scratch-ing himself until his skin was raw. He had a terrible rash on his chest; it makes me itch just to think about it. He blamed my cooking, but he was lying to himself again. Anyone could see it was a nervous rash.

I remember one of the electronic bulletins going around the Good News steeple over the summer. Ask and ye shall receive! If only life were so easy. We needed help, but there was no one to ask. Our closest friends had their own troubles, not to mention the children.

I called my younger boy in July while Sid was out fighting legal windmills with the other Don Quixotes. Zoot first brought me up to date on the music business: he'd just spent his last few dollars on that Selmer Mark VI, then used it for a gig in SoHo where all the people on the dance floor gave him the energy he needed to funk it up.

My mind must have wandered because it suddenly dawned on me that the subject had changed. And changed it had. Zoot was telling me that he'd finally taken the teachers' exam. Yes, after all those years of arguing with Sid. May wonders never cease!

"Now, this isn't what you think it is," he said. "I'm going through some changes, but I'm not doing a one-eighty. I can still cat around at night after punching a time clock during the day."

In other words, he intended to keep his night job, playing jazz, but he'd have a steady day gig to pay the bills—that is, if he passed the exam.

"The written part was a real head-twister," he said, "but I blew the hell out of tenor and clarinet."

Meanwhile, Dewey had barely lowered the iron curtain. We called him a few times in June and July, but he only wanted to rake Sid over the coals. We didn't hear any gossip from him until August when—for goodness' sake!— *he* phoned *us* from Zsa Zsa's home in Beverly Hills.

He began by giving his father the business again, saying Sid was like a giant vacuum cleaner that sucked the life from people. After getting that out of his system, he dished the dirt on Zsa Zsa's latest—hubby number eight—a prince this time, Frederick von Whosis und Whatsis.

"He got his title from a dowager in Germany. He was plain Freddie before she adopted him. Now he's peddling his own titles."

Dewey was at Zsa Zsa's home, the old Howard Hughes place, to write up the wedding for *People*. He was getting a few hundred dollars as a freelancer, the only money he'd earned since his ill-fated trip for *Vanity Fair*, don't remind me. I think Eva was boycotting the ceremony, but Zsa Zsa's other sister, Magda, was there.

I always made sure to ask after Fleur when I was on the phone with Dewey. I hadn't heard from her since that awful call and wanted to find out if I was still persona non grata.

"Did you tell her how sorry I am, Dewey? Now, I don't expect us to be Naomi and Ruth, but isn't it about time we made up?"

"Fleur's got a lot on her mind now," he said. "Anyway, she's more teed off at herself than at you, as she should be. After what she did, she ought to turn in her Nobel Prize in Economics."

CHAPTER 37

WHEN THE CEMENT HARDENS

Didn't Mrs. Roosevelt say a wife has to hiss like a serpent and coo like a dove? Well, Mrs. Waxler did more hissing than cooing the night Purdy got us together again, the people led astray by Arlee Sparlow. We were at the Club House in Pelican Pond this time because the VFW Hall had been booked by the Connecticut Yankees for their annual clambake.

Purdy spent an hour going over our depositions for the civil case in Titusville. Then he tried to answer our questions about the criminal trial in Melbourne, but he had to refer most of them to the State Attorney's office in Coco, which was handling the prosecution.

After he'd gone, we drifted into the Card Room, the smart husbands in smoking and the Merry Wives in non. The accordion door dividing the room kept down the stench of tobacco but did nothing about the noise pollution.

As usual, the men were consoling one another about the fickleness of fate. If one itched, the others would scratch. As for the wives, none of the us knew the whole picture, but each one had a part of it. For the first half-hour, we'd exchange information, my little tidbit for yours. It was the only way to find out what was really going on that September.

I tried to ignore the wheelers and dealers on the other side of the accordion door, but I couldn't help hearing them. Everybody else was to blame, especially the wives.

"Maybe we didn't all come out with diamonds and gold fillings," Sid was saying. "But this wasn't some get-rich-quick scheme that promised you King Solomon's mines."

"That's what I've been trying to tell my wife, but she doesn't want to hear," Mo Bialer said. "She's ready to string me up like the salamis hanging in the window."

"You should listen to my wife," Heshy Liebowitz said. "I married a Chihuahua and ended up with a pit bull. The only way I can shut her up now is to turn off my hearing aid."

Muriel and Loretta were redder than the ink we were all swimming in. Everyone at the table avoided their eyes.

Now, it was Bernstein's turn. His rental bungalow was still the Divided Kingdom with invisible territory lines his wife wouldn't let him cross. Carlee, the granddaughter, had visited for a week, then began drawing pictures of half-houses for her sixth-grade class on Long Island.

"Millie has no right to treat me like a leper," Bernstein said. "Do you know what Georgie Jessel called marriage? A mistake that every man should make. He never met my wife."

Mildred excused herself from the table and went to

the ladies' room. I was wondering how she could face any of us, when all of a sudden Sid was exercising his lungs again.

"Selma has a big mouth, too. She's like a black widow spider that wants to eat you alive. But I don't let her get away with it. Whenever she opens her mouth, I let her have it."

My jaw hit the card table. All the other wives gasped, but nobody said a word. It was a struggle to keep my composure, let me tell you.

Thank God for one thing. The rest of that miserable meeting is a blank. If you held a loaded gun to my head, I couldn't tell you one more thing that was said on either side of the accordion door. All I heard was the thumping of my heart in my chest.

I gave Sid the silent treatment as we left the Club House. It wasn't until we were in the front seat of the Toyota with the doors slammed shut that I exploded.

"Where do you get off insulting me like that? I've never been so humiliated in my life."

"What's eating you now, Selma?"

"I'm talking about you and your lecture on the taming of the shrew. Finally I know how you talk about me behind my back. Over forty-five years of marriage and this is the loyalty I get."

"You were spying on me!"

"I didn't have to spy. All the wives heard. I won't have you insulting me in public."

"Stop exaggerating. You take one kernel and blow it up into a bowl of popcorn."

"I didn't lose all that money. I didn't flush our life savings down the drain. And I'm not an old windbag with delusions of grandeur."

"I warned you not to aggravate me, Selma. Do you want to give me a heart attack?"

"What about me? My heart is pounding. And another thing. I'm sick and tired of your making excuses for that crook Arlee Sparlow. One more excuse and I'll scream."

This was the turning point for me. It was like one of those near-death experiences where your life passes before you. Everything flooded back, all the latest indignities as well as the old skeletons in the closet.

"You act like I'm a bad person," Sid said as he pulled out of the Club House parking lot and went around the Olympic pool. "I always wanted the best for us."

"That may be so, but you ruined us all the same. Who knows if we'll have a bed to sleep in next month? And it's all because of that bloodsucker."

"There was no reason to doubt him, not in any way, shape, or form. If he did something wrong, it was a case of Dr. Jekyll and Mr. Hyde. I only saw the good side of him."

"Admit it, he was rotten through and through. As my mother would say, the fish stinks from the head down. All these excuses for him, I want them to stop here and now."

For once, Sid was speechless. That was progress, anyhow. I let him stew in his own juices until we were back in our breezeway. With the engine idling, I caught him staring at me out of the corner of his eye as if I were a total stranger.

"It's me, Sid."

"I never saw you like this before, Bubbie. You're as hard as concrete."

Sid was still giving me strange looks a few weeks later when our forty-sixth wedding anniversary arrived. Kitty had wanted to give us a party, but my heart wasn't in it. I didn't feel like making believe I was enjoying myself with my friends. As luck would have it, Sid and I had an excuse to beg off.

We were one of three couples to win the Labor Day raffle at Beth Shalom, a champagne dinner for two at the Polaris Lounge. At first, I didn't want to set foot in Arlee's crooked restaurant, but then I thought better of it. Why shouldn't we see where our stolen money went?

We were picked up in a pink Cadillac with the top down. It was your typical Space Coast restaurant—stuffed sailfish behind the bar, Titan swizzle sticks, gator tails for the appetizer. The swordfish steaks were fourteen inches long. I couldn't finish mine, but Sid kindly helped out.

The waiter was filling Sid's champagne glass a third time when you-know-who swaggered in like the lord of the manor. As Arlee made his way toward the bar, with a tip of his Panama hat to all and sundry, a sudden change came over Sid.

"Look at that guy, Bubbie. I'm spending my days sticking all ten fingers in the dike and he comes to the scene of the crime to celebrate."

Sid noticed me staring at him. "I know what you're thinking, Bubbie, but I have more hindsight now. The nerve of that guy! Not an ounce of shame!"

Arlee almost tripped over himself when he spotted

Sid and me. He gave us that big, toothy grin and weaved his way over to our table. He started talking while he was still ten feet away.

"Hey, good buddy, you're a sight for sore eyes. And how's the pretty lady? I always knew you fine folks would pay no heed to that pack of agitators barking like mongrels in the pound."

Sid began to get up, but I grabbed him by the arm and held on for dear life.

"I have only one thing to say to a liar and a cheat like you." Sid spit out the words like carpet tacks. "Good riddance when they put you behind bars where you belong."

Mr. Sparlow stopped in his tracks.

"I know you're hurting, old friend. We have a country saying here that a cut dog barks. But I never lied to you. I'll swear up and down on it."

I couldn't hold Sid any longer.

"You never lied?" he said as he sprang from his chair. "Selling the same package to six people at a time. You should burn in the electric chair. I'd like to strap on the electrodes myself."

"Where did I have a hand in one crooked thing, Sid? That's just dead false."

The waiter hurried over to our table, then froze when he saw Sid's face.

"You had a hand in it up to the elbow. I'd throw the switch myself. I taught at Gompers. I know what two thousand volts at five amps can do. You know what your brain would be like in two minutes?"

"You're drunk, Sid. You better sit down before you

say something you'll regret. Waiter, I wouldn't serve this man any more champagne."

Sid clenched his fists. His chest was heaving up and down. I was afraid the veins and arteries would burst.

"You should drop dead, you maggot-infested pile of dung. Come on, Selma, let's get out of this greasy spoon. The company makes me sick."

CHAPTER 38

ALLIGATOR TEARS

I've always hated left turns. I'd rather make three rights than a left, especially during the morning rush hour. All those extra turns must have added ten or twelve minutes to our trip in October, but I still got us to the Melbourne courthouse in plenty of time.

Sid had been too nervous to drive. He was very anxious to be there for Arlee's sentencing. I was, too, if truth be told. It was revenge, revenge pure and simple. I'm not ashamed to admit it.

Judge Laffler was a tough cookie, not like that old fool at the arraignment. She was a no-nonsense black woman with clumps of white hair, a beaked nose, and feathers that were easily ruffled. As she glared down from the bench, she looked like a bald eagle thinking about lunch.

The defense lawyer, a good old boy named Buford something or other, tried every trick in the book. He was an ugly little thing, as pockmarked as a pineapple, but he had the gift of gab.

"What did Arlee do that was so bad, your honor? He

didn't rob Fort Knox with a Tommy gun. What he tried to do was help a few people make a better life. It didn't turn out that way, but there isn't a shred of evidence to show he profited personally from their misfortune."

This Buford person was wearing a crumpled suit about three sizes too large and a scruffy pair of shoes even Zoot would have thrown out. He did everything he could to muddy the waters. It reminded me of what Harry Truman used to say: If you can't convince them, confuse them.

"Mr. Sparlow is the poorest man in this courtroom, Your Honor. If you had him up against the car and went through his pockets, you wouldn't find a red penny."

He was good, but he couldn't disguise the plain, unvarnished truth. Not even Perry Mason could have gotten Arlee off, no matter how often he shouted incompetent, irrelevant, and immaterial—or was that the other one, Burger, the DA?

The woman from the State Attorney's office, I think her first name was Yolanda, didn't look like any prosecutor I ever saw on TV. She was a Southern belle, but not your usual magnolia flower.

"Listening to a country boy like Buford try to defend Mr. Sparlow is enough to make your dog sick," she said. "Oh, gee whiz, all Arlee did wrong was this one little itty-bitty thing. Well, you can put perfume on a skunk and call it Miss Florida, but it's still a skunk."

How do these Scarlett O'Hara types do it? Somehow she managed to sound syrupy no matter how angry she got. She was very good—as good as Buford, if not better.

"This is an open-and-shut case, Your Honor. Mr.

Sparlow is a vile man who stole from dozens of honest working people. He should be put away for a long, long time, but even when you get rid of a skunk, the smell lingers on."

I think the judge liked that, the part about the skunk. She didn't exactly smile, but she toned down the glare a degree or two.

Arlee had been convicted the week before of racketeering and defrauding investors. The jury found him guilty on all counts. I think there were eighty-eight of them, two counts for each of the phony mortgages. Now he had the gall to plead for mercy.

"I'm sorry, Your Honor, bitterly remorseful." His hands were clasped as if in prayer, tears rolling down his cheeks like what's-his-name, the TV evangelist caught with his pants down. "Believe me, I'm truly, truly ashamed of my actions."

He was wearing a striped shirt with his white suit. I hoped he liked stripes. There was something wolfish about him even from the back. He looked as if he were about to get up on his hind quarters and howl at the moon.

"I don't know what possessed me," he was saying. "I'll swear up and down on the Bible, I didn't know what I was doing."

"I'm not your exorcist, Mr. Sparlow," the judge broke in. "You weren't possessed by an evil spirit. You knew exactly what you were doing."

"Excuse me, ma'am. I'm truly repentant. I'm as sorry as any sinner who took a breath of pure air and defiled it."

It was the Goebbels theory of the big lie. You tell a lie, repeat it often enough, and maybe someone will believe you. Not that the judge was buying any of this.

"You're more full of it than a Christmas turkey, Mr. Sparlow. You're a deliberate, manipulative, and unblushing liar with no moral fiber. There's a feeling among white-collar criminals that they won't be incarcerated. This has got to stop, and it will in my courtroom."

In the end, the crook got ten years. Even that wasn't enough for Sid.

"It's a slap on the wrist," he said. "The law doesn't have teeth. It doesn't even have gums."

Actually, you couldn't help being a little impressed by Arlee, even when you knew he was concocting one lie after another. How could he say such things with a straight face? In the end, you had to accept he wasn't the worst person in the world, no matter what Sid now thought. He wasn't Dr. Jekyll before and he wasn't Mr. Hyde now. He was bad enough, mind you, but no worse than a lot of others.

Well, the sentencing didn't solve our financial problems. Crabbe never stopped calling. One day it was Ready Credit, the next Checking Plus or Visa or MasterCard. We were running out of excuses, but phone calls wouldn't be a problem if we missed another payment to Southern Bell.

Worst of all, Beachview was threatening to take away our home unless we caught up with the mortgage payments. We got a letter from the bank's law firm in Orlando—Wiley & Fowler—but we couldn't scrape together enough money to consult Dunaway about our rights. We still owed him a few hundred and he was pressing us, too. I was afraid to open the mail each morning. Somebody else would be asking if the check was in the mail.

The debts were swallowing us up like Jonah and the whale. Depew, the nervous fellow who sold us our home, called to ask if we wanted to sell. Birdella was now coming every other week and who knew how long we could afford that? Once I was ten dollars short and had to pay her the next time. By now, even Sid had to face facts.

"In a million years, I wouldn't have figured this to happen, Bubbie. It was so easy at first. You put your fishing line in the barrel and came up with a twenty-inch bass. I didn't realize the barrel would run out of fish."

Sid developed an ulcer in October and had to check his stools whenever he went to the bathroom. If they turned black—pitch black, not just dark—that was a bad sign. I got constipated myself and had to take Metamucil.

I'm not a doom and gloom person, but I felt like somebody in a Russian novel, waiting for the next slap from the hand of fate. We needed help, but I didn't know where to turn. The boys? Rose? Forget them. The only one left was Kitty, but she had worries enough of her own. Anyway, Sid wouldn't consider it. He'd never ask Kitty for help.

"I'd rather go on welfare than have her lord it over me," he said.

"We have to do something, Sid. If not Kitty, then something else. You can't just take the temperature of a sick person over and over. Sooner or later, you have to give him medicine."

I think it was in October that Kitty asked me to go

with her to Silvercrest—Leo's nursing home—and help give mambo lessons to the patients. My mambo was rusty, especially that part with the hips—the swivel—but I always enjoyed dancing to a syncopated beat.

Kitty was a terrific teacher. In no time, she had them dipping and twirling like Latins from Manhattan. Dr. Bidwell was even doing it. Everybody got a kick out of it, especially Leo, but my feet were black and blue from his clumsy shoes. I finally got him Poppy Rappaport as a partner. She'd been in Aquacise with me before she began forgetting her routines.

Dr. Bidwell couldn't thank Kitty and me enough. Do you know what she told us on the way out? There's value in living the moment even if you can't remember it five minutes later.

"Jesus, I'm beginning to feel my age," Kitty said as she backed out of the parking lot.

"Tell me another. I'm the one who's been mamboed to death."

"Thanks for coming, Selma. I really appreciate it."

"Don't mention it. I enjoyed myself. It took my mind off my own troubles."

"It helps if you think of life as a mambo," she said, turning onto A1A at a break in the traffic. "Two steps forward and one step back."

There was a workman on a cherry picker in front of the House of the Sizzling Fajita. He was fixing one of the lights in Pancho Villa's sombrero. All of a sudden, I felt Kitty's hand patting me on the knee.

"I don't want to mix myself in where I don't belong, but when have I ever let a thing like that stop me?"

I knew where this one was heading. I got out a hanky and blew my nose.

"I should have said something months ago, Selma, but I've been feeling sorry for myself. It took Rose of all people—Rose with her troubles—to point out to me that you and Sid were drowning and needed somebody to throw you a life preserver. Can you forgive me?"

She wanted me to forgive her? Kitty went on before I had a chance to say anything.

"Now, tell me what I can do for you two—and I don't want any false pride."

"Oh, Kitty."

"Goddamn it, don't get mushy with me or I'll break your foot—the other one. I don't intend to sit on my rear end while an old friend is in trouble."

"Who knows when we'll be able to repay you?"

"What the hell are you talking about? Money's like a puddle; some people step in it and others don't. A thank you will do just fine."

"You can't put a thank you in your pocketbook."

"Look, honey, I have more money than I know what to do with, but I don't have friends to spare. I'm too old and mean to make new ones."

I blew my nose loudly, then we started to laugh. We hadn't had a good laugh together since God only knows when.

"There's one problem," I said as we turned into Pelican Pond. "Sid will never—"

"Let me handle it."

Sid was on the chaise longue in the Florida room, looking as moody as the slow movement of the *Moon-*

light Sonata. I made a pitcher of lemonade and brought out three glasses. Kitty had already opened two beach chairs and pulled them over to him.

"If I were your wife, I'd make you wear a dunce cap and sit in the corner," she was saying. "But who am I to argue with Selma? She'd let you get away with murder. Wake up, Sid. She's nuts about you. You may be broke, but you have a treasure living with you. Come on, tell Selma how much you appreciate her."

Sid looked so forlorn lying there. I handed him his glass of lemonade. He started to thank me, then shook his head.

"I feel like such a horse's behind, Bubbie. I tried to be a big shot, but if you want to know the truth, I'm nothing but a king-size nobody."

"You're a terrific human being," I said. "But a human being is only human."

"Face it, Bubbie, I was just an old Jew making a fool of himself. I had no right to get you involved. Bubbie, Bubbie, I can't tell you how sorry I am."

"Oh, Sid, don't say any more. You'll just talk foolishness. Now sit there and listen a moment. Kitty's got something to say."

To make a long story short, Kitty offered to help with the debts until we were back on our feet. It was a loan, of course, but we could pay her whenever. Not that any amount of money could have repaid her for lifting the stone off my heart.

She also got us a smart lawyer from Rockledge, Goldfarb. He found a way to save one more package, a big one on a warehouse in Melbourne, then use the proceeds to pay off the mortgage on our own home. It was a very complicated thing. We were still in debt up to our eyebrows, but none of the other creditors could touch the Chalet now, not even Southland.

I know what you're thinking. If everything turned out all right in the end, what was she complaining for? Well, I'm sorry, my dear, but all's not well that ends well. What about the aggravation? The sleepless nights? The stomach upsets? And my story isn't over yet. You can finish ninety-nine miles out of a hundred-mile race, but the last mile is the killer.

CHAPTER 39

THE CHILDREN'S TABLE

If children aren't the way you like, you're supposed to like them the way they are. That's a nice sentiment, but the theory is a lot easier than the practice.

I always knew Dewey was no Woodward or Bernstein, but not in three lifetimes could I have guessed what he'd do next. He had offers that fall from any number of places—*AP*, *UPI*, *USA Today*. So how could such a talented person take a job with a filthy rag like *The National Enquirer* just because the editor offered him a few lousy dollars more?

I should have held my tongue when he called in October to tell us about his latest career move. Being who I am, I couldn't help needling him about Dolly and Madonna and Princess Di, not to mention all the Elvis sightings and other nonsense.

"Wise up, will you?" he said. "News is news, no matter where you work in this business. I'm not paid to be Albert Schweitzer."

"You're no Schweitzer, my dear. I remember when you were six and we took you to *Peter and the Wolf*. Do you know what you liked best? The part where the wolf ate the duck."

"If I want to dredge up my childhood, I'll call a shrink, not my mother."

"All I want is for you to be happy, Dewey."

"What makes you think I'm not? I sat down in the tenth grade and wrote out what I wanted to do with my life and it looks like I've checked everything off."

The *Enquirer* sent Dewey all over the country. He had to live out of a suitcase for weeks at a time—not luxury places like the Breakers, or even the Hilton, but a Day's Inn here and a Great Western there.

He stayed at a Howard Johnson in Manhattan while he was on the Jackie beat. He and his photographer, an old-timer named Smiley, shared a double with twin beds. The two of them would sit in their rental car all day and watch her apartment house on Fifth Avenue.

When Jackie emerged, they'd chase after her. Maybe she'd go to her butcher on Madison or jog around the reservoir in Central Park. Smiley got a picture of her coming out of the Colony Club with what's-his-name, her constant companion. He was Jewish, not so good looking as Kennedy nor so rich as Onassis, but he had a nice smile.

She didn't have her Secret Service agents anymore, which should have made it easier to follow her around, but that wasn't always so.

Dewey called us after one wild-goose chase in New Jersey. This was just a few weeks after he got the job. He and Smiley had followed Jackie out to Peapack, where she had a horse estate and hunted foxes. Smiley had done this dozens of times. You couldn't get near her home, but he knew all the best spots to wait. There was a back road where you sometimes caught sight of her galloping by with the fox hunters, but not this time. Maybe they were out of foxes.

Anyway, Jackie was out of sight, if not out of mind, until Sunday afternoon, when the two of them waited at the corner gas station until she passed by on the way home to Fifth Avenue.

"It's pouring rain and she's hauling ass like you wouldn't believe," Dewey said. "I'm trying to save the paper money so I'm driving this two-bit Honda rental. Suddenly, she pulls away from me like I'm standing still. I don't know what she has under the hood, but I get the big message that nobody is going to keep up with her."

Jackie got on the Jersey Turnpike, which takes you to the tunnels under the Hudson. She was doing eighty-five in the pouring rain and Dewey was putt-putting after her in his little rental.

"We're at a toll booth. It was about a buck, but all I had was a five. Thank God it wasn't a twenty. I just tossed this bill into the basket and peeled off after her. The guy at the booth started yelling, but he shut up when he saw that he'd picked up a four-buck tip."

It was a waste of money. Dewey lost her in the rain and his editor was furious. He was an Englishman, over six feet tall and two hundred and fifty pounds. By the time my thin-skinned son finished talking back to this Beefeater, he was an unemployment statistic again.

"Why the hell do they have to go to London to find

a jerk with an IQ that's smaller than his shoe size?" he told us. "I thought there were enough morons in this country."

For somebody in his line of work, Dewey was far too sensitive. Oh, who was I to complain? I was only his mother. If he wanted to take his marbles and play in another sandbox every other month, it was his business, not mine.

I finally got a call from Fleur herself later in the fall. Was she tough on me! Who was I, anyway—Tammy Wynette standing by my man? I won't repeat the rest of it. Well, better an honest slap in the face than a false kiss, as we say. Fleur made me grovel for fifteen minutes before she finally agreed to make up. Then she told me all about her latest decorating job. It was in Beverly Hills and there was a very formal dining room.

"I want them to have a feeling of being godlike. Everything is classic. Think of ancient Greece. I tried to contrast the stateliness of the dining room with the chaos in the world outside."

Someone once said the strongest mother-in-law in the world isn't strong enough to hold her tongue for five minutes. Well, I managed to hold mine for ten. The subject of you-know-what never came up—not in that conversation, anyhow.

Meanwhile, we had an interesting call from Zoot around this time—collect, but who was counting? Sid and I were both on the line. As usual, Zoot took his time coming to the point. He'd played the night before with a rehearsal band at the Vanguard. He didn't get paid for this one, but he was still very nervous—a lot of music had been played up on that stage.

Finally, Zoot got to the real news. He'd passed the teachers' exam and was working at an elementary school in the Bronx.

"I'm only a temporary per diem, but the bread is pretty good. I have a master's plus, which is a hundred and fifty bucks and then some for a six-hour day. If I dig it, I can go for my permanent license. Mr. Fernandez, the principal, thinks it would be a finger snap."

It was hard work teaching kids from the projects how to play, but Zoot didn't mind the headaches. "These kids come in expecting a vaudeville show," he said. "You have to psych them out by giving them a reward for doing what you want."

"I always preferred the carrot to the stick in my classroom, too," Sid said. "You give them a little show: Abbot and Costello; who's on first?"

"Mr. Fernandez says sometimes you have to grab a kid, but he doesn't want to hear about it. I haven't had to do that yet. Once a kid threw a recorder on the floor in frustration. You don't concentrate too long when you're young."

Sid offered to speak to a few people at Gompers. He still knew the principal, Guerrini, and two of the shop teachers. But Zoot knew a guy at the school board—Eddie Lipman—an old friend from the music business who could get him per diems whenever he wanted.

Zoot still had a few misgivings about teaching. You could tell from the anxiety dream he was having, something about leaving his Mark VI on the subway and not realizing until the doors slammed shut behind him. It was cheaper to use Sid and me as his sounding board than a shrink.

"I was always one of those guys who never had heavy questions about what I wanted to do. But one day I said to myself, hey, wait a minute, is this happening to me? It was like, man, playing jazz is cool, but I also have to do something with my life."

Sid let Zoot talk himself out before offering his opinion. He was very tactful, and modest, too. I guess the Disaster had taught him more than one lesson.

"Who am I to be giving advice? Not after the way I made a foul-up of my own life. But for what it's worth, I think you're doing the right thing."

That's what Zoot had been waiting to hear all these years. It was like when Jacob fought with the Angel all night. They were still wrestling at the break of day, but Jacob wouldn't let go until the Angel blessed him.

"Hell, I won't be like any other music teacher you ever knew," Zoot said. "I'll still be me. There's only one Zoot Waxler to the box."

Oh, Zoot had a few dates with Myra, but nothing came of them. The problem was cats. He had a gig in Buffalo that autumn and left Billie with Myra for the weekend. Unfortunately, she had a black cat of her own, Ella, and the two didn't get along. Zoot took this as a bad sign.

"She's much too grounded for me. It could be hip for a while, but it wouldn't last. I guess maybe I'm growing up. I don't want to waste my time learning the wrong charts."

CHAPTER 40

THE THREE WITCHES

Sooner or later, the time comes for the Greek chorus to sum things up. What can I say? It's like cabbage borscht. You throw in a handful of brown sugar to sweeten it and a drop of lemon juice to make it sour. Like life, except the portions are usually reversed.

I went trick-or-treating with True Sisters on Halloween. We were collecting for the melanoma research lab at Holmes Regional, the hospital in Melbourne. I had to go door to door from one end of Pelican Pond to the other—my poor feet swelled up like balloons.

Otherwise, I felt fine for a youngster of seventy-one, and don't ask how many years ago this was. Let's just say I won't be seeing my seventies again, not unless Einstein was right and we all end up back where we began, if we should live so long.

I did have one thing wrong with me, a white fungus growing in my mouth. It hurt when I ate, and gave me bad breath, but Ramsool prescribed an antibiotic that cleared it up in a few days. He said I had the constitution of a horse. I should have kicked him for that.

Well, Sid was still feeling sorry for himself, but he wasn't Hamlet pacing the stage anymore. He was back to his old ways, lying in the La-Z-Boy as the television droned on. I wasn't going to let it bother me now.

At first, his nose was glued to CNN again, but after a few months he got bored with politicians talking out of both sides of their mouths. "Politics is like life insurance, Bubbie. You may need it, but you don't want to hear anything about it."

Next came the religious channel. It helped to get Sid's gastric juices flowing. The guy he loved to hate the most was that Bible thumper from Hollywood, the one who chain-smoked cigars. Every time he appeared, Sid would glare at the screen and mutter to himself.

"Get a load of this guy. Isn't tobacco a sin? He must think he's George Burns. Look at him. He's got another outfit on every five minutes. Is he supposed to be Johnny Carson, too?"

Religion may be the opium of the people, but it didn't hook Sid for long. In a few weeks, his viewing habits changed again, from the other world back to this one—the food channel.

He hadn't lost his interest in eating. Just the mention of food would make him salivate like Pavlov's dog. And what he found on cable! A recipe for Hawaiian wedding salad. You mix pineapple chunks, mandarin orange slices, shredded coconut, and maraschino cherries into a bowl of cooked macaroni, then cover the concoction with brown sugar and Cool Whip.

I wouldn't make such a thing, but that didn't stop Sid. He did it himself while I was at Aquacise, using canned black cherries instead of maraschinos. What a mess! It took me over an hour to clean up the kitchen. Well, at least I had Birdella back to once a week.

Sid would remain in his Fruit of the Looms all morning, even on Tuesdays when she came to clean. Birdella was a very religious person and it bothered her plenty to see him in boxer shorts.

"You should be ashamed of yourself. How can I do the windows when you look like that? I'm getting my Windex from the broom closet now and I want you decent when I come back."

"I've had enough trouble without you starting in on me, too, Birdella."

"My, my, Mr. Waxler is feeling sorry for himself. One time I had my bursitis so bad I couldn't even bend over to do the tubs, but I found a way. If you do your best, the Lord will do the rest. Now, where is that Windex hiding?"

I tried to get Sid to take more of an interest in life. I invited him to go with me to see Charo in *Hello, Dolly!* at the Cabaret, but all he wanted to do was dwell on his failures.

"I'm an old fool, Bubbie. I had my head so high in the clouds, I couldn't see my feet."

"What's wrong with being old? I don't see why everything has to be new. You put new on a box of Tide and that's supposed to make it better."

"Excuse me, Bubbie, I have to go."

Whenever he didn't want to talk about something, he had to go to the bathroom. He always had to go. He had to go more than any man in the world.

To be fair, he had an enlarged prostate now and would spend half his day in the toilet. He didn't bother closing the door unless Birdella was there. I was used to seeing him like that, of course. A woman knows she's married when her husband stops bothering about the toilet door.

Sid would stand over the bowl for ten minutes and all I'd hear would be a dribble here, a dribble there. Age was catching up with him—as with all of us.

Rose developed a problem with her thyroid or parathyroid in November, the one that affects your energy. If she walked more than a few steps, she'd be panting like a dog. The oncologist, Butcher, said it had nothing to do with the cancer. After consulting Ramsool, he had her get a walker. She could still walk on her own, but it took too much out of her.

Butcher insisted he was happy with the progress of Rose's chemo. Everything else might be going wrong, but the cancer was under control, if you know what I mean. Needless to say, he wasn't the one who had to live with the side effects.

Rose became more and more withdrawn as her last few wisps of hair fell out and her eyebrows dropped off. Even on good days, she didn't want to be seen in public now. I knew it would be a hard sell, but I tried to get her to come with Kitty and me to *Stage Door Canteen* in December. One of the McGuire Sisters was making a guest appearance.

"Come on, Rose, it'll be like old times—boogie-woogie, boogie-woogie, eight to the bar."

"I don't want strangers staring. Every time I go out, I

feel like somebody is following me around with a bull-horn and yelling look, look, she has cancer."

"Oh, Rose."

I let her be for another week, but I knew this couldn't go on. In the end, I took matters into my own hands.

"You can't stay cooped up in here all day," I said, arriving on her doorstep just before the holidays. "It's time to get out and face the world."

"I can do whatever I want, Selma. I'm seventy-one years old. I have half my lungs kaput and I can't get around without a walker."

It hurt me as much as it hurt her, but I stood my ground. After an hour of coaxing, she finally went with me to Ginza Wig on Okeechobee Boulevard. We found a very nice one, a little wavier than her real hair but quite natural looking. I wouldn't be embarrassed to wear such a thing myself, if the situation warranted it.

A few days later, Rose agreed to put on her new wig and go with Kitty and me to the Hanuka show at the Cabaret. Art Linkletter was going to be there. No sooner had we gotten Rose into the Roadmaster than Kitty opened her big mouth.

"Where'd you get the rug, Rose? It looks like something Teddy Roosevelt shot on safari."

"Kitty, really!" I gave her a stare, and turned to apologize to Rose, but she was—believe it or not—laughing!

"Oh, it's all right, Selma. Everywhere I go it's Rose, I'm sorry, and Rose, are you all right? Yes, I'm all right. Rose is just fine, thank you very much."

As for Kitty, she still had a strong constitution, but

she was having trouble with her kishkes. They were coming out of her, something to do with the Caesarean she had when her baby, the brain-damaged one, was born. Now she had to wear one of those gadgets that hold the uterus in place and keep it from slipping down. I don't know, the word is gone.

Oh, there was something else that happened to her. Kitty had shingles in a very embarrassing place. I'd have kept it between me and my doctor, but she had to inform the whole world. As Ramsool was examining her down there, she told him it was a good thing she wasn't a hooker.

Otherwise, she was holding up fine. She might have a bad spell now and then, but she'd snap out of it. She visited Leo at the nursing home every day. I'd go with her once or twice a week. We usually sat outside on lawn chairs and sipped lemonade as we tried to get through to him.

"I can't say he's any better," Kitty warned me in December as we waited for a nurse to bring him down. "But he's at peace after all that turmoil. Do you know what I got him for Hanuka? Calvin Klein's Obsession. The whole enchilada—cologne, body powder, and shampoo."

Actually, Leo looked much better than the last time I was there. He was wearing a velvet smoking jacket and a silk ascot, quite the gentleman. In fact, he looked terrific.

"He could be the same old Leo, couldn't he, Selma? I got him that jacket from Saks for his sixtieth birthday."

Kitty removed a piece of lint from the shawl collar. She straightened the shoulder pads and smoothed out the sleeves.

"Leo, say hello to Selma."

He didn't recognize me at first. I was wearing my new toreador pants and top from Byron's. He stared as if I were a stranger. But then Kitty opened her pocketbook and took out her wallet. She showed Leo the picture of Kitty, Rose, and me at Times Square, the one with the whiskey bottles and shot glass on the bar. Can you find her, Leo? No, don't look on the left, look in the middle. Finally, a light came on, and Leo smiled.

"Hello, Selma, that's a great bolero you have on."

I think that's what he was trying to say. You could barely make him out. Not that it mattered. I did most of the talking. Leo was going in and out. He wasn't there most of the time.

"Go on," Kitty would prompt me. "If he goes off into his own world, you just keep talking and he'll come back again. Dr. Bidwell says each little memory gives him dignity."

I chatted on for the rest of the visit, even while we were taking him back upstairs, but Leo didn't respond. I felt like such an idiot. I even apologized to him as we were leaving his room.

"I'm sorry, Leo, I'm such a bore. I'll think of something more interesting next time."

My hand was on the doorknob when he called after me—clearly now, in his old voice.

"You don't have to apologize, Selma. I wasn't exactly the life of the party myself."

I once read that the greatest curse in life is the ability to get used to anything. If my mind ever goes, I hope somebody puts a pillow to my face. I tried to talk to Sid about proxies and medical directives, but he wouldn't listen to me. Not now, Bubbie, I have to go.

It was Christmas again when Annette raised her prices at the House of Aloha. She needed more money to pay off the IOU's Rocky had saddled them with when he lost the Villa Romana.

She was going to charge old-timers like us the same as before, eight dollars for a wash and blow dry, but I usually gave her ten. That was only fair. It wasn't a tip. She was the boss, so you didn't have to tip her, but I wouldn't take advantage.

Theresa always did Rose's nails while the wig was under the dryer. Rose was very embarrassed about being bald in public, but Annette used to wrap a House of Aloha towel around her head like a turban. I remember asking Rose why she wanted to spend money to get her wig done when she could wash it at home.

"It's always important to do your hair right, Selma, especially before you go into the hospital for chemo. The doctors try harder if you look good."

I'm running on, I know, but parting is such sweet sorrow. Was that Romeo or Juliet? My God, it was so many years ago, Miss Cowper and the rest of it.

Annette had a luau on New Year's Eve so her customers could say good riddance to A.D. 1986. It was at the beach where Rabbi Nathanson took us to throw bread on Rosh Hashana. The husbands were invited, too, but none of them wanted to hang out with the wahines.

Kitty found an old lava-lava at home to wrap around her hips, but Rose and I rented grass skirts from Nick's Costume Shop in Palm Bay. We spread our blankets on the sand by a dune overgrown with sea oats and sea grapes. The ocean was turning dark and the sea oats were starting to stir in the breeze. Behind us, the sun was about to set over the Banana River.

Everything tasted good after two mimosas and a mai tai, even the poi. I never heard this before, but Rhonda said mai tai means out of this world in Tahitian. Theresa couldn't leave the children, but her sister Rhonda came to help Annette at the luau table.

Kitty gave everybody a hula lesson with all the bumps and grinds: Oh, we're going to the hukilau, huki, huki, huki, huki, hukilau. I still remembered a little from my hula class in the mountains, but that must have been the G-rated version.

I was the one-woman orchestra. Millie had borrowed her husband's ukulele for me while he wasn't looking; it was made by the same guy who did Arthur Godfrey's. She still went to the House of Aloha for cuts, but she was doing her own color now to save money. Do you want to hear her favorite joke? She was a suicide blonde—dyed by her own hands.

Rose had to hold on to her walker as she did the hula. I tried to help her over to the luau table after the dance lesson, but she wanted to do it herself. She was very sensitive.

Oh, Rose gave us some bad news as we helped ourselves to the mahi-mahi. Not about herself, thank God, but Lettie what's-her-name, the girl from Healthercise. She died of breast cancer at Cape Canaveral Hospital; there was going to be something in *The Orbiter*.

After gossiping with the rest of the girls, I found myself sitting with my two old friends on our beach blankets. I must have had one mimosa too many because I was apologizing to Rose for the thousandth time and thanking Kitty for the thousandth and first. Kitty waved a hand as if all that she'd done for me amounted to nothing.

"Christ, you're embarrassing me, Selma. Your problem is you think too much."

Rose tried to speak, but she had a coughing fit. I caught only a few words, something about how she and Sol had been Siamese twins joined at the heart. Suddenly, the coughing stopped and her voice was clear again.

"For everything there's a season—Ecclesiastes. One minute you're alive and a minute later you're so much fertilizer for the grass."

"Jesus, that's a cheerful thought," Kitty said. "Well, for people so close to feeding the worms, we're still a pretty lively bunch, if I say so myself."

"I remember something," I said. "Charlie Chaplin, baggy pants, taught the girls the hula dance. Where does that come from?"

Everybody was tipsy now. I think Loretta was chasing Millie Bernstein across the sand and squirting her with an old seltzer bottle that belonged to Mo Bialer. Muriel, Mo's wife, was doing the thing about a little song, a little dance, a little seltzer down your pants.

Kitty stood up now and did a Spanish dance in her bare feet, kicking up the sand as she clapped her sandals together like castanets. I helped Rose to her feet and we stood looking at the waves. Kitty joined us and touched me on the shoulder.

"Do you remember the dime your mother gave me for dance lessons when we were girls?" she said. "You can't imagine how much that meant to me. It might have been a million dollars."

"You couldn't keep it, though. Your mother made you give it back."

"I never told you this, but Tante Zissel wouldn't take it back. She made me promise not to tell anyone, not even Selma. She didn't trust you to keep your mouth shut."

"No! Really? I don't believe you never told me, Kitty."

"I never told you a lot of things. I know you're watering that goddamn plant."

Rose was gripping the crossbar of her walker—a Palm-Pusher. She wasn't wearing her diamond ring. It must have been too big for her finger now.

I bent over to rub my creaky knees. As I looked up, the sea oats were fluttering like lavender streamers. I remembered so much, too much, things best left in the past. We're born in one world and die in another. Thousands of years, all those billions of people, forgotten people. Soon I'd be forgotten, too, a figment of my own imagination. Kitty interrupted my reveries.

"Selma? Earth to Selma? You've got the strangest look on your face."

"Do you remember May Day, Kitty? You were Mother Goose and we were your geese. Imogene Coca used to have a song: Did I walk away from the May Walk or did the May Walk walk away from me?"

Wanda was doing the hula barefoot in the surf, tossing macadamia nuts into the water: And we'll throw our nuts out into the sea, and all the ama-ama come a-swimming to me.

"I was looking at my latest driver's license and didn't recognize myself," I said. "I don't feel like an old woman."

"Maybe we're not as young as we used to be," Rose said. "But we're younger than we're going to be, God willing."

"All I know is the little man winds me up in the morning and I go," said Kitty.

She finished her mai tai, ate the pineapple wedge and maraschino cherry, then stuck the miniature orchid in her hair.

She held out the glass and waved her free hand over it. "Double, double toil and trouble."

"The three witches," Rose said.

There was a burst of red over the Banana River as the sun fell below the horizon. I put my arms around my dearest and oldest, kindest and wisest friends. I felt the blood warming in my body. I smelled the sea grapes, the salt of the sea, the life and the living all around me. I didn't want to let go.

CPSIA information can be obtained
at www.ICGtesting.com
Printed in the USA
LVHW041133020619
619867LV00002B/562/P

9 780980 153286